PRIVATE NIGHTMARES

Another gripping case for Bluebelle Investigations

Geoff Palmer

PODSNAP PUBLISHING
WELLINGTON, NEW ZEALAND

Podsnap Publishing Ltd., 17 Moir Street, Mt Victoria,
Wellington 6011, New Zealand.

Published by Podsnap Publishing Ltd., 2020

ISBN: 978-0-473-51931-5

1

Bor-ring!

Jane Child sighed as she tossed aside a battered copy of *Country Life* and looked out at the view across the street. It wasn't much of a view since one of the window's triple bombproof-glazing layers was slightly misted, but she did spot a segment of the Thames and a corner of Lambeth Bridge. A small insect had been trapped between the multiple panes and lay on its back, desiccated, its legs in the air. She was beginning to understand its last moments, trapped in an airless no-man's-land.

'Are you sure we aren't supposed to be in Legoland?' she said to her companion, referring to this building's more famous cousin at Vauxhall Cross.

Matt Healy's long hair, despite being brushed and tied back neatly, looked out of place combined with the near-new suit Jane had found him in one of her charity shop expeditions. He was really a jeans and T-shirt man, not "corporate" at all.

'Avery said MI5, not MI6,' he replied, referring to the phone call he'd received the day before from his old friend and former colleague at the National Crime Agency. 'Besides,' he added, glancing up from his own magazine, 'we wouldn't have got past the front desk if we weren't expected.'

"Front desk" was something of a misnomer, Jane thought. There wasn't much "desk" in evidence amid the collection of electronic barriers, x-ray scanners, and taciturn guards that occupied the building's unwelcoming entrance. Entering had been more like undergoing a rigorous airport security check.

'I bet Legoland have more up-to-date magazines.' She gestured at the one she'd discarded. 'According to that, Queen Victoria's due to open the Great Exhibition at Crystal Palace next month.'

Matt grunted, continuing turning his own pages, barely glancing at them as he did so. He hadn't slept well the last couple of nights and was clearly not in the mood for banter.

Jane studied the wood-panelled waiting room with its metal-legged chairs and framed photograph of a Royal Navy battleship. The dried arrangement in the corner might have been someone's abandoned bouquet, and the mustard-coloured carpet had its heavy-traffic areas protected by a series of transparent plastic mats. 'I love the ambience of this room,' she said. 'That hint of grim despair mixed with a dash of desperation. Abandon hope all ye who enter.'

'Careful,' Matt said, 'the place is probably bugged.'

'Well if it is, *perhaps they'll get a bloody move on!*' she said.

Another ten minutes passed before they heard a clack of heels on the plastic matting. The waiting room door opened, and a young man with a polished face and a crisp side-parting looked down his long, patrician nose at them. His rich black hair was so well oiled it seemed more ploughed than combed, and he raised an equally well-groomed eyebrow at them. 'Bluebelle? This way, if you please.'

He turned and they followed him down a long, wood-panelled corridor, past a series of identical doors, each one numbered with a small gold plate. He paused outside the last of them, gave two short knocks, then opened it and ushered them in.

A middle-aged man with a polished pate rose from behind a cluttered desk and came around to greet them. He was tweedy and avuncular, with a smile that mirrored the shape of the lower edge of the half-rim glasses he wore. 'Ms Child, Mr Healy. Welcome. Marius Fennel. My apologies for the delay. Things tend to pop up unexpectedly in this office.' He glanced at the young man who hesitated a second, returned a curt nod, then backed from the room, closing the door behind him.

'What office is this, exactly?' Jane asked, looking around the windowless room at the floor-to-ceiling shelves crammed with books and binders.

'We're a sort of crossover between intelligence gathering and analysis. Now, please ...' He gestured to a pair of seats in front of the desk and resumed his own.

'I'm very pleased to meet you both. You come highly recommended.' He looked over the top of his half-rims at Matt. 'I understand you've made a full recovery, Mr Healy, after your little stint in London Bridge Hospital?'

'Yes, thank you.'

'No lingering after-effects?'

'None at all.'

'I'm not just talking about physical effects. Getting shot is a traumatic event that can have other manifestations.'

'I'm not diving for cover every time a car backfires, if that's what you mean. I did work undercover for many years.'

'Nerves of steel, eh?' Fennel sat back and crossed his arms. 'But I do think you could do with a holiday. The pair of you.'

Matt frowned. 'I'm sorry, but I don't see that that's any of your business.'

Fennel beamed. 'Quite right. It isn't. Which is why I asked Detective Inspector Avery about you two. The fact that you are *not* employees of this organisation – or indeed, of any organisation but your own – is one of the reasons I asked him to suggest this visit.

'After the remarkably successful completion of your last case – albeit with unfortunate side-effects for yourself, Mr Healy – you may recall that the National Crime Agency picked up the tab for your private medical treatment and rehabilitation. A token of appreciation for the apprehension of that murderer the pair of you uncovered. Now, while the NHS is a fine institution staffed by many caring and compassionate individuals, in my experience there is no ailment that quite so galvanises a medical man's attention as one that's accompanied by the glint of a little extra coinage.'

Matt and Jane said nothing. They both knew the NCA hadn't actually picked up the tab for Matt's treatment and rehabilitation. Colin Avery told them so himself, perhaps overstepping the bounds of what he should have said. So they both affected surprised looks when Fennel added, 'It may surprise you to learn that the NCA was just a convenient conduit for those funds, which actually came from the Foreign Office. The FO is very grateful for that tip-off about their stolen data. Obviously, they can't say so publicly because, obviously, there was no actual data stolen.' He tapped the side of his nose. 'But that, at least indirectly, is why you were asked to pay me a visit this afternoon. And why I'm suggesting the pair of you might like to take a holiday.

'But before we get into that, tell me what you know about the Foreign Office.'

'Britain's marketing department, isn't it?' Jane said. 'Headed by the Foreign Secretary.'

Fennel nodded. 'And you, Mr Healy?'

'What Jane said. They promote British exports and investment opportunities abroad. Oh, and they run our consular offices too.'

'Quite correct, both of you, but they also have another lesser-known function.' He glanced at a document on his desk. 'That of "safeguarding the United Kingdom's national security by countering terrorism and weapons proliferation".'

'I'm sorry, isn't that your job?' Jane said. 'I mean, MI5's?'

'Yes, and yes, although we're a bit more counter-intelligence focused. But there is some overlap.' He sighed. 'MI5 report to the Home Office, MI6 report to the Foreign Office, but MI6 are a *foreign* intelligence agency and this is a *domestic* matter. Look, to be perfectly honest, I've been in this organisation twenty years and even *I'm* not quite sure where the boundaries lie. The point is, the Foreign Office love your work and would like to employ you again, unofficially, in your capacity as private investigators.'

'And they'd ... like to employ us ... to go on holiday?'

'Precisely! Avery said you were quick on the uptake. You've got it in a nutshell.'

'Where, exactly?' Jane asked.

'The client will provide the details. We want this to look like a regular job, but you're to give it your utmost priority – without appearing to do so, if you catch my drift.'

'We do have a number of other cases,' Matt said.

'Then may I ask you to conclude them as swiftly as possible? Defer or reschedule anything non-urgent, perhaps? In my purely non-medical opinion, you both look like you could do with a little R&R – especially if it were combined with a spot of simple sleuthing.'

'To be clear,' Matt said, 'this non-holiday holiday is actually a job: one to be charged at our usual hourly rate?'

'Plus expenses?' Jane added quickly.

'Yes and yes.' Fennel beamed. 'And you're to bill the client in the usual manner. In fact, apart from this little chat and the request that you give it priority attention, you should treat it in the same manner as you would treat any other of your cases.

'Will we need our passports?'

'No, it's a local job. By which I mean Britain, not overseas.'

'When do we meet the client?'

'You will do so tomorrow in the normal course of business.' He stood and offered his hand, indicating the meeting was over.

'But ... what if we get two or three clients tomorrow? How will we know it's the right one?'

'Oh, I think a couple of sharp-eyed detectives like yourselves will know at once,' he said, holding the door for them.

2

'That was weird,' Jane said as they left the building and walked along Millbank, heading towards Westminster Station. She adjusted the collar of her overcoat. The air was cool, and autumn's approach was already showing in the trees across the road.

'They're all a bit weird in Five,' Matt said, taking a deep breath.

'You've been there before?'

'No, but I have had dealings with them.' His mood seemed lighter now they'd left the building. 'I think it's all those TV and movie portrayals. They have a sort of inflated sense of themselves. They're very much into knowing nods and winks and all that Secret Squirrel stuff when in fact, most of them are just pen pushers.'

'Pen pushers?' Jane grinned. 'Hark at granddad! What's a pen, Gramps?'

'All right then, keyboard clackers.'

'Better, but it's still a bit Nineties.'

'Touch-screen twitchers?'

'I like that!'

Seconds later, one such twitcher collided with them. A tourist, following directions on her phone and not looking where she was going. 'Sorry. I'm so sorry. Do excuse me.' An American accent. Jane wondered if her memories of London would simply be of the different views shown on Google Maps.

'Like Fennel playing at Mystic Meg,' Matt continued. 'What could possibly be wrong with telling us who to expect tomorrow, or when? And you were right to ask about jurisdiction. The boundaries are blurred. There's the Home Office, the Foreign Office, the Security Service, the SIS, GCHQ, the Joint Intelligence Committee – and that's without the police and the so-called "friendly" foreign agencies working here too. Frankly, I don't trust any of them.'

They crossed the road at Great College Street and continued past Old Palace Yard, where the tourist crowds began in earnest. Middle-aged Americans, for the most part. A sea of beige overcoats and blue-rinse hair.

'We could do with a break though,' Jane said. 'It has been pretty full-on since we started.'

In her old job at Bartley's Bank, Jane would have managed at least a few days off over summer, but now, working for herself in her own business – *their* own business – even weekends were becoming something of a luxury. Still, better to be turning work away than having to beg for it. A couple of high-profile cases solved in quick succession had set them up, and their reputation would have soared even higher if the full details of the last one had been revealed to the general public.

'Depends what the job is,' Matt said grimly. 'Why don't they give the job to their own people? We could end up spending weeks in Milton Keynes.'

'Oh God, I spent a month there one day.'

'Or maybe somewhere classy like Scunthorpe or Hull.'

'Oh, shut up!'

'What about Oldham? Gravesend?'

'There's a branch of Bartley's up the road. Perhaps they'd have me back ...'

Matt continued teasing her as they crossed to the station – 'Rochdale? Bradford? Sunderland, perhaps?' – where he was finally and mercifully drowned out by the roar of the Underground.

Emerging at Elephant and Castle, heading back towards Jane's place, Matt ducked into a pound shop and emerged carrying a blister pack of ping-pong balls. Jane groaned. 'Oh, Matt. Not more!'

'She keeps losing them.'

'They're not lost, they're down behind bookshelves and underneath the sofa. Every time I vacuum, I find a cache, and the poor old Hoover practically has a hernia.'

Matt ignored her and patted his pocket. 'Best cat toys ever, pingers.'

The subject of their conversation was waiting for them on the step of Jane's townhouse, right below the brass plaque that read:

Registered office of
Bluebelle Investigations

The tortoiseshell cat from whom the business took its name got to her feet and stretched languidly as they came up the path. To Jane's annoyance, she went straight to Matt.

'Hello, me old flowerpot,' he said, getting down on his haunches and rubbing her ears. 'Guess what Daddy's got for you. Woo-hoo, yes. Look at this ... Lots of fun and games tonight, eh?'

'Don't be fooled, Bluebelle,' Jane told the cat as she reached into her pocket for her keys. 'Men are all the same. He used to talk to me like that, you know.'

'Just let me get one out of the packet ...'

'Those words exactly!'

As she brought her keys out, a card fluttered out with them. Bluebelle lunged for it, bringing it to earth, then pawed it briefly before deciding it was dead. The cat returned to her adoring fan while Jane picked up the card. The front showed it was from one of London's fancier hotels. There was a handwritten message on the back:

To: Bluebelle Investig.

From: Susan Burdon, Room 727.

Plse excuse this intro, but I need help. Am under close surveillance so do not call or approach. At wits' end what to do. Plse, plse help me!

SB

3

Bluebelle – after a nibble of kibble and a disdainful look at the unpacked ping-pong balls – sat on the windowsill cleaning herself and keeping an eye on the new neighbour, a ginger tom perched on the brick wall between the gardens. Matt cooked. Jane paced, a glass of white wine in one hand, the hotel card in the other.

'It must have been that woman who bumped into us on Millbank. The one with the phone.'

'It's not dated,' Matt said. 'It could've been there before.'

'I'd have noticed when I pocketed the keys. Besides, I haven't worn that overcoat in months. In fact, I don't think I've worn it since I quit the bank.'

'She used to dress posh for me once,' Matt told the cat. 'Now all I get is track pants and sweatshirts.'

'That's not true, Matt Healy! I *never* dressed posh for you. Anyway, I thought you preferred my too tight T-shirt and running shorts over a business suit.' She gave him a hug.

'Whoa, yeah. Any day. But ... stop it, woman! ... not right now. Unhand me, damn it. This is a delicate stage of the operation.'

'I had no idea deep frying was such a challenge.'

'Well it is. The temperature has to be just right. Too cool and you'll be eating pink chicken, too hot and it could spontaneously combust and burn the house down.'

'You make it sound like rocket science.'

'Cooking is a sort of science, you know. Or it can be. You only get consistent results—'

'If you work in a consistently boring manner,' Jane finished for him.

'Not quite, but you're getting there.' He grinned and clapped the tongs at her like a pair of castanets. 'Now, if you don't want to dine on Crispy Buttermilk Chicken there's some kibble in the cat bowl. I'm sure Bluebelle won't mind sharing, especially as she doesn't seem very keen on that new stuff. Besides, your overcoat might appreciate it.'

'What?'

'Look.' He held up the bag of cat biscuits. 'It says right there it's good for your coat.'

Jane groaned and shook her head. 'That chicken had better be damn good, Healy!'

It was. Better than good. Jane pushed back from the table with a contented sigh and toasted the chef. 'To consistency.'

He clinked her glass. 'Boring though it may be.'

Sipping her wine, Jane considered the hotel card propped on the table beside them. 'So how do you speak to someone who says you mustn't contact her?'

'Find out if she's real for a start. A quick call to the hotel's reception desk will tell you that.'

'Just what I was thinking. Why don't I do that while you rustle up something for dessert? Consistently.'

'Hey, you're on desserts tonight. Anyway, how long does a phone call take?'

'From a call box? About ten minutes.'

'We do have those things now, Grandma.' Matt gestured to their mobiles lying on the breakfast bar.

'I'd rather use a public phone. More anonymous.'

'Just to talk to the front desk?'

'And ask about a woman who says she's under close surveillance? How would that call be different from one asking to be put through to her room? It's still going to draw attention – to her and the caller. Besides, this could be our new VIP client.'

'Too soon.' Matt shook his head. 'Fennel said tomorrow and "in the normal course of business". This is hardly a knock on the front door.'

Jane picked up the card and studied it again. She had a bad feeling about this, and for a moment was tempted to ignore the plea for help. It would be easy enough to overlook or put it down to some crank or pretend she hadn't seen it. But she couldn't do any of those things. She just hoped she wasn't making a mistake.

*

The little light left in the sky was masked by banks of cloud and the air smelled of impending rain. Jane raised the collar of her jacket. The nearest public phone was by the shops at the top of her road, but that was too close, too convenient, too easy to link with Bluebelle Investigations. So she ignored it and carried on to the main shopping centre.

It was hard to say what disquieted her most about the message: its hurried content, the message itself, or the manner of its delivery. Whoever Susan Burdon was, she clearly knew who they were and where they'd be. It was too much to expect the collision was a chance encounter – that card had been prepared beforehand – which meant Burdon must have followed them.

Jane wished now she'd paid more attention, but she'd been talking to Matt and her guard was down. All she recalled of the encounter was a dark-haired woman focused on her phone, her accent, and her words: 'Sorry. I'm sorry. Do excuse me.' Perhaps that should have alerted her. Most touch-screen twitchers seemed to think their inattention was *your* fault.

Slipping a card into a stranger's pocket would take some skill. A slip-up could see you accused of pickpocketing. She'd done it left-handed too, Jane recalled. Her phone had been in her right hand.

A bunch of young football fans in Tottenham colours hung around the corner by the off-licence opposite the phone, swilling from cans and catcalling at passing cars. Jane gave them a wide berth and crossed the road.

The phone was wall-mounted and open to the elements except for an enclosure so skimpy that it wouldn't even shelter a child. The gunmetal grey keypad hadn't been properly cleaned after someone had been sick on it, and Jane gingerly tapped out the number with her little finger, holding the receiver an inch from her ear as she did so.

'Good evening, Pimlico Heights Hotel. You're speaking with Martin. How may I help you?' The voice was rich and reassuring.

'Oh, hi there.' Jane put on a nasal American accent. 'My name is Abigail Kowalski. I'm looking for a friend of mine. I know she's staying in a London hotel beginning with a P, but I can't for the life of me remember which one it is. Can you believe a brain like mine? Numbers, no problem: room 757. But which goddamn hotel?' Jane laughed uncertainly as the lads across the road bellowed and hooted. Perhaps Martin would think she was in a bar.

'And guest's name, please?'

'Susan Burdon. That's B-U-R-D—'

She heard the tapping of a keyboard, then, 'That's quite correct, madam. You have the right hotel. Would you like me to put you through?'

'No, but thank you. Sue's expecting me. I'll grab a cab and come right over. Thank you so much.'

Jane put the phone down, lost in thought. That part of the story was true, at least. A light rain began falling and a black cab drew up beside her. The driver called through the passenger-side window, 'Need a lift, love?'

Surprised and a little unnerved by the cab's sudden appearance – as if he'd overheard her on the phone – Jane thanked him and declined. Zipping up her jacket, she re-crossed the street and headed home, moving at a modest jog as the rain increased, and thunder rumbled in the distance.

A sudden flurry of stinging rain drove into her face, forcing her to shield her eyes and keep her head bowed. If it hadn't been for that, she might not have noticed the headlights reflected in the puddles up ahead. A car seemed to be keeping pace with her about ten yards behind.

At first, she thought it was someone looking for an address or the cabbie hoping she'd changed her mind, but when she turned a corner and the car turned after her, still keeping its distance, she began to wonder.

Rather than quicken her pace, she slowed instead. It was difficult to judge from the reflections in the shop windows up ahead, but it looked like the car did too.

Pausing at the phone near the top of her road, she pretended to make another call, noting how the car pulled up ten yards behind her. No one got in or out.

After punching the keypad at random, she talked to the number-unobtainable tone, turning idly as if lost in conversation, sweeping the street for a clearer fix on the car. It was parked between streetlights with its headlights on so all she could see of it was its general shape, a sedan of some sort. The headlight's glare and the rain hid its registration plate.

She hung up the receiver, retrieved her phone-card and set off at a brisk pace, crossing the top of her street and moving on at right angles to where she really wanted to go. Twenty yards behind, the car moved off too.

The rain picked up, the night was turning foul, but that was good, she thought, that was to her advantage. It didn't matter now, she was already soaked, a bit more rain wouldn't hurt, but it would reduce the driver's visibility. Besides, she had two other advantages: local knowledge and flexibility.

Her house backed on to a school playground. The school's main entrance was on the far side of the block, but a number of cycle lanes provided shortcuts between the houses. There was one coming up.

She passed it without slowing then began counting her footsteps. *Forty-eight, forty-nine, fifty.* About thirty yards, she guessed. That should do it. She turned abruptly and doubled-back, breaking into a run.

The driver reacted slowly. From the corner of her eye she saw the car's brake lights reflected in the rain. A BMW, dark green, single occupant, four doors. Registration plate still indistinct.

We'll see about that!

Passing the cycle lane at full stride to let him think she really had reversed direction, she then doubled-back a second time, keeping to the shade of an overhanging tree. By now, he'd started a hasty U-turn, his reversing lights clearly illuminating the rear number plate despite the pounding rain.

Only then did she edge away down the cycle lane, repeating the number to herself as she went.

4

Unobserved, Jane watched from the shadows as the car raced past. What would the driver do now he'd lost her? What would she do in his place? Race ahead then pull up somewhere, lights off, disguise his vehicle amongst other parked cars, and hope she'd catch him up perhaps. Or if he'd followed her from her street, go back there and lie in wait there till she returned. *Good luck with that!* she thought, continuing down the tarmac path that led towards the school.

The playing field was muddy and masked by rain, but her general direction was clear enough: a line of lighted houses in the distance. Partway across, stopping in the middle of a particularly muddy puddle with the water overlapping the tops of her trainers, she turned her face to the sky and let the rain run down her cheeks and forehead. It felt glorious, a benediction, even the runnels down her neck and back that made her shiver. A year ago, buttoned up in her buttoned-down life at the bank, she'd never have dreamed she'd be standing out here in the middle of a downpour and revelling in every moment of it. Oh, there were frights and fears in her new life, certainly – like just now – and stretches of routine and boredom. But there was mystery too. Puzzles and challenges, excitement and variety. Right now, she wouldn't swap this muddy puddle for all the comfortable offices in the world. Not only that, she had someone at home waiting for her: a partner and business partner.

Actually, she had two someones ...

One of them regarded her inscrutably as she dropped into the back garden, landing with a soggy squelch. Jane smiled at the feline silhouette watching her from the dining room window as she dusted off her hands. Hardly the right term, she thought, since the "dusting" consisted of smearing the contents of one muddy palm with the other. The sliding door and back door were locked – increased security was one of the minor irritations of living with an ex-policeman – so she knocked and stood back from the step as the outside light came on.

'What the devil ...?'

'Can Matt come out and play, please?' she said, grinning.

'Where the hell have you been, Jane? You said ten minutes. It's been more than half an hour. I tried calling your mobile only to discover it's in the lounge.'

'Seriously, who goes out to a public phone with a mobile in their pocket?' She held out her arms to the falling rain. 'Especially on a night like this.'

'And what are you doing in the back garden?'

'Come out here, and I'll tell you.'

'No way!'

'Go on, you know you want to.'

'Unhand me, woman. You're not just wet, you're filthy!'

'I thought you liked me like that.'

'Ga-aah!' Jane caught his hand and pulled.

Bluebelle watched their antics with a mixture of surprise and curiosity. They were strange creatures. Great providers, purveyors of warmth and shelter, good company when you felt like it, fun playmates too. A great source of massages, rubs and cuddles. And then there were times like this when they went totally out of control. Feline intuition told her there was nothing she could do but wait them out. They'd come in eventually: wet, bedraggled, apologetic. It wasn't always easy looking after humans.

*

Matt and Jane returned to the kitchen after they'd showered and towelled off.

'You missed dessert.' Matt pointed to a bowl on the breakfast bar.

'Apple pie and melted ice cream?'

'You said ten minutes, and I know you like ice cream runny.'

'Not quite *that* runny.'

He looked at the bowl. 'That's odd. I'm sure there was more in it when I put it out.' He looked across at Bluebelle, who was assiduously licking one paw then using it to wipe her whiskers.

Jane saw the direction of his look. 'Oh great. Apple pie with cat-spit flavoured ice cream!'

He picked up a spoon. 'Come on now, eat up.'

'Get off me, you loon!' She laughed, dodging away. 'I'll settle for a cup of tea instead.'

'Let me see if we have any cat-spit flavoured milk ...'

Jane settled at the breakfast bar while Matt put the kettle on. 'Can you get Avery to trace that green BMW?'

'I'll ask, but I don't want to overdo the favours thing. DVLA checks are recorded. He needs just cause to request one, and he really shouldn't be giving out the details to members of the public.'

'We're not members of the public, we're MI5 agents.'

'Not until tomorrow. And then only unofficially.'

'The car was being driven erratically, and the driver was acting suspiciously. How's that for just cause?'

'That'll do.' He paused. 'But the big question is, *why* was he following you at all? Following a pedestrian with a car is a pretty blatant move, especially this time of night with little traffic about. Whoever it was must've realised they'd be spotted.'

'Well?' Jane arched an eyebrow. She could see it was a question for which Matt already had an answer.

'Intimidation. Someone wanted to send you a message. Warn you off.'

'Off what?'

'The only thing I can think of is Susan Burdon.'

Jane had already considered that. Burdon's "collision" had

been carefully planned. The card with her help request had been prepared earlier and was already in her hand. That meant she must have been following them. Not overly difficult in that part of London with the Houses of Parliament and Big Ben forming a mecca for tourists.

'If she was following us while being followed in her turn ...'

'When she bumped into us, her followers guessed the collision might not have been as accidental as it looked ...'

'So they checked us out by following us back here.' Jane thought about the plaque on the front door announcing the nature of their business. 'But then what? Sit around all night and watch the house?'

'Intelligence gathering is all about watching who comes and goes, and when. The fact they moved so quickly suggests they have a team at their disposal.'

'A team?'

'No one can watch a house all night. People need toilet breaks, food, sleep. Believe me, I've done it. You glaze over after a few hours, start missing things, even nod off. Twenty-four-hour surveillance requires at least two people, spelling each other every four hours.'

'Is this it then, the start of our big new case?'

His brow furrowed. 'It's certainly the start of something.'

*

Matt jerked awake, his first thoughts about Jane. Had he disturbed her? She was a light sleeper. Bluebelle jumping on a corner of the bed was often enough to wake her, and, in his dream at least, he'd cried out.

Had he really done so?

Lying in darkness, listening to the regular sound of her breathing, he decided no, it was just that dream again, more vivid than ever this time. Why did his mind keep tormenting him like that? What was it trying to tell him?

He drew another long, slow breath, closed his eyes and tried to relax, but it was a long time before he went back to sleep.

*

Jane woke with a start. Matt had been twitching again and muttering under his breath. She tried to catch his words, but couldn't quite grasp them. It was like listening to a whispered conversation in a foreign language.

Her first thought had been to watch and wait, perhaps even wake him, but it would do no good. Neither strategy worked, and she'd tried both over the last few nights. He'd wake, sweaty and sheepish, saying he'd instantly forgotten whatever it was that was haunting him. Then his eyes would slide away from hers, and he'd put his arms around her and mutter something like, 'Couldn't have been important then, eh?'

But it was, Jane sensed it, and it showed in the tired lines around his eyes the following day. It was something he didn't want to talk about, something he didn't want to tell her, despite their earliest promises to each other.

Suddenly he spoke again, clearly this time. Out loud. Three plaintive words that chilled her despite the mild night and the warm duvet. Then he jerked awake. She could feel the tension in his body, sense it in stillness of the bed. He was holding his breath, listening, checking on her. He knew she was a light sleeper.

She didn't let on, keeping her own breathing slow and steady. No point in trying to force the issue. He would talk about it when he was good and ready. Or perhaps not at all. But she couldn't help the hollow feeling in the pit of her stomach as she turned the three words over in her mind. One of them was a woman's name.

She kept her eyes closed and her breathing steady, but it was a long time before she went back to sleep.

5

Jane left Matt sleeping and wrote him a note. He'd had a restless night. They both had. She fed Bluebelle and was back over the back wall and into the school grounds before first light.

The rain had passed, but the air was still misty and damp. Dressed in running shoes, shorts, T-shirt and a light grey jacket with a hood, she'd already done her stretches and set off across the playing field at a steady pace. She had considered running all the way to the Pimlico Heights Hotel. It would be an easy stretch – around three miles – and she loved London's early morning unpopulated streets, but there was contact to be made once she got there, a delivery, all manner of unknowns. So she relented and took the tube.

Coming out at Victoria station, she got her bearings and headed off at a gentle jog, spying the hotel in the distance. The frontage was all copper-coloured glass and spotlights. A uniformed doorman stood at the apex of a semicircular drive. The backage – was there such a word? – was less imposing, and she felt more comfortable there dressed the way she was.

The rear of the hotel was closed off by a security gate. A couple of early birds stood smoking out the back of the kitchen while a colleague rearranged the wheelie bins. The gate was controlled by a man in a small white hut, and she breezed straight up to it.

'Hi there!' she called in her best American accent.

She startled him, catching him in mid-yawn. A young, bland face looking forward to the end of his night-shift.

'My friend's staying here and left her phone at my hotel last night. I'm heading out for a run and thought I'd drop it off. I wonder if you could get it to her, please?'

Jane took a burner phone from her pocket. They kept half a dozen of them in the office – essential equipment when anonymity was important.

She could see the young man was on the verge of telling her to drop it at the reception desk when she took a twenty-pound note from her other pocket. 'Would that be enough for your trouble?'

The promise of a portrait of the Queen was enough to convince him.

'Er ... yes. Certainly, madam.'

'Oh, great! I even have an envelope. Here.' She pulled out a small padded packet, slipped the phone inside, added her business card, and sealed the self-adhesive flap. It was important he saw what he was accepting. A closed packet could contain anything: drugs, explosives ...

'May I borrow your pen? It's for Susan Burdon in Room 757.' She echoed the words as she wrote out the details in big, cursive letters, adding a personal message below: *Guess what you left behind last night? Love, Bluebelle.*

'Would you see she gets it personally, please? It's got all her stuff on it. You know what phones are like.'

'I don't get off shift till nine.'

Jane waved dismissively. 'Oh, that'll be fine. She's not an early riser. Thank you so, so much!'

She pushed the packet and the banknote through the narrow slot at the bottom of his window, gave him a wave, and headed off. Mission accomplished, she decided to run home.

*

Wednesday morning was a regular workday at Bluebelle Investigations, and a busier one than normal because they had a number of ongoing cases to wrap up, or defer pending the arrival of their mystery visitor. Both Jane and Matt were strict about their time-keeping. Both knew the dangers of working from home in their own small business. "Commuting" might involve simply going up to the office in Jane's spare bedroom, but it was too tempting to take a half-day here or have a lie-in there and tell yourself you'd catch up at the weekend. Keeping timesheets kept them focused, and from the hours they'd been putting in lately – all dutifully recorded – they were certainly due some time off.

'I've written up that insurance investigation,' Jane said. 'The report's on the shared drive. If you check it, I'll get it away this afternoon.'

'Swap you for the Mason case. The guy's got a gambling problem, but there's no evidence of another woman. If Mrs M wants us to continue, it's going to cost her big bucks. Check it out. I've phrased the letter as politely as I can, but you're better at telling people to stop wasting our time.'

Jane laughed as she read through Matt's draft. 'I'm not sure about that final line: "Now sod off!"'

'I shouldn't have used an exclamation point?'

'No, it should be in bold, uppercase italics.'

A rhythmic tapping echoed the sound of Jane's corrections, then a ping-pong ball shot across the carpet and out the door, rapidly pursued by Bluebelle. Their home office did make one concession to its location: it permitted pets – and their playthings.

'See that?' Matt chuckled. 'Best cat toys ever, pingers!'

'Head down, Healy,' Jane growled, grinning herself.

They took a break at 10:30.

'Nothing from Burdon yet,' Jane said, glancing at the burner phone paired with the one she'd delivered earlier.

'Assuming your tame guard didn't nick it.'

'You always assume the worst in people.'

'Years of experience.' Matt took out his own phone and put in a call to Colin Avery.

'Well?' Jane asked, switching on the kettle.

'He's busy on a murder enquiry, but he'll look up the index

number of that beemer when he gets a chance.'

'It's not a problem then?'

'Doesn't seem to be. I think we're still in the NCA's good books after that last bust. He did want to know about our visit uptown, but we don't know what that's about ourselves yet.'

The downstairs doorbell chimed.

'Our mysterious new client?' Jane asked.

'Or someone looking for a parking spot for a green BMW.'

Matt returned, directing a young man in a sharp suit in ahead of him. Jane recognised him at once. The immaculate grooming, the side parting with its comb-over and the long, patrician nose: the young man who'd showed them into Marius Fennel's office.

'Sebastian Harroway.' He extended a hand.

Jane shook it as Harroway looked around the office, and for a moment she saw it through his eyes.

It might only be a temporary office in the spare bedroom of her South London townhouse, but it was still a proper office. Once the business was firmly established they'd look at finding a more suitable space, but in the meantime it was a relatively central location and had the great advantage of being rent-free. They'd furnished it with good secondhand equipment – desks, chairs, credenza, conference table and computers. Even a small fridge and office kettle. What's more, it *looked* like a proper office. The metal filing cabinet was filling with files, the corkboard beside her desk was pinned with maps and papers, and the whiteboard beside Matt's was covered with notes and reminders. Perhaps the old floral bedroom curtains could do with replacing, but that was about all.

Harroway sniffed. Matt gestured to the conference table and he took a seat, but only after inspecting it first.

'How can we help you, Mr Harroway?'

'My uncle is missing.'

'Your uncle?'

'Terrence James Araton, a maternal uncle. It happened ten

days ago. He went missing on a coastal walk in Wales, and nothing has been heard of him since.'

Matt said, 'I take it the police have been informed?'

'Of course. They made enquiries and even sent a couple of searchers to cover the route he took but found no sign of him. He's an experienced walker, was properly equipped, and the weather there has been flawless for a fortnight. There's no chance of him getting lost or falling down a cliff in the fog.'

'Was he travelling alone?'

'Yes.'

'And he's been registered as a Missing Person?'

'By my mother, yes. She's his nearest relative. He's a widower. He and his late wife had no children.'

'Any other close friends or family?'

'My uncle lives for his work.'

'Which is ...?'

'A senior research chemist at Porton Down.'

Jane raised an eyebrow. Porton Down was Britain's most secretive military research facility. MI5's interest suddenly became clearer.

'Do the police know of this connection?' Matt asked.

'I believe so. There was a little initial over-enthusiasm, but my department specifically requested they treat the case as an ordinary missing person. The last thing we want is a public appeal and a blaze of publicity.

'We did consider asking them quietly to upscale their enquiries, but local forces leak like sieves. It would only be a matter of time before the national press got wind of it.'

'There's always the NCA.'

'We're talking Welsh villages, Mr Healy. The back of beyond. The arrival of even a small squad would attract comment and speculation. The last thing we want to do is draw attention to his disappearance.

'As there's a family connection, Mr Fennel thought the next

logical step would be for the family to instigate their own enquiries through a private agency. Your name came up, so here I am.'

'I understand.' Matt took out his notebook. 'Well, let's proceed on that basis then. Is this disappearance out of character?'

'Absolutely. He's a most punctual and punctilious man. He promised to keep my mother informed of his movements every two days, and did so at precisely 7:00 pm each night. At least, up until the Saturday before last.'

'That would be the fifteenth.' Matt glanced at the calendar. 'How, precisely, did he keep in touch?'

'Text messages from his mobile phone. And before you ask, yes, we checked the locations of those calls from the phone company logs, and they all match his planned route.' Harroway took a manila folder from his briefcase and placed it in front of Matt. 'All the details are in there.

'When he missed a call two days later, the Monday evening, my mother wasn't overly concerned. It could have been anything: a dropped phone, a flat battery, out of the cellphone coverage area. But when there'd been no word by the following evening, she began to get concerned.'

'This is Tuesday the eighteenth, two weeks ago yesterday?'

'Correct. She tried his mobile several times, but all calls went straight to voicemail. She left several messages on his home phone too.

'After another day without word, she drove over to his house. She's only an hour away in Bournemouth and has a key. She thought he might have been injured or taken ill and returned home. The place was closed up, and the neighbours hadn't seen him for more than a week. That's when she contacted the police.'

Matt studied his notes. 'So to clarify: his last contact was Saturday the fifteenth – eleven days ago. He missed the Monday evening catch-up call, and was reported missing on Thursday the twentieth?'

'Around lunchtime, I believe.'

'There are no other friends he might have called or gone to stay with?' Harroway shook his head, saying they'd checked all his close contacts. From the sound of his reply, there weren't many. 'When was he due back at work?'

'Next Monday. He had three weeks off.'

'So technically he's still on holiday. His workplace has had no contact, I take it?'

'None at all.'

Matt looked through the file. 'I see your uncle is sixty-one years old. Is he in good physical health?'

'Very much so, yes.'

'No medical conditions?'

'No.'

Jane asked, 'What about his mental health?'

Harroway looked as if his own mental health had been questioned. 'He's perfectly fine. There's no history of depression or anything like that in our family. Obviously, working where he does, those sorts of things are closely monitored.'

'Do you know what he was working on?'

'No idea. He never speaks about his work. Ever. To anyone. It's all TOP SECRET – NATSEN. National Sensitivity,' he added for Jane's benefit. 'His employers are as puzzled as anyone by his disappearance. In fact, they're the ones pressing for a more thorough investigation.'

'Are they?' Jane said. 'Any particular reason for that?'

Harroway frowned. 'He's one of their top people. They look after their staff.'

'So there are no TOP SECRET – NATSEN considerations then?'

'Certainly not. We wouldn't have involved you, an outside party, if there were.'

'I presume you've done checks on his phone and computer usage, bank accounts, car movements and so on,' Matt said.

'All negative. It seems his mobile phone was switched off shortly after that last text to my mother. Computer and bank accounts haven't been touched, nor has his car, which was still in the village where he left it. He was walking a portion of the Wales Coast Path. He's done some of the more northerly segments on previous holidays.' Harroway gestured at the manila folder. 'You'll find full details of the investigation to date in there, along with photographs, contact numbers, his itinerary and so forth.'

'So you want us to go to Wales?'

'That would seem the logical place to start since that was where he was last seen.' Harroway straightened. 'My personal contact details are in the file, but I will, of course, be liaising with Mr Fennel. Is there anything else you require?'

'Just one thing.' Jane leaned across and plucked a printed form from her desk. 'Your signature on our standard Terms of Engagement. I've made it out for a one-week minimum. Usual hourly rates plus expenses.'

'Of course.'

'Do you need a—'

Harroway produced a fountain pen and signed the form without a second glance.

'We'll keep you informed of progress.' Matt rose with him. 'Let me show you out.'

When he came back up the stairs he said, 'I take it that was our premium rate, spy services special contract?'

'Absolutely.'

'Lovely jubbly.' He rubbed his hands together. 'Ready for a holiday in Wales, boyo?'

'You're very cheerful all of a sudden.'

'It's a misper – a missing person. All very straightforward. Trace Terence Araton's movements, talk to people who last saw him and check out the possibilities. No cloak and dagger stuff involved.'

'Still, I have a feeling there's more to dear old Uncle Terry than Harroway was letting on. I mean, why employ us?'

'It's the age of the contractor, Jane. Governments outsource everything these days. Besides, I can understand how a bunch of English coppers turning up and asking questions in a quiet Welsh village would arouse interest.'

'Why? People go missing all the time.'

'You're right. One every ninety seconds on average. And most of them turn up again, days, weeks or sometimes months later. The police don't have the resources to look into every case. The ones you hear about get high-profile treatment: kids, suspicious circumstances, people off their meds ...'

'But not missing weapons scientists.'

'There's no evidence that's what he was working on.'

'Harroway said his employers are keen to get him back, and we both know what Porton Down is famous for. Bombs and guns are amongst Britain's biggest exports.'

'You can't judge a man by his employer. I suggest we familiarise ourselves with that file, finish up here, rent a car and head west ASAP.'

'Except ...' Jane looked at the silent burner phone on her desk.

'Except, nothing,' Matt said. 'Potential clients don't pay bills.'

6

Sally Thompson dropped wearily into the seat opposite Jane, settling her bulk with a sigh. She was seven months pregnant and showing every inch of it. 'I swear, after this I'm giving up men altogether. If Paul comes near again me with that thing, I'll cut it off and throw it in the blender!'

'I seem to remember you saying something similar last time.'

'Yeah, but this time I actually *have* a blender.'

The waitress appeared. 'We have a special today on strawberry smoothies,' she said cheerily, and was slightly perplexed by the strangled snorts from her customers. Both women ordered coffees.

Jane said, 'I have a favour to ask. Matt and I have to go away for a week. Would you mind calling in and feeding Bluebelle?'

'Mind? Nothing would give me more pleasure. Dylan's playgroup's only a mile from your place so I can pop in and feed Bluebelle after I drop him off. And I might just use your house as a refuge at the weekend.'

'Is Paul still on his home-handyman kick?'

Sally rolled her eyes. 'I told him to get someone in, we can afford it, but he's come over all man-the-provider again. He was the same when I was carrying Dylan. I don't mind the hammering and banging, it's all the swearing. And the injuries. He managed to drill into his own thumbnail last weekend.'

'Urgh! Is he all right?'

'He's fine. His thumb's bandaged up like the hitchhiker from hell and he's on antibiotics, but we did manage to give the A&E staff a little variation. They'd had a rush of sliced-off fingertips from mandolines apparently, so this was bit novel.'

'It was an A&E job?'

'Not like the old days either when it was into the car and away. Now there's a car seat to find and secure, a squealing child to catch and placate, a squealing husband to stop bleeding on the upholstery.'

'Oh God!'

'So if I can slip away for a few hours and leave the menfolk to it, it'll be a blessing.'

'I should warn you though, the house is full of ping-pong balls.'

'Ping-pong balls?'

'Bluebelle's latest passion. She bats them all over the place. We're forever fishing them out from under the furniture, and Matt keeps buying more and more. Just be careful where you tread!'

Sally patted her stomach. 'You really think a ping-pong ball is going to unbalance me and this? You'd better tell Bluebelle that if she knocks any my way she'll have to prise them out of the carpet.'

Their coffees arrived and Sally proposed a toast to strawberry smoothies. They both giggled.

'How are things going with you and Matt?' Sally asked.

'Fine. Why do you ask?' Jane was aware she spoke a little too quickly though Sally affected not to notice.

'It's just that you're over the honeymoon period now, and I know what you can be like.'

'I don't know what you mean.'

'You know, the first six months of a new relationship: how the sun shines out of the other person and even the birds seem to chirp his name when he walks by. Then you start to discover all his nasty little habits. Like he cuts his toenails in bed or wears the same pair of socks for a week. Then all the little niggly things start to niggle away at you.'

Jane sipped her coffee and stared into the cup. Sally waited. Eventually she said, 'It's nothing like that.'

'But there is something?'

'He's been having dreams. Nightmares, I suppose, though he won't admit it. They make him twitch and mutter and jerk about in his sleep. It's frightening enough to see it, like he's having a fit. God knows what he must be going through. But if I wake him, or ask him about them in the morning, he always makes a dismissive comment and says he can't remember. He's lying, Sal. I can tell.'

'How long has this been going on?'

'They've got worse in the last few days, but they started a couple of months ago, after our last big case. After Matt came out of hospital.'

'Getting shot by a Russian hit-man would be enough to give anyone nightmares, I'd have thought!'

'Absolutely. Which is why I don't think it's that. He'd just come out and say so if it was.'

'Well, he was an undercover cop for what, fifteen years? Most of them don't last half that time. There must be stuff in his past he's had to do but isn't proud of.'

'We've talked about that too. A lot of it, at least.'

'And you talk about everything, do you?'

'We made a deal at the outset: no secrets. It was Matt's idea. He'd lived half his life concealing things, even from people he was close to. It was like turning over a new leaf for him, a parting of the ways, but ...'

'Old habits die hard.'

Jane sighed.

'And this is everything, is it? You tell each other everything? Past mistakes, past relationships?'

'Everything.' Jane set down her cup. 'He's been talking in his sleep. Muttering and mumbling, mostly. Stuff I couldn't catch. But last night he spoke clearly. He called out in a sort of pleading voice saying, "Please, Penny. No!"'

'Penny?' Sally repeated the name quietly. 'Are you sure?'

Jane nodded.

'Do you know—?'

Jane shook her head. 'But I've been thinking about it. After he was shot, he spent over a fortnight in hospital. One of his nurses, a pretty young thing, was called Penny.'

*

The paired burner phone didn't ring until mid-afternoon, startling Jane with its unfamiliar ringtone. The caller ID showed as "Phone 1", exactly as she'd programmed its mate, so she answered, 'Bluebelle Investigations, Jane Child speaking.'

'Ms Child?' The voice sounded furtive. 'My name is Susan Burdon.'

'Ah yes, I believe we bumped into each other yesterday.'

'Indeed we did. Thank you for getting this phone to me.'

'I must admit I was intrigued by your approach.'

'A necessary precaution, as you may yet discover.'

As I may have already discovered. Jane kept the thought of the green BMW to herself.

'I'm sorry, I can't say too much here,' the quiet voice continued. 'I'm in the Reading Room of the British Library. I wonder if we can meet.'

'Can you give me some indication of what this is about, Ms Burdon.'

'My children. They're in the company of a dangerous woman and a very unpleasant man. And before you ask if I have been to the police, the answer is no, I have not. Number one, because I am an American citizen and don't believe they have any jurisdiction in the matter. Number two, because the man concerned is my former husband and he has, technically at least, legal custody of the children. And number three, because he is attached to the American Embassy here in London where he is ostensibly working as a trade representative. I say "ostensibly" because, in case you are not familiar with the parlance they use, it means he works for the CIA.'

The CIA? Two intelligence agencies in as many days? We're

private investigators, not a club for secret agents!

Burdon continued in her measured tone. 'My husband is having me followed, Ms Child. And God knows what else. That's why I'm being cautious.'

'I'm afraid you've caught us at a bad time, Ms Burdon. We're going to be closed for the next week.'

'Oh, why's that?'

'My partner and I are taking some annual leave, but perhaps I can suggest another agency.' Jane swivelled to the noticeboard where the cards of several other private detectives were pinned.

Burdon said, 'I really would like to meet with you, Ms Child. I'm nervous about saying too much on the phone, but perhaps if you were to hear the full details in a face-to-face meeting ...'

Jane said nothing.

'Please ...?'

'You said you're in the British Library.'

'Yes.'

'Look, I can't come right away, but I may be able to arrange something for this evening.' She checked her watch. 'Most of the reading rooms have study carrels – little booths where you can work in private.'

'I'm right across from some now. But they have to be booked in advance.'

'I have a contact there who may be able to wrangle one for me.' Jane brought up the library's web page. 'The place is open till eight tonight, and the last hour's usually the quietest. I'll book a carrel in the Humanities section and text you the number and time. If there's any problem or change of plan, I'll call you back on this number. All right?'

'That sounds great. Thanks so much. I'll see you this evening.'

Jane hung up, then made a call on the office phone.

'Alistair Downley speaking. How may I help you?'

'You know, you almost sound like you mean that.'

'Jane, darling! How's my second-favourite private dick?'

'Second-favourite?'

'The lovely Matt *has* to get top billing. Any time you're tired of him just flick him my way.'

'Not a chance! Anyway, how's the new job going?'

'Oh God, I can't *begin* to tell you. The bliss, the glory, the delight of working with civilised people!'

'Is that a dig at me and Barry?'

'You two were the only civilised people in that whole fucking edifice. Once you left ... well ... rats and a sinking ship, darling.'

'Barry's still clinging to the wreckage, isn't he?'

'Not very tightly. Between you, me and the gatepost, he too is casting around for a lifeline.'

'Really?'

'Astounding, isn't it? I thought he was like a stick of rock: chop him in bits and it would say Bartley's Bank all the way from his soles to his scalp. But no, your wicked influence has corrupted another stout heart. He too has seen the light; there is life outside that fucking place. *Hallelujah!*'

Jane, Alistair Downley and Barry Tonks had shared cubicle space back in her banking days – which were starting to feel like ancient history.

'Are you allowed to swear in the British Library?'

'I have a proper office all to my fucking self, so I can fucking well say what I fucking well please.' Alistair laughed. 'Besides, the word is Old English or something, isn't it?'

'How would I know? You're the one with all the books.'

'A hundred and fifty million of them, so they reckon.'

Alistair's former role in the bank's Retail Division and his experience with their web platform made him a shoo-in for a senior role in the management of the library's online services.

'Now, tell me how you and the adorable Matt are doing, and when are we all going to catch up again for drinkies?'

Jane lost herself in small talk and banter. It was one of the few things she missed about her old job: the casual camaraderie of colleagues. Hearing Matt's key in the door downstairs brought her back to the real reason she'd called him. 'Look, I need a favour ...'

She waited, listening to the clack of a keyboard on the other end of the line. 'Sorry, darling, booked solid. I could get you one later in the week.'

'It has to be tonight, Alistair. It's very important.'

'Behind on your homework again, eh? Hold on a sec ...' She heard a door open and some background chatter before he came back on the line. 'OK, I'm about to make a newbie mistake ...' More keyboarding sounds. 'There, I've accidentally booked you a Disabled Access carrel for seven o'clock tonight in Humanities, so bring a fucking walking stick or something or they'll disable *me*.'

'You're an absolute treasure, Alistair. *Mwah!*'

'Don't thank me, darling. Get that hunk of yours to do it for you.'

Jane hung up as Matt entered, studying his mobile.

'If that's Google Maps, your desk is three feet to your right,' she said.

Matt frowned. 'It's a message from Avery about that index number from last night. According to the DVLA, that green BMW's a company car registered to some crowd called Anglo-Ameritech Import-Export Ltd.'

'Who are they?'

'I've no idea.' Matt put down his phone. 'Maybe I've read too many spy novels, but a name like that sounds like it's a front for some nefarious organisation.'

'Import-export?' Jane repeated, thinking of what Susan Burdon had said about her ex. 'You mean, someone like the CIA?'

'You can't be serious,' Matt said after she told him about Burdon's call and her plans to meet with her that evening. 'For a start we're not in a position to take on new cases right now. We've got one already, a big important one, remember? We're supposed to be off to Wales this evening. I've got a rental booked and everything. Plus, if this is beyond the jurisdiction of the local constabulary, then it's *certainly* beyond ours. And last but not least, if it really does involve the CIA, I don't want anything to do with it. Those bastards are unscrupulous.'

'Oh come on, they're not going to ship us off to Guantanamo Bay. It's obviously a domestic matter; a marital dispute.'

'They can be the nastiest kind.'

'Anyway, I haven't actually taken the case. I think she just wants to talk to someone, woman to woman. Once I know more about it, I can recommend another agency, but I need to know the details first. Besides, dropping that card in my pocket is such an oddly desperate way to make contact that it's got me curious.'

'You know what that did to the cat.'

'Good job I'm not planning to take Bluebelle then. Look, I know it's going to put back out departure time, but we'd probably spend half the evening sitting in traffic anyway. If we go a bit later we'll get a clean run. And I thought we could stop off halfway, find a nice little inn or something. Bath, perhaps ...'

Matt relented. 'Actually, I was thinking of stopping off partway, but not in Bath. Bournemouth. I'd like to know more about our missing man.'

7

The rental car was parked on the street several doors away. Matt scooted ahead with her bags while Jane said farewell to Bluebelle. 'Aunt Sally will pop in and check on you every day, and we'll only be away a week at most.' She kissed the top of the tortoiseshell head. 'You be a good girl now.' Bluebelle yawned and stretched and made herself more comfortable on the sofa.

After one last check of the windows and doors, Jane followed Matt. She hated leaving the cat. Even an absence of a few days felt like a betrayal. But Bluebelle would be happier at home than going to a cattery, and cats were very self-reliant.

'What on earth ...?' she stopped dead as Matt squeezed the boot lid shut and rushed around to open the passenger door for her.

'Madam's carriage awaits.'

'I thought you'd get a ... a Toyota or something ...'

'That's what I thought too. Then I thought, to hell with it, it's on expenses.'

Jane giggled as she looked over the gleaming red Jaguar F-type with its sunroof down. 'How much?'

'A little under fifteen hundred for the week. I know James Bond drives an Aston Martin, but I thought that might be a bit showy.'

'Well, I have only one thing to say about this ... acquisition of yours, Mr Healy.' He raised an eyebrow. 'If you haven't included me as a designated driver, *you are dead!*'

The trip to the British Library was exhilarating if somewhat chilly as Matt insisted on travelling with the top down. 'It's a sports car,' he told her. 'It's early autumn!' she replied. Still, the admiring looks they got at traffic lights, even in the early evening light, made the discomfort worthwhile. And the heater blowing across her legs helped.

Matt dropped her off at the corner of Euston Road before heading off in search of a car park. 'Somewhere covered. Got to look after Precious,' he said, patting the dashboard.

'I'm starting to feel like an optional accessory in this car,' Jane said, extracting a walking stick from the narrow space behind the front seats.

'Ignore her, Precious.' Matt stroked the centre console before activating the electric sun roof. 'Let's see if we can find you somewhere safe and warm ...'

Technically, the walking stick was a proper forearm crutch with an anatomical grip. It had been cluttering up the hall cupboard ever since Jane had badly sprained her ankle some years earlier, but now, in deference to Alistair's new job, it was proving a useful prop.

The Humanities reading room was on the first floor. Jane checked in at Reader Registration, made her way up in the lift, then hobbled across to study booth B12. The room had an extra-wide door to accommodate a wheelchair but the interior space was tiny, with just enough room to accommodate two people sitting side by side. The walls and adjustable-height desk were a beige wood veneer. Jane took a book from her shoulder bag and settled in to wait.

Matt parked in a basement car park, taking his time keying in the parking bay's number and slotting coins into the machine. It gave him a chance to inspect the two vehicles that had followed him in. Ever since Jane's report of being followed the night before he'd kept an eye out. Not openly. Discreetly. As only a former undercover cop could.

One of the drivers – a middle-aged man from a grey Volvo – joined him at the pay station, remarking on the cost of parking. 'If you pro rata what they charge per hour, you could rent a bloody flat for less.'

'And still have nowhere to park,' Matt said ruefully as he took his ticket. The driver of the other car – a blue Audi – hadn't yet emerged.

Matt put the ticket on the dashboard, locked the doors and ambled towards the lift. As he approached the blue Audi, the driver leaned across to the glove compartment obscuring his face and form, possibly looking for change for the machine. Or possibly not.

Matt's pace didn't falter. He reached the lift, hit the Up button then stepped back, taking himself out of view of the blue Audi. The indicator panel showed the lift was still five floors up.

There was a stairwell to one side, even further out of the Audi's line of sight. Matt snatched the door open and took the stairs two at a time.

Following people in a car wasn't difficult. All you had to do was stay back and remain unobtrusive – ideally keeping one or two vehicles between you and the target. But when the target stopped, when one of its passengers alighted, you were faced with a dilemma: ditch your vehicle and follow them, or stick with the person in the car? Parking being what it was in London, there was no real choice.

Which was why Matt hadn't dropped Jane off outside the library's main entrance – no point giving any watchers a clue to her destination – and why he hadn't opted for the nearest parking building. Racing up the stairs to the exit, he was now reasonably confident neither of them had any unexpected followers.

Someone had left a copy of Mary Shelley's *Frankenstein* in the carrel. Jane was leafing through it when there was a faint tap on the door. The long glass panel on one side showed a stooped woman in a brightly patterned headscarf and grey overcoat. Her dress and posture suggested someone in their seventies.

Jane opened the door, assuming it was the woman who'd left the book. 'Did you leave—?' Her words froze as a much younger, sharper face winked back at her and pushed her way inside.

'Ms Burdon?'

'Ms Child. I saw you arrive. You're not really injured, are you?'

'No, it's just a disguise.'

'I guessed as much. To get the room, right? So is this.' She pulled off her scarf, letting loose an abundance of auburn hair, and squeezed out of the overcoat – not an easy manoeuvre in the tiny space, before bundling both and stashing them in a tote bag. Underneath, she was wearing jeans and a dark blue sweatshirt. 'I changed in the bathroom in case anyone was following me.' She took off her leather shoes, exchanging them for a pair of trainers. 'Keep them guessing, right?'

Jane looked on, bemused by the activity. The woman was in her early forties, lightly tanned, with a firm, no-nonsense figure. Her sweatshirt was baggy, but Jane could see that she was trim and fit. The set of her shoulders, sinewy neck muscles and the firmness of her handshake suggested someone who regularly worked out with weights.

Her complexion was unblemished. She could have passed for someone ten years younger at a modest distance, although up close in the little study booth there was a hint of tautness and artificial stretching about the corners of her mouth and eyes. The result of Botox, Jane guessed. Or possibly more serious, more permanent work.

'Tradecraft.' Burdon stowed the tote bag under a seat. 'They drum it into you so hard it becomes instinctive. Once learned, never forgotten.'

'Does that mean you're also with the CIA?'

'I was. Before I met my husband, now my ex. We were both operational. That's a liability in a couple, so I took a desk job. Then we had a family, and I had to give that up too. The sacrifices I've made for that creep!'

Jane took a notebook from her bag. 'And that's what this is

about, your family?'

'My daughters. Twins aged three, and the eldest aged five.'

'You said on the phone he has legal custody of them.'

'We broke up eighteen months ago. Barty – that's Bartram Horovitz – has friends in high places. What you English call an Old Boy's Club. After the twins, I had a severe bout of post-partum depression. Our marriage was already getting shaky so that really didn't help. Barty was looking for a way out and ended up using it against me.'

'How do you mean?'

'In one or two cases per thousand, post-partum depression slips into post-partum psychosis, a psychiatric condition that can lead to infanticide. Nothing was specifically alleged, he and his friends are too clever for that, but he did manage to have me committed to a mental institution for observation. Having done so, it was easy to convince a judge that he should be granted custody, especially as he'd been offered a senior government position overseas – which is to say, here in London.

'I spent eight months in that damn nuthouse trying to prove I didn't want to kill my kids. Have you any idea how difficult it is to prove a negative? Especially as half the people running the place seemed crazier than the patients.

'I got out four months ago. Since then, I've been trying to put my life back together. It's been difficult. I have no firm proof, but I suspect Barty and his pals have put out the word about me around Washington. I can't even get an interview for jobs I could do in my sleep.

'Naturally, you're sitting there thinking this woman's fresh out of the funny farm, and now she's showing signs of paranoia. Maybe I am imagining it, but from what I've read about you, Ms Child, you're a woman of the world and know how these things work. How the system can close up against you, especially if you're a woman.'

Jane gave her a quizzical look.

'The Trotter case. There was a feature about it in the US edition of *Vanity Fair*. I'm surprised you haven't seen it. There's a full-page picture of you and your business partner.'

Jane had no idea their notoriety had spread that far, but it did explain how Burdon came to recognise them in the street.

'As I told you on the phone, my ex was recently promoted and made deputy head of the CIA station here in London. He pulled some strings and got temporary custody while he was here. His initial term is two years, and that might get extended. The kids are three and five. I'm scared they'll forget all about their mom.' The words were plain enough, but Burdon's expression barely changed as she uttered them, and for some reason Jane was reminded of an actor on the first read-through of a new play.

'He has a new woman,' Burdon continued. 'Brought her over with him. She's from a rich, lawyered-up family, and they all love my kids. I'm afraid they'll steal my girls away from me.'

'What makes you think that?'

'When I called him and said I was coming over and that I wanted to see them, he said no way. He said I couldn't, that this is a foreign country and that if I tried he'd call the diplomatic police or something and have me expelled. Plus, he's had me followed since I landed at Heathrow.'

'How can you tell?'

'The Agency has a long reach. He probably knew I was coming before I arrived. Charges to my credit card, airline tickets; remember, I used to be an operative myself. I spotted someone at the airport, and I've spotted several someones since. Which is why I contacted you the way I did.'

'I must admit your approach was ... unusual.'

'Part of his job here is to train new operatives. I think he's using me as a soft target.'

'You mean, for practice?' Burdon nodded.

Jane was tempted to tell her she was right, but there was something in the woman's manner that made her cautious. Here was a mother desperate to see her kids, yet when she mentioned them there was no catch of the voice or misting of the eyes. She might have been talking about items on a supermarket shelf.

'I'm not sure there's anything we can do for you, Ms Burdon. I'd have to look into the legal aspects first, and that might get complicated. Plus, as I mentioned, we'll be away for at least a week.'

'I understand. Where are you going?'

'Heading west. Wherever the road takes us.'

'Sounds nice.'

No, that was too easy.

'I can recommend someone else to see in our absence though.' She handed Burdon a business card. 'Brickell and Mason are very good, and they specialise in custody cases.' Burdon took it with barely a second glance. 'May I ask how you came to us in the first place?' Jane added.

'Oh, from the *Vanity Fair* piece. I was visiting your Parliament Square and happened to see the two of you go past. I recognised you at once and noticed you went into a building up the street, so I waited around till you came out again. Played the tourist, got a coffee, and wrote that card.

'It was a spur of the moment thing. I don't know anyone here, and I figured I could do with an ally. I'm sorry if my approach was a little unorthodox, but I do appreciate your time and effort.' Burdon rose, dug in her pocket and produced a folded wad of fifty-pound notes.

'Oh. No, that's all right,' Jane said.

'Please. For your trouble.' When Jane refused a second time, Burdon placed them on the desk beside the book. 'I'll just leave them there then. Now, I suggest you give me a couple of minutes in case Barty's trainees have tracked me down.'

'What are their names, by the way? Your twins?'

Burdon held her gaze a moment. 'Did I not tell you? I thought I did. Mary and ... er ... Shelby.'

'Lovely names.'

'Thank you. Goodbye, Ms Child.'

8

Matt paused at the entrance to the reading room, casting a casual eye around the expansive, airy space with its white-painted columns and neat lines of study desks, each with its own downlight. Most were occupied. Some of the seated figures were hunched over, studying, while others sat bathed in the subsidiary glow of laptops or phones. An L-shaped mezzanine floor projected out over aisles of books and a handful of study carrels. More lined the outer walls. Jane had chosen well, he thought. It was a difficult place to surveil. If either she or Burdon had been followed, their conversation in one of the tiny, box-like rooms would be difficult to monitor.

In another sense, however, he couldn't imagine an easier spot from which to watch a target's comings and goings. There were dozens of people about, most of them stationary. To track who the target met and for how long, all one had to do was pull up a seat and pretend to read.

Or lean on the mezzanine railing and pretend to study your phone.

Matt spotted the figure directly across from the carrel Jane had booked. A young man in a beige wind-breaker, check shirt and jeans. Clean-shaven, short dark hair, a faint swarthiness that looked more than a light tan. Southern European, perhaps. Then he glanced up and Matt saw the bushy eyebrows and the set of his jaw. Or maybe Middle Eastern.

Matt found an empty desk and took out his phone.

The library closed at 8:00. Just as the warning chimes sounded at 7:45, the door to carrel B12 opened and a woman carrying a tote bag stepped out, walking away without a glance to her left or right. On the mezzanine, Beige-jacket leaned on both elbows studying his phone more intently. Matt spotted a telltale movement of his hand, a widening motion of thumb and index finger used to zoom the phone's camera. He wasn't interested in the departing figure so much as the other occupant of the little room.

A quick text to Jane – "Stay put!" – then Matt began to move.

He'd already determined the quickest way up to the mezzanine and took the stairs two at a time, but when he reached the top, he saw there was no need to hurry. Jane had received his message. The carrel door remained closed and Beige-jacket was still waiting for his photo.

Matt caught his breath and prepared a second text, only hitting Send as he sidled up to the man. 'Excuse me, but aren't you Bob's brother?'

The man glanced at him without a hint of recognition, the phone still in position.

'It is! Remember me, Dave Armitage.' Matt held out his hand.

The reaction was instinctive. The man straightened, switched the phone to his left hand, and looked directly at Matt.

'Oh no! I'm so sorry. The profile ... it's uncanny ...' From the corner of his eye, Matt spotted movement across the other side. Jane had got his message.

The man spotted it too and made to follow, but Matt blocked him briefly. 'Really, I'm so sorry to have ...'

'No worries,' the man said, edging past him.

American, Matt thought, and began following the man who was now following Jane.

*

After a moment's hesitation, Jane picked up the wad of fifty-pound notes. She'd give Burdon a minute or two to get clear as she'd suggested, and was still thinking about her odd encounter when Matt's first text arrived. Burdon must have been followed despite her precautions.

Jane waited, adjusting the fit of the crutch, one eye on her phone. Then the second text arrived: "Go! Back stairs."

Jane went, moving with no pretence of an injury, and headed for the stairs beside the lift.

From the corner of her eye, she glimpsed a figure in a beige jacket keeping parallel with her as she headed across the mezzanine, moving as though he meant to intercept her. She reached the stairwell ten seconds ahead of him, raced down the first flight, then reached up and jammed the end of the crutch through the metal bannisters.

Beige-jacket didn't spot it till the metal stick caught his outstretched foot. He tripped, made a grab at the railing, missed, fell sideways down six of the stairs and landed heavily on his right ankle.

Matt was seconds behind him. He took in what had happened, leapt over the fallen man and gestured for Jane to carry on.

Jane was still holding the walking stick. She tossed it back up the stairwell, assuming Beige-jacket's need was now greater than her own.

*

Matt paused at a pound store on the way back to the car. 'Not *more* ping-pong balls?' Jane said, but when he came out he tore the wrapping off a cheap pair of side-cutters, explaining the situation as they went.

'Just a backup. In case he's still there.' He handed her the keys.

Jane took the lift, Matt took the stairs and emerged out of sight of the blue Audi. It was still there, its driver still in place.

Jane went to the Jag. The Audi driver straightened and watched as she got in, revved the engine and eased the sleek red car out of its park. The burbling throb of its supercharged V6 echoed off the concrete. That was Matt's cue.

Keeping low, moving between parked cars, he made his way

to the rear of the Audi – which had just started its engine. Taking out the side-cutters, Matt reached through the open spokes of the rear mag wheel and snipped off the tyre valve. The sudden hissing rush was lost amidst the burble of the Jag's engine.

Edging back to the stairwell, Matt straightened and pocketed the side-cutters as Jane drew up level with him. The Audi driver hadn't noticed his sinking rear wheel yet.

Jane sped out of the car park. The Audi followed as far as a judder bar at the exit, took it painfully then stopped.

'You might have cost an innocent man a new tyre,' Jane said, checking the rearview mirror.

'And you might have put an innocent man in A&E.'

They glanced at each other, then laughed.

9

The mid-week streets were emptying of traffic, but Jane kept her focus on her driving and the unfamiliar car while Matt programmed the satnav. They didn't really speak till they eased on to the M25 heading for Heathrow where Jane found an empty lane and floored it. The acceleration pressed them back in their seats before she eased off at just over seventy miles an hour.

'Woo, that was nice!'

'Nought to sixty in 4.8 seconds,' Matt said.

'What's our top speed?'

'A hundred-and-ninety. But don't even think about it with all the speed cameras around.'

'Don't tell me you got the reduced excess but forgot the speed cam waiver?'

'Damn, I knew there was something else!' His grin faded. 'Still, I wish I'd gone for something less conspicuous now – like a white van.'

'That's your East End upbringing coming out. We are *not* going on holiday – even a working one – in a white van. Ever! Understand?'

'We could have brought Bluebelle. And a ton of camping gear.'

'*Or* going camping!'

'If this thing had a tow-bar, we could pick up a caravan.'

Jane hit him.

'Both hands on the wheel, please. You know I'm a nervous passenger.'

'You should be with suggestions like those.'

They drove on into the night as Jane filled him in on her meeting with Susan Burdon. 'She's odd, definitely odd. Not the motherly type at all. She's flown across the Atlantic desperate to see her kids – remember that note? – *Plse, plse, help me!* – yet when I tell her there's nothing we can do at the moment, it's like, "OK, never mind." I gave her Brickell and Mason's card, but she barely glanced at it.

'Plus, I didn't buy the way she claimed to have chanced across us in the street either.' She told him about the *Vanity Fair* article. 'OK, maybe she did see us go into MI5, but we were in there for ages.'

'You think she was deliberately targetting us?'

'Definitely. But why? Oh, and get this. Someone left a copy of *Frankenstein* in the carrel. It was sitting on the bench right where she left the money, and when I asked her what her twins' names were, guess what she said?'

'Not Mary and Shelley?'

'Not quite. Mary and *Shelby*. But the author's name was in an ornate font. I can see how you might make a mistake like that.' Jane drove on. 'She didn't even have photos of them. You know what parents are like, always flashing around pics of their kids. Sally's even got the ultrasound of their second on her phone.'

'So why approach us in the first place?' Matt said. 'If I didn't know about the CIA connection, I'd have shrugged her off as a harmless nutter. But the CIA don't concern themselves with harmless nutters, only dangerous ones.'

*

They stopped at motorway services an hour into their trip. Jane went for coffees while Matt checked out the car. She returned carrying a cardboard tray, two takeaway cups and a large paper bag to find him leaning against the bonnet tossing a black box the size of a packet of cigarettes from hand to hand.

'Look what I found up inside the rear wheel arch.' He held it out to her.

'What is it?'

'A GPS tracker. Magnetic. I couldn't work out why Burdon wanted to see you in person when she knew you were going away. Maybe this is the reason.'

'So she can track our movements? But why would she want to do that?' Matt shrugged. 'Besides, I thought Blue-Audi-Man was tailing us.'

'I suspect Blue-Audi-Man placed this. He was parked up all the time we were away and had a clear view of the car.'

'That's a bit belt-and-braces, isn't it? Tailing *and* a tracker.'

'That's the other thing: he followed us out because the GPS wouldn't kick in till we came up to street level. They don't work underground. Once he confirmed it was up and running, he'd have turned off and let us go our merry way.'

'So you cut his tyre valve for nothing.' Matt made a face. 'Does that mean Blue-Audi-Man is working for Burdon, not the CIA?'

'The library guy was CIA. The one you tripped on the stairs. He wanted to see who she was meeting.'

'Which means that if that green BMW last night was also CIA ...'

'They've now confirmed she contacted us,' Matt said, finishing her sentence for her.

'Well, whoever she is and whatever she's up to, she's still one step ahead of them.'

'Or thought she was.' Matt went over to a parked delivery truck, glanced about to see he wasn't observed, then reached underneath briefly before coming back empty-handed.

Jane settled the cardboard tray on the Jaguar's sunroof and passed him a coffee. 'So we'd have been just as conspicuous if you'd rented a white van.'

'Would've made it worse, actually. A lot more places to search.' He patted the car. 'See? I told you Precious was a good investment.'

*

Susan Burdon looked down on the lights of London from the balcony of Room 727 of the Pimlico Heights Hotel, sipping from a bottle of tonic water. The minibar had a selection of more intoxicating drinks, but this was all she'd allow herself.

Overall, she judged the evening a success. Jane Child had been all she'd expected: lively, smart, quick on the uptake, and nobody's fool. And her partner, Matthew Healy, was clearly no slouch either. According to the report from Reaves – a sealed envelope slipped under the door of her hotel room – he'd quickly spotted and dealt with one of Barty's boys in the British Library. Apparently, the kid was limping and leaning on a crutch when he finally emerged from the building. Burdon smiled. Even Reaves' tubby sidekick had come through too, despite getting a flat tyre.

Returning to the laptop open on the desk beside the sliding door, she took another swig of tonic water and entered the pass-phrase to a special Virtual Private Network. The added encryption and layers of security protocols slowed down the hotel's free Wi-Fi, but they ensured no one else could see her traffic.

Interesting, she thought, studying the screen. They were taking the M3, not the M4, which meant they were doing exactly what she'd expected them to do. It was a logical diversion, almost certainly an unnecessary one, but they were still her best chance of finding what she was seeking. If anyone had the wherewithal to locate Terence Araton with the least amount of fuss, it was those two.

And once they did? Well, omelettes, broken eggs and all that. Her instructions were very clear: there must be no one left alive to connect her to Araton.

*

Matt blinked awake. Light. Where was that coming from? Then Jane leaned across him, the ends of her long auburn hair tickling his arm. He rolled on to his back and looked up at her.

'You OK?'

'Yeah, why? What was I doing?'

'Talking in your sleep. Twitching. It looked like you were having a nightmare.'

'No, no, just ... dreaming.'

'Well, it didn't sound like a pleasant one.' She traced the scars on his chest. Scars on top of scars now.

He blinked. 'Funny, it's all slipped away now. What was I saying?'

'Just mumbles and grunts. Nothing I could make out.'

Except you mentioned Penny again.

He sighed.

'Are you sure you can't remember anything?'

He shook his head.

'You would tell me, wouldn't you? If anything was bothering you?'

'Of course.' He reached up and drew her close.

Only then, as she nestled against him, did he furrow his brow and bite his lip.

10

The idea of the Barleycorn Loft was intriguing, but its execution left something to be desired. Jane woke with a crick in her neck, and Matt nearly knocked himself unconscious returning from the bathroom.

'Oh, God! Are you all right?'

He slumped onto the mattress beside her holding a hand against his forehead. 'I really did see stars there for a moment.'

'Come here, let me see ... Well, the skin's not broken.'

'Great. So I won't bleed to death, just die from internal injuries. And ...' he fidgeted, '... it won't be a comfortable death.'

'You're right about that. This straw mattress is rubbish. And woollen blankets instead of a duvet? I think they've overdone the "Ye Olde England" thing. Giving the punters a taste of what a sixteenth-century inn was really like doesn't mean you can't supply an electric heater.'

'Or a beam-free ceiling.'

'That's your fault. You shouldn't be so tall.'

'You're right, I should stop that immediately.' Matt lay back, staring up at the underside of the thatched roof and the heavy oak timbers that supported it. They were blackened with age, split in places, but as hard and cold as steel to the touch. 'Seriously though, were they all bloody midgets when Shakespeare was around?'

Jane cleared her throat theatrically. 'I believe the correct term is *vertically challenged*.'

'I do beg your pardon. I'll rephrase that: Were they all bloody midgets when vertically-challenged was around?'

'Hmm,' Jane said, bending over him. 'There seems to be some damage to the political correctness cortex. I think I'd better give you a thorough physical, Mr Healy.'

He groaned. 'Oh, if you must ...'

Sometime later, flushed and fully recovered, they made their way down to breakfast to be greeted by their host, a jolly, rubicund man who, despite his middle age and thinning hair, reminded Jane of a cherub.

'Good morning, good morning! How was the loft? Everything to your satisfaction?'

'Fine, thank you,' Jane said.

'And you slept well?'

'Perfectly, thanks.'

'Splendid, splendid.'

They took a table by the window. Matt gave her a disapproving look as their host moved on to interrogate another set of guests. Jane shrugged. 'I won't actually make a complaint. I'll just moan about it for the rest of my life.'

He nodded. 'Fair enough, I suppose. It is the English way.'

*

Bluebelle was sunning herself on the front doorstep when Sally Thompson arrived, looking forward to five hours of freedom. Dylan's thrice-weekly playgroup sessions – Wednesday to Friday – were to give her time for grown-up pursuits like catching up with former colleagues or continuing the advanced online marketing course she'd begun in a flurry of optimism shortly after discovering she was pregnant for the second time. Today, she had an assignment to complete and cursed her lack of foresight at not bringing her laptop with her. She could have kicked back at Jane's place, finished the assignment, then leisurely collected Dylan at 3:00 pm. Instead, she'd have to shuttle madly back and forth through London traffic.

Bluebelle regarded her remotely as she hurried through the

gate. 'Yes, yes, I know. Breakfast's late today, but look on the bright side. We'll make up for it with an early dinner when I collect Dylan.'

The cat yawned and stretched and moved aside as Sally unlocked the door, then bustled in ahead to get to her food dish. 'Anyone would think you'd been locked out all night!'

Bluebelle had two cat flaps – one in the front, one in the back – but much preferred to let tame humans do the opening and closing of the main doors for her. From a cat's perspective, they must seem like the automatic doors in office buildings, Sally supposed.

Bluebelle reached the kitchen, glanced at her food dish, then shied away as if it formed the opposite pole of a magnet. She turned back to Sally and began rubbing around her legs.

'You are a trier, I'll give you that,' Sally told her, squatting awkwardly to retrieve the dish before topping it up from a packet in the pantry. 'But this is all they've left you. Here.'

She replaced the dish. The cat eyed it disdainfully then shied away again.

'Sorry, I don't have time to debate the matter,' Sally said, thinking of her assignment. She gave Bluebelle a quick pat and hurried out again.

*

Matt drove with the sunroof down, taking a circuitous, scenic route to their destination. They'd lingered over breakfast, browsed the shop windows of the tiny village where they'd spent the night, then moved on a few miles and stopped at another thatched-roof town for morning tea and scones on the village green. It already felt like a proper holiday.

Matt stuck to the quieter B roads. The day was sparkling fresh with pockets of coolness in the shadows and beneath the branches of overhanging trees. Jane tilted her seat back and looked straight up as they passed beneath a long avenue of maples, sunlight filtering and flashing through green leaves already edged with the gilding of autumn.

Back on the A338, they hit roadworks and a long tailback on the road into Bournemouth. Matt puffed and snorted at the delay. Jane took out Araton's file and studied the photograph on the inside cover of a mild, shaggy looking man with unkempt hair and a beard. He wore round wire-framed glasses and had the air of someone whose thoughts were elsewhere.

There were more photographs of the inside of his house taken by the search team – for what purpose she couldn't imagine. They showed a sparsely and somewhat randomly furnished home. It was tidy and neat, but clearly a house too big for a single man as he seemed to have confined himself to a handful of rooms and abandoned the rest. She recalled Sebastian Harroway's words about how his uncle lived for his work.

Matt glanced at her as she drew the page closer and squinted at one of the pictures. 'Trying to read what's in the bottom corner,' she said. 'The photocopying's not great. I thought it was a date, but it can't be. It looks like 10/10 or 10/18. Same on all the shots. Must be a job number or something. I wonder who took them?'

A toot from behind alerted Matt that the traffic had moved on all of six feet, and there was now a gap in front of them that must be closed up immediately. He sighed and inched forward.

Jane turned the page then started flicking backwards and forwards between two separate sections of the file. 'That's odd. The text message log is incomplete.'

'What do you mean?'

'This part's got copies of the messages to and from his phone, but it doesn't match up with the metadata.' She turned to the back of the file. 'Here, for example. Thursday the thirteenth, a week before he was reported missing. The metadata shows he sent three messages to his sister that evening, at two, six and eleven minutes past seven, yet the log only shows the first one. "19:02 Good progress today. Eleven miles. Weather glorious." To which she replied a minute later, "I look forward to seeing the photos."'

'Must be an oversight.'

'Must be. There's also a number here with no caller ID. Someone who called repeatedly in the days before he disappeared. The first time it looks like they left a message, see? "Status: unanswered. Duration: 0:42." But the rest of the calls are all unanswered with a duration of around fifteen seconds.'

'And Araton never called them back?'

Jane turned the page and ran her finger down another printout. 'Nope.'

'Well, we can ask Jean Harroway about the missing texts, at least. She may still have copies on her phone. *If* we ever get through this bloody traffic!'

*

Their destination was a modest, well-presented house with a long front garden behind a dry stone wall. Jane had called ahead – the traffic only slightly delayed their projected arrival – and Jean Harroway opened the front door to them as they walked up the path. A pair of red setters bounded out around her to provide a lolloping escort.

'Claudio! Cosworth!' She called them to heel, and the dogs responded immediately.

Harroway ushered them through a house smelling of primroses with an undertone of dog and out to a paved patio at the back where the long garden continued down a slight incline to a leafy stream.

'What a lovely spot,' Jane said.

'The dogs like it,' Harroway replied indifferently.

She was a fine-boned, thin-lipped woman with the same patrician nose as her son. She wore brown slacks, a white blouse, and an old tweed jacket with a pair of secateurs in the breast pocket, but despite the informality, Jane sensed an air of preparation about her. The fine grey hair was brushed and set just so, and the lipstick and powdered cheeks seemed a little too much for a casual day in the garden.

The dogs lolloped off as Jane and Matt were directed to seats around an ornate metal table. The white-painted iron chairs were heavy, and scraped against the concrete paving stones as they made themselves comfortable. No sooner were they settled than a young woman appeared bearing a wooden tray laden with cups, saucers, teapot, milk jug, and sugar bowl. Perhaps it was heavier than expected because she set it down smartly and earned a look of rebuke from her mistress.

'Thank you, Maria. That will be all for today. You may go now.'

The young woman looked surprised. 'But your lunch, and the ironing, Mrs—'

'I can manage. And don't worry, I'll sign your sheet for the full morning.' She turned back to her guests. 'My day help,' she explained as they heard the front door close.

They took their tea in china cups. There was no question of them not taking tea. There were no other options, and they weren't even asked.

'I'm not sure what more I can tell you. I understand from Sebastian that you have all the details of my brother's disappearance along with the report I made to the police.' Jean Harroway's words were addressed to Matt. A typical assumption, that the man was in charge, and it might have irked Jane if it hadn't presented her with an opportunity.

'Oh, sorry, I left the file in the car.' She gestured at the house. 'Do you mind if I duck back through and get it?'

Jean Harroway gave her the same dismissive wave she'd given the day help.

Jane retrieved the file and found Maria unlocking a rusty bicycle propped against the dry stone wall. 'Early finish today then?' The young woman wrapped the plastic-coated chain around the bike's seat post and nodded. She was about eighteen, with dark eyes and thick, dark hair that showed a liveliness and life of its own despite its short cut. 'Is that unusual?'

She shrugged. 'Make up for all the time she keep me late. The agency say I should finish at one o'clock, but sometimes it is half-past or more, and she will not sign for extra. Say I am too slow.' Her English was good, her accent slight. Spanish or Italian, perhaps.

'My name's Jane Child. I'm a detective.' Jane handed her a card. 'Would you mind if we spoke later?'

'What about?' Maria glanced back at the house.

'Just a little background about the family. Have you worked here long?'

'Over one year.'

'Would it be all right if I gave you a call? I can't really talk now, my tea's getting cold, but maybe later?'

Jane took her number and returned to the house, taking her time to examine each room she passed through. The framed photographs in the hallway, the plushly comfortable sitting room, the kitchen with its marble worktops. Outside, Matt said something and she heard Jean Harroway laugh politely. That was her cue. If he was playing Good Cop, there was only one role left.

She took her seat and flicked through the file, drawing out a copy of the Missing Persons report. 'I understand your brother texted you every two days. Was that usual when he went on holiday?'

Jean Harroway gave her a haughty look. 'He liked to keep in touch, that's all.'

'That wasn't quite what I asked,' Jane said gently.

'My brother and I have always been close. We lost our parents when we were young, and since Terence lost his wife, we've become closer. There's no one else in his life. We normally speak or text or exchange emails every day. Two days was a sort of holiday joke. Besides, he loves walking the wilds, and one can't always get a signal in out-of-the-way places.'

'Yet you left it four days before you reported him missing. He should have texted you the Monday before last, the seventeenth.'

'I thought there might be some problem with his phone or the signal. The places he was going aren't exactly on the beaten track.'

'But you didn't hear from him, did you? Or the next day, the Wednesday, when there should have been another two-day call.'

'That's why I drove up to check his house last Thursday. I thought he might have taken ill and gone home early. He can be like a bear with a sore head when he's unwell. He hates company and sympathy and fuss. But when I found the house empty and still couldn't reach him, that was when I contacted the police.'

'You drove all the way to Salisbury to see if he was there?'

'It is only an hour.'

'You didn't try emailing or calling him first?'

'Of course I did. Several times. But my calls and messages went unanswered.'

'Was that normal?'

'Possibly. As I said, if he's unwell he retreats into himself. He dislikes fuss and attention.'

'Still, you had no real reason to expect he'd be there, yet you drove up anyway.'

'It was ... something to do. I was concerned. Anything might have happened. He lives alone. I hope you're not suggesting I'm somehow involved in my brother's disappearance.'

'My colleague is just trying to get a fuller picture of events,' Matt said soothingly.

Harroway sniffed. Jane persisted.

'What about the texts you exchanged while he was on the walk? The file contains metadata about the calls – the times sent, the sending locations and so forth – but the message content didn't come from the phone company, did it?'

'No, I provided that myself.'

'Is that the full content of the messages you exchanged?'

'What do you mean?'

'Looking through the file, it seems there were other messages that haven't been documented.'

'The rest were just chitchat. Family matters. Things that couldn't possibly concern the police.' Despite her smooth response, Jean Harroway coloured slightly.

'Would you mind if we looked at the full content of those exchanges?' Jane asked.

'I most certainly would! Those messages are private. They're nothing to do with you or anyone else. What possible relevance could they have?'

'We're not just looking for your brother, Mrs Harroway. We're also looking into reasons why he might have disappeared.'

'Are you suggesting he has deliberately absented himself?'

'It's not unheard of.'

'That's ridiculous! He's a middle-aged man, sound in mind and body, not some flighty teenage girl who runs off to London after a row with Mummy.'

'So there is nothing in those messages indicative of a troubled state of mind or suggesting that he might go on somewhere else?'

'No, and no,' she replied firmly. 'If there had been, I would most certainly have informed the police. Look, he knows that coastal path, he's walked it before, and he very clearly didn't go anywhere else. They found his car exactly where he left it.'

Jane nodded. 'They did, yes. I'm sorry for the questions, Mrs Harroway, but we need to get as much background information as possible. We are all on the same side, and we're as keen as you are to find him.'

The older woman pursed her lips and blew out of her nostrils, but seemed to accept Jane's climb-down. That was Matt's cue.

'So you went to his house in ... Plover Place last Thursday,' he said, glancing at the file. 'Can you tell us about that, please?'

'What do you want to know, precisely?'

'Everything. From the moment you arrived, which was just after eleven, I believe.'

'Yes, I remember because the news on Radio 4 was just finishing as I pulled up the drive. I could see he wasn't home right away. No car. He doesn't have a garage, you see. But I thought he might have popped up to the shops, so I let myself in.'

'You have a key?'

'We both do, to each other's houses. As soon as I opened the door I could tell he hadn't been back. The mail was piled up in the hallway. Still, I checked the house. There was no sign of him. That's when I went to the police and reported him missing.'

'That was the Stratford Road station?' Matt asked, studying the file.

'It's the nearest one to his house.'

'How far away is that?'

'About a ten-minute drive.'

'What did you do in the interim?'

'I beg your pardon?'

'The Missing Persons Report is timed at ten minutes past one. You said you arrived at your brother's house just after eleven. If the station's only a ten-minute drive away, that leaves a two-hour gap.' Matt's manner and voice were mild, but Harroway coloured again.

'Oh, I ... um ... well ... of course, I didn't go there right away. I wanted to check first. To be absolutely sure. So I spoke with his neighbours in case they'd seen anything, and ... and phoned his work number thinking he might have been called in on an emergency or something.'

'Who did you speak with?'

'No one. He has his own office with a direct line. I just got a voice message saying he'd be back on the thirty-first. I left a message and hung up.

'I wasn't sure what else to do, Mr Healy. It's not an everyday occurrence, is it, a loved one going missing?'

'No, I understand. And after you filed the Missing Persons report?'

'I drove back here. I was in a bit of a daze, to be honest. His work called when I was halfway home. Someone from their security department.'

'His work? I thought you just left a message?'

'I did. I never spoke with anyone. I suppose the police must have contacted them. They seemed to know all about the report. But there was nothing I could add.'

'You don't happen to recall who called you?'

Harroway shook her head.

'Do you know what your brother does at Porton Down?' Jane asked.

Harroway bristled. 'He isn't at Porton Down, not in that place anyway. He works for DSTL – the Defence Science and Technology Laboratory. He has a PhD in chemistry and does a great deal of research work. Beyond that, I couldn't say. He's not permitted to speak about his work and never does. And I never ask.'

Matt and Jane exchanged a glance. Jane closed the file.

'Well, thank you for taking the time to see us, Mrs Harroway,' Matt said. 'And thanks for the tea.'

They got to their feet, and she followed them through the house, seeming to relent a little as they approached the front door. 'If there is anything else I can do ...'

'Actually, there is one thing. Would you mind if we borrowed your key and had a look around your brother's house?'

'What on earth for?'

'We're heading past there anyway, and it might help us get a fuller picture of the man himself. Background, interests, hobbies, that sort of thing. A wall covered in hip-hop posters suggests a different personality to one lined with bookshelves, for example.'

She gave him a sceptical look but took a key from a peg beside the coat rack. 'I can assure you my brother's house is *not* papered with hip-hop posters. Good day, Mr Healy.'

As they walked back up the path, Jane said quietly, '*I* didn't get a goodbye.'

'That's because she's rattled,' Matt whispered as dog barks saw them out, and the door closed behind them. 'She's hiding something.'

11

Mick Rosten wasn't sure what he was doing in Bournemouth, but the call had come in early, and Reaves had shouted a lot.

'Where the hell did you stick that tracker?'

'Up inside the left rear wheel arch,' Rosten replied calmly. 'Exactly as you suggested. And I confirmed it was operational when they drove off.'

'It's fuckin' operational, all right. They're going all over bloody Hampshire, and have been since seven o'clock this morning.'

'So?'

'The client's suspicious. Wants me to check 'em out. Reckons they *should* be heading for Bournemouth, so get your arse there pronto. I'll text you the address.'

Rosten, who was only a sub-contractor on this job, sighed as he hung up the phone. Technically, that made Reaves his boss, but he'd never liked the young punk. The kid was full of himself. One of those people who thought the way to make an impression was to throw their weight around and shout a lot. Rosten preferred a softly, softly approach. He was slow to anger, but when something did finally rile him he'd lash out. As a certain sergeant on the police force had discovered to his surprise. That little slip-up had cost Rosten an unremarkable but steady career, so here he was now, a freelance "security consultant", working for a little prick like Reaves.

At times like this, he reminded himself of the advantages of his new career. It was varied, the hours might be unsociable but the money was good – always cash-in-the-hand so none of that tax or

VAT nonsense – and occasionally you got cruisey rides like this late-model Audi. The drive was as smooth as silk and the seats seemed to be made for a man of his generous proportions. Electrically adjustable and electrically heated too. So an early morning run to Bournemouth wasn't much of an imposition.

As he turned into the quiet country lane and the in-car GPS told him his destination was four hundred feet away on the left, he spotted the red Jag nearby, swung into a car park and stopped.

After double-checking the index number he called Reaves. 'OK. They're here. Where are you?'

'Gosport!'

'What are you doing there?'

'I'm following a fucking delivery van trying to get my fucking tracker back!'

'What?'

'And when I do, I'm going to shove it so far up your fat fucking arse that—'

'A little professionalism, please, Roger.'

The line went quiet.

'Don't *ever* call me that,' Reaves said in a low voice.

'Why not? It's your name, isn't it?'

He'd arrested the young punk once, back in his former life, though Reaves didn't remember him. Rosten knew all about the loathed Christian name and how he told people to refer to him as "The Reaver", (no one did), or his second preference being for his surname. With a policeman's knack for needling a suspect, he'd quickly discovered that using "Roger" was a sure-fire way to get the young punk's attention.

Rosten spoke into the silence on the line. 'Now, as I told you, I put the tracker on the Jag last night and confirmed it was operational.'

'*Where* did you put it? In the middle of the fucking bonnet?'

'I told you that too if you'd been listening. They must have found it.'

'How?'

'Maybe they got a flat tyre.'

'Yeah, well, you'd know all about that, wouldn't you?'

'They're here, now, and you're in Gosport. And I'm awaiting your instructions, oh mighty leader.'

'Fuckin' obvious, isn't it? Stick with 'em! Don't let 'em out of your sight till I catch up with you, all right?'

'Understood.'

Rosten hung up, smiling. The young punk sounded like he was about to burst a blood vessel. Just then, Matt and Jane emerged from the target address, closing the gate behind them.

*

Matt drove as Jane counted off the unexplained items on her fingers. 'First, there's the text messages. Jean Harroway says the missing content is just family stuff, but if it's so innocuous, why won't she let us see it? It's got to be more than "The bathroom needs repainting" or "The dogs have uprooted the dahlias". And that's important. It gives us a clue to his state of mind. If they had a row, maybe he did toss himself off the Welsh equivalent of Beachy Head.'

'Agreed,' Matt said.

'Second, why did she drive to his house if she wasn't getting answers to her calls or emails? She seems to know his neighbours. Why not call one of them and have them check the place out? And that business about them texting or talking or emailing every day strikes me as a bit odd. I've got brothers, and I barely contact them once a month.

'Third, there's the two missing hours between her arrival at his house and going to the police.' She closed her eyes, trying to picture the scene. 'You push open the door through a pile of mail, call out just in case, then check all the rooms. That's two minutes, tops. It's obvious he's not there so you ask the neighbours; say, one either side and two across the road. That's, what, no more than twenty minutes? Especially if you keep drawing blanks. Then a call to his work, leave a message, then drive to the police station. She said herself it's only ten minutes away. That leaves at least an hour unaccounted for.'

'There is the shock factor. The plain old not-knowing-what-to-do.'

'Jean Harroway doesn't strike me as the dithering type. Anyway, she must have been bracing herself on the drive up. The whole reason she went was because she half-expected to find him stretched out dead from a heart attack or something.'

'And finally, why did she chase her home help away the moment we arrived? The girl told me she usually works till one. It's like Mrs H didn't want us talking to her.'

'Maybe she didn't want the girl listening in.'

'Again, why? What could be scandalous about a missing brother?'

'Hopefully, we're about to find out,' Matt said. 'Oh, while you were out chatting to Maria, I enquired about Mr H. There is one. Husband's name is Philip, and he's been out of the country for the last few weeks.'

'Doing what?'

'You ready for this? Selling weapons systems to Saudi Arabia.'

'What a family. The son's a spook, hubby sells bombs, and brother plays with chemicals in a secret weapons lab!'

'Speaking of spooks, I was thinking about those missing texts. We can probably get them from the phone company via MI5. I'll give Sebastian Harroway a call. And didn't you say something about an unidentified number?'

Jane flicked the folder open. 'This one: blah-blah-7453. They called five times in a row over a period of two hours, but Araton never replied.'

'Calls or texts?'

'Calls. First time it looks like they left a message. There were a couple more calls that evening, and two the following day, but the only number Araton called was his sister's.'

'What day was that?'

'Friday the fourteenth, a couple of days before he disappeared. The first call came in at 09:03 – he might have been out on the trail by then – but the last one that came is timed at 23:17.'

'Sounds like someone was keen to get hold of him.'

'So much so they tried again at 06:53 on the Saturday morning. Then at regular intervals throughout the day.'

'But he never replied.' Matt tapped the steering wheel thoughtfully. 'Interesting. Does the police report make any reference to that number?'

'Ah, good thought.' Jane rifled through the pages. 'Here we go: "Caller excluded from enquiries".'

'Without saying who the caller is? Now that *is* interesting.'

'Why?'

'Look at the wording. They say "excluded", not "eliminated". A witness is eliminated from enquiries if they have an alibi. The only people ever excluded are other law enforcement agencies.'

'So ... you think it might have been the police or MI5?'

'I really don't know.'

'It could have been Sebastian, I suppose. But why use a work phone to call his uncle?'

'And at eleven o'clock on a Friday night?' Matt drove in silence for a while then slapped a hand on the steering wheel. 'Something else just occurred to me. Susan Burdon claims she happened to spot us going into a building not far from Parliament, then hung around and waited for us to come out again.'

'So?'

'She's not stupid. She had a mobile phone and Google Maps. She must have known where we were.'

'You mean Thames House? MI5's HQ?'

'Their location's not exactly Britain's best-kept secret. And she is ex-CIA.'

'OK, but what does that mean?'

'I don't know, it's just ...' He sighed. 'It's like that "caller excluded" business. There seems to be too much spy stuff in this case.'

The satnav directed them to a whitewashed stone building with a cafe on the ground floor and flats above. Jane spotted Maria's bike chained up outside, then the young woman herself sitting at one of the tables. She'd changed out of her day-help smock into an embroidered cotton blouse and jeans. She recognised their car and waved.

'My flat is small, the day is nice, so ...' she gestured them to seats. 'Is OK to talk here? Not busy at this time. I work here in the evening, sometimes very late, so is convenient, yes?'

'Very,' Jane said. 'I really wanted to ask you about your other employer, Mrs Harroway.'

'Of course. For her, I work more than one year now. Three mornings every week.'

'What do you do, exactly?'

'Clean, tidy, hoover, laundry. Can get messy with the dogs, especially winter time with the muddy paws. Also, make her lunch and sometimes food for the evening. Things she can put in oven or heat in microwave.'

'What about Mr Harroway?'

'Often, he is not here. Away much. Only home some weekends, so I do not see. Since I work there, I meet him maybe five, six times.' Her face dimpled with a shy smile. 'I only recognise him because there are photos I must dust.'

'What about her brother, Mr Araton?'

'Mr Terence? Again, I do not meet much, but he come regular. Two, three times some weeks.'

'Weeks, not weekends?'

She nodded, colouring slightly. 'I must make up the spare room, but he is very clean, tidy, does not make mess. He does not live far, I think.'

Matt glanced at Jane. She could tell what he was thinking: far enough.

'So Mr Araton and Mrs Harroway are close?'

The young woman looked down at her hands. 'I think ... yes. At first, I did not even know he is the brother.'

Sensing her hesitation, Jane asked, 'Who did you think he was?'

'Maybe family friend or ...' She left the sentence unfinished and looked down at her hands again. 'Then one day I see them in the garden from the upstairs. They do not see me. First, they argue. Then stop, make up. Then ... they ... hold each other close and kiss most passionate. Long time. With tongues.'

12

'*Eew!*' Jane said as they returned to their car. 'Just ... *eew!*'

'Gives that phrase "a close family" a whole new meaning,' Matt remarked as his phone rang. He checked the caller ID and added, 'Our new client,' before putting him on speaker-phone. 'Good morning, Mr Harroway.'

Sebastian Harroway spoke without preamble. 'I understand you just visited my mother.'

'That's correct. We're building up some background on your uncle.'

'I wish you'd spoken with me first.'

'Oh, why's that?'

'She's in a delicate state at the moment. My uncle's disappearance has hit her hard ...' Jane made a face '... and I don't appreciate her being cross-examined.'

'It was hardly a cross-examination.'

'That's not what she told me. There were implications she withheld information from the police. That she might even be involved in my uncle's disappearance.'

'I can assure you there were no such implications, Mr Harroway, and if she took it that way, it was certainly not our intention.'

Jane held up the file and pointed to the texts. Matt shook his head as Harroway continued.

'My mother's currently seeing the doctor for her nerves, Mr Healy. She's taken all this rather badly. It seems she blames herself for not alerting the authorities sooner.' The pitch of Harroway's voice fell as if he was running out of steam. 'If you'd spoken with me first, I could have warned you to tread carefully.'

'I'm sorry now we didn't,' Matt said. 'Please pass on my apologies if she took things the wrong way, but my colleague did tell her we're all on the same side. That we all want to find her brother.'

Sebastian Harroway muttered something indecipherable and hung up. 'You didn't ask him!' Jane said.

'No, for two reasons. If he hasn't noticed the discrepancy, and the missing texts do contain hints of what we think they contain, it's a hell of a way to find out. And if he does find out – or if he already knows – he's hardly likely to tell us, is he? "Oh, by the way, Mummy and Uncy are at it like knives." Besides, we don't know how long it's been going on. How old do you think Sebastian Harroway is?'

Jane stared at him in horror. '*Eeewww!*'

Matt laughed and guided the Jag out of the car park. Ten seconds later, a blue Audi let them pass then fell into line two vehicles behind them.

*

They took the A338 to Salisbury, crossing the Avon, then circling the ancient city centre anti-clockwise, heading for the former village, now suburb, known as Stratford-sub-Castle. The sky was misty grey and the air mild, but they drove with the sunroof down, making the most of the novelty of having a sports car.

Jane acted as tour guide, courtesy of her phone. 'Did you know the cathedral used to be north of the city at Old Sarum? It was only moved to its current location 800 years ago.'

'I always thought Salisbury was a bit *nouveau*.'

'Funnily enough, up until 2009 the place was officially known as New Sarum ...'

'There you go.'

'... when the Salisbury City Council was established.'

'I quite like the sound of New Sarum. Very *Lord of the Rings*.'

'Interesting you should mention that because the book was written by a man who wasn't born anywhere near here.'

'Tolkien? Where was he born then?'

'South Africa.'

'Really? I thought he was as British as bulldogs. Next, you'll be telling me that chap who made the films isn't one of us either.'

'Brace yourself ...'

Matt checked the rearview mirror. 'You should brace yourself too. I think we've picked up a tail.'

'What?'

'Call me superstitious, but there's been a blue Audi one or two cars behind us for some time now.'

'You mean, like the blue Audi you vandalised in an underground car park?'

'I prefer the phrase "temporarily inconvenienced". It is the same model, but I haven't been able to clock its index number yet.'

'What do we do? Floor it and try to lose him, or stop him and let down some more tyres?'

'Neither for the moment. Let's not let on we know he's there.'

*

'Is this your vehicle, sir?'

The voice made Roger Reaves jump and bang his head on the van's exhaust. He'd just spotted the tracker too, wedged in a gap between the fuel tank and the floor. Whoever had placed it, knew what they were doing.

Sliding out again, he found himself staring at a pair of black boots and the cuffs of a pair of blackish-blue trousers. There were another pair standing further back.

'Er ... no. I was looking for my cat,' he said, dusting off his hands and sitting up.

'Really, sir? All the way under like that? With a torch and all?'

'It's a ... small cat. Gets ... up inside things.'

'A small cat. You mean a kitten, sir? What's puss's name

then?'

Reaves licked his lips, only now noticing the van's driver standing off at a distance behind the second policeman. *Damn that tracker being so well hidden!*

'Er ... Rosten. Rosty, for short.'

'Rosty, sir?'

'He's just been neutered.' *Or just about to be.*

'Well, no wonder he ran off. You'd be local then, sir?'

'What?'

'Local, sir. From around here.' Reaves said nothing. 'I mean, you must be if your newly neutered cat has just run off.'

The policeman stood looking down at him, hands on his hips. It was the tattoos round his neck, Reaves thought. People always judged you if you had tattoos.

He heard the van driver say to the second policeman, 'Been going on for weeks, this. Rival firms interfering with our vehicles.'

The first policeman said, 'If you could provide some identification, sir, proof of address and such like, we can clear this matter up right away.'

'Er ...' Reaves said, 'I don't have anything on me.'

'Then perhaps you can show us where you live, sir. You'll have your keys, of course.'

Reaves bit his lip and shrugged helplessly.

'I take that as a no, sir. I think you'd better come along with us. This way, please.'

13

'That street there, on the right,' Jane pointed, but Matt carried on up Goose Green Grove. 'Where are you going?'

'It's one-way. I want to see where it leads.'

In addition to Plover Place, they passed Dotterel Drive and Lapwing Lane before coming round in a broad semicircle and passing them again in reverse order.

'It seems the developer was into ornithology,' Matt said, noting the names.

'To say nothing of alliteration.'

The houses were all 90's New Builds, semis with neat front gardens, mock timber framing and double-glazing. Araton's was an exception. A two-storey Edwardian pile squatting in a tangle of ankle-deep weeds, it looked like a confused elderly relative lost in a swarm of youngsters.

Jane paused at the gate. 'Whoa, flashback! I remember a house like this when I was a kid. My aunt's place. I bet it's gloomy and cold inside.'

'A house like this? In Leicester? I thought they all lived in caves up there.'

A concrete path led past a rusting iron fence to the front door. Two bare earth strips to one side provided drive-on access, but there was no garage.

'Not much of a gardener,' Matt said.

'Pot, kettle, black,' Jane muttered. Matt had a place in Greenwich with a back garden – at least when she first met him – that was in a state of what he euphemistically described as "overgrowth".

'To be honest, I prefer this to polished pavers, plastic bird baths and lawns trimmed with nail scissors,' he said, opening the front door with the key Jean Harroway had given him.

Jane gathered up the handful of letters on the mat – bill, bill, bank statement, postcard, a flyer about a local fete – and took a second look at the postcard. There was a picture of Tower Bridge on one side and a message on the reverse reading, "Everything well. Expect to see you soon." She slipped it and the other correspondence into the padded envelope they'd use to return the keys.

The house was silent and the air smelled stale. All the windows were closed. All had locking catches. No keys.

'He takes his security seriously,' Matt said.

The lounge was tidy but haphazardly furnished. A large brick fireplace occupied one side, its hearth filled with an ugly gas appliance. Before it, sat a modern leather rocker-recliner and an antique sofa and chairs. The mix of old and new continued in a beautiful rosewood bookcase with hand-carved cornices that was packed with a tattered collection of paperbacks. Jane ran her eye along the titles. Science fiction mostly, secondhand, though a newer looking selection of improve-your-memory type books was wedged in one side. One half of the shelf below was filled with old VHS tapes, the other with DVDs. No dramas or comedies though. They were all documentaries or history sets: *The First World War*, *The Second World War*, *The Vietnam War...*

The kitchen contained the usual appliances, older models mostly. An ancient coal range, painted an unconvincing lemon colour, stood in an alcove beside an only slightly newer gas cooker and served as a de facto shelf. There was a carton of stale milk – unopened, bulging slightly – in the fridge. It sat beside a block of Edam with a greenish fuzz on its exposed face. The cupboards were mostly empty.

'He doesn't seem to spend much time here,' Jane said, picking up a note on the breakfast bar.

Call me. <u>Please</u>.
Jean

'Want to check upstairs while I have a word with the neighbours?' Matt asked.

'I love what he's done with the living area. I can't wait to see the bedrooms. See you in a bit.'

The photographs in the file hadn't captured the oppressive emptiness of the place. It was as soulless as a motel room. As she went up the staircase, Jane noted the absence of ornaments or pictures or decorations of any kind.

There was a box room to the right full of flattened cardboard boxes. 'Seems appropriate,' she muttered, wiping a finger over one of the dusty cartons. Araton might have moved in yesterday instead of owning the place for more than two decades.

The master bedroom had the same empty, storage-space feel as the rest of the place, and the only room with any real sign of regular use was the second bedroom, which served as Araton's office. A large, old-fashioned bureau sat against one wall, the roll-top cover was up, the sliding desktop extension drawn out and locked in place. A thick green plastic mat covered the surface, which was covered with books and papers. The larger slots in the back of the bureau acted as a rudimentary filing system for bills and accounts, while the smaller nooks and crannies contained a selection of office stationery: sticky notes, paperclips, a stapler, staple remover and all manner of pens and pencils. There was one absence. The coiled cord of a laptop power supply was wedged in place by a couple of paperbacks, but the PC itself was nowhere to be seen.

Jane leafed through the books and papers. The former consisted of technical or reference works, the latter contained a three-week-old copy of the *Daily Telegraph*, pages evidently printed from the internet on subjects ranging from bad puns to newspaper articles, and one heavily amended page looked like he was editing the Wikipedia entry for Methylphosphonyl difluoride. Its presence seemed to underscore the laptop's absence.

A check of the cupboards under the bureau revealed a carry case branded Asus like the power supply, but still no machine. Would he have taken it with him on holiday? Possibly. But surely not without the power supply. And wouldn't he have taken the bag too? It was a big machine though from the look of it: a 17-inch screen. That meant it would weigh around five pounds. A lot of dead weight for a walker, even without the case.

Jane wandered back through to the master bedroom, still with no clear picture of the inhabitant's temperament or interests. Araton was more a collection of negatives. Not a gardener. Not bothered about the appearance of his property, even to the extent of having someone come in and mow the lawn. The interior showed a similar disregard for both décor and possessions. Nothing on the walls, no ornaments or clutter, an almost empty fridge. *My uncle lives for his work.*

Perhaps he's a clotheshorse, Jane thought, tugging at the handle of the walk-in wardrobe. The door was stiff and opened with a jerk. She gasped and stepped back, finding herself face to face with a grey, goggle-eyed monster.

*

Matt drew a blank with Araton's easterly neighbour – no one home – but the westerly one was a woman about his own age preparing for the school run. She could only spare him a few minutes, enough to confirm they knew Araton by sight, barely ever exchanged more than a polite greeting, hadn't seen him for some time, and that the kids called him Mr Weird behind his back.

Mrs Chufney, directly across the road, proved much more helpful. She was a curtain-twitcher and spent her days in the front room with one eye on the telly and the other on the street. Yes, she knew Terrence Araton as well as anyone hereabouts, which is to say not well at all. 'Keeps himself to himself, that fella, and his garden's a disgrace. It's all right for him with those heavy curtains. We've got to look out at it! My Billy says it depresses property values. Depresses me, all right.'

'Does he get many visitors?'

'Nary a one. There's a sister, I think. Looks a bit like him at any rate. Silver Toyota. One of them mini truck things they all drive these days. Like they have to drive up a mountainside to get to work.'

'Have you ever met her?'

'No! She looks as standoffish as him in her tweedy skirts. She was here last week though. Parked up that drive for an hour or more. Mind, you need a mini truck to get up that track. Why can't he put a proper driveway in? It's a disgrace. And we have to look out at it!'

She crossed her arms and nodded at the departing school-run mum. 'They're the ones I feel sorry for, Ross and Jenny. Three little 'uns with that fella next door. I'll not say anything against him, but you never know, not these days.'

'Who lives on the other side?'

'Steve and Amanda Brent. They're like him: hardly ever home. Work all week then away most weekends. But at least they keep their garden tidy.'

'The sister, the one in the silver Toyota. Did she take anything with her when she left last week?'

'Oh, I couldn't say. She was carrying a bag, wasn't she?'

'A handbag?'

'No, no, one of them gym bags. Big thing.' She gestured with her hands. 'Heavy and all, by the look of it.'

'And she took it from the house?'

'She took it both ways, in and out.' Mrs Chufney frowned. 'Actually, come to think of it, it looked heavier going in than coming out.'

'So she took something *into* the house?'

The woman made a face, staring into the middle-distance as she recalled the scene. 'It was sitting on the passenger seat when she arrived. I saw her open the door and take it out. It were a strain. Like it were full of weights or something. You know, like dumbbells. But when she came out again, she was swinging it light as a feather. Didn't open the passenger door, neither. Just slung it in from the driver's side. Must've left 'em in there, I expect.' To Matt's quizzical look she added, 'The dumbbells.'

'Did anyone else visit that day?'

She considered for a moment. 'The big black ranger came round about three o'clock.'

'I'm sorry ...?'

'Another of them truck things, but even bigger.'

'You mean a Range Rover?'

'That's what I said. Came round about three and parked up the drive. Two men, nice looking fellas in suits and all. Went straight round the back. They must've had a key 'cos ten minutes later they came out the front.

'I'm not nosy, mind. I only kept an eye on 'em 'cos the schools had just come out. The way they was parked, they had to back into the road and there were kiddies everywhere. I don't know how they can see behind 'em in them big truck things, especially with all that coloured glass.'

'It had tinted windows?' She nodded. 'Two men?'

'Like *Men in Black,* I thought, what with them suits and sunglasses.'

'Did they take anything in with them, or bring anything out?'

'I couldn't really see. But they made sure to lock up after themselves. I remember 'em trying the front door.'

'I noticed you said *the* black ranger, like you'd seen it before.'

Mrs Chufney nodded. 'They must be friends of his, keeping an eye on the place while he's away. Haven't seen 'em for the last few days, but they seem to come regular. They was there a couple of days before his sister, and my Billy spotted 'em the weekend before that.'

'So that would be the previous Tuesday, and before that the Saturday or Sunday?'

'I can't tell you what time Tuesday, but it would've been Sunday morning 'cos I was away at church.'

Matt thanked her, declined the offer of a cup of tea, deflected a string of questions, and headed back across the road.

*

Jane caught her breath. The last thing she expected to find hanging on the inner door of a domestic wardrobe was a hazmat suit. Not one of the modern, bright yellow ones with a large, transparent faceplate either. They'd look positively cheerful beside this. The whole head-covering was a thick, grey rubber mask with two circular glass disks for eye holes. The bottom of the mask tapered to a drain-like stainless steel fitting connected to a thick black rubber hose that ran down the chest to some sort of filtration device worn around the waist. The remainder of the suit was a brackish, brownish grey and hung in saggy folds like the skin of a monstrous Shar-Pei.

When she'd recovered from her shock, Jane reached out and touched it. The fabric was thick, rubber-lined with something. Lead? It was the real McCoy all right. It must have weighed a ton. It was certainly no Halloween costume.

The remainder of the wardrobe contained no further surprises. A handful of mid-range, mid-priced suits, a few casual clothes and shoes, but like the rest of the house, most of the available space was unused.

She closed the door again, the weight of the hazmat suit making it drag across the carpet, and stood considering what she'd learned about Araton and what her intuition suggested. She was still deep in thought when she heard Matt's voice downstairs.

'You still up here?' He found her in the master bedroom. 'Anything interesting?'

'Check out the wardrobe.'

He did so. 'Jesus!'

'That's pretty much what I said.'

He looked closer, fingering the air hose and the rubber mask. 'This thing's for real. At first, I thought it was a fancy dress costume.'

'So did I.'

'Cold War era by the look of it. Russian, judging by that lettering on the gas mask.'

'What's he doing with a hazmat suit in his wardrobe?'

'This is for more than just hazardous materials. It's the whole nine yards. It's an NBC suit: protection against nuclear, biological, and chemical contamination. These things were made for Soviet troops. See the boots? They didn't all have size-20 feet. They're made to fit over the top of combat boots.'

'But what's it doing here?'

'Historical artefact? I imagine these things are collector's items to a certain type of person.'

'Right. And the house is full of other little knick-knacks and collector's items.'

Matt glanced around the spartan bedroom. 'I see what you mean.'

'You said NBC, the C being chemical. Given his line of work, is it possible he was worried about something?'

'This thing?' Matt fingered the heavy fabric. 'It looks functional, but I'm sure there are better, more modern equivalents.'

'But I don't imagine an NBC suit is the sort of thing you could perk from work.'

'True. Whereas, you could pick up something like this on eBay. Have you checked his browsing history?'

'No computer.' Jane told him about the power supply and the carry case and how he was unlikely to have taken it with him, given its apparent bulk.

'You think his sister took it?'

'The one he texted, phoned, or emailed every day? That would be my guess.'

Matt shook his head and told her what Mrs Chufney said about the gym bag.

'*Delivered* something? But there's nothing here!'

'Dumbbells, she suggested.'

'Araton doesn't seem like a workout kind of guy.'

'So what was Jean Harroway doing here in the time before she went to the police? Because she certainly wasn't chatting to the neighbours.'

'That's what she told us.'

'She's telling porkies. The neighbour across the street's got eyes like a spy-cam. She remembers her coming and going last week, but that's all she did. No wandering about knocking on doors.'

'So she dropped off something the weight of a pair of dumbbells and did what – tidy up?'

'She might have thought it prudent given the nature of their relationship.'

'You think he had pin-ups of her on the walls and used her undies for lampshades?'

'Who knows? But I don't think we're going to get anything more here. Time to move on.'

'Aye aye, skipper. Where to next?'

'A chat with Araton's employers if I can arrange it.' He took out his phone. 'Then it's westward-ho.'

'Fun fact,' Jane said as they headed downstairs. 'Did you know there really is a town called Westward Ho!, complete with exclamation mark, somewhere in Devon?'

'Really?' Matt said. 'You are full of it, aren't you?'

'Fun facts?' Jane asked brightly.

'That's ... one word for it.'

14

Part of the pleasure of playgroup was the exhausted child one collected at the end of the session. Dylan would usually prattle on about all he'd done that day, then suddenly lapse into silence, lulled to sleep by the comfortable car seat and the rhythm of the traffic. Back home, Sally would carry him up to his room and be guaranteed at least another hour's peace and quiet before he re-emerged.

Not today. It seemed as if his teachers had fed him coffee laced with cocaine because he fairly bounced out of class and was only kept in his car seat by a buckle he couldn't yet manage to undo. Perhaps it was the excitement of visiting Aunty Jane's – despite the warning that she wouldn't be there – because he charged into the house and caught Bluebelle by surprise. Unused to small, noisy humans in any form, especially those thundering towards her, Bluebelle leapt from the sofa and attempted to flee. Dylan pursued her with a delighted whoop and grabbed at her tail.

'Dylan!' Sally shouted, but too late. He had it.

The cat yowled and rounded on him. Startled but undaunted, Dylan let go, and Bluebelle, out-numbered, out-sized and frightened, dived for the rear cat door and disappeared into the back garden.

'Kitty gone!' he announced, continuing the pursuit and peering through the still swinging cat flap.

'She didn't scratch you did she?' Clearly not. 'I've told you before about pulling cats' tails, haven't I?'

Dylan gave a cheeky laugh and ran off through the kitchen.

Sally checked the back garden, but there was no sign of

Bluebelle. It seemed like a wasted visit as she'd hardly touched the biscuits Sally had left for her that morning.

*

Sebastian Harroway studied a copy of the file he'd given Bluebelle Investigations, unsure what had upset his mother. She hadn't said exactly, just that she didn't like their tone. 'They spoke to me like I was some sort of criminal. I won't have it, Sebastian. The least you could have done is warn me they were coming.'

Why would she need a warning?

He didn't believe Matt Healy and Jane Child had gone hot and heavy on a witness without reason, and it was that alone that took him back to a file he was already familiar with. He had asked to lead the investigation into his uncle's disappearance, but Mr Fennel refused for reasons that hadn't really surprised young Harroway: he was too close to the subject, inexperienced in the procedural aspects of such an enquiry, and altogether too new in the job. Still, it had felt like a rebuke.

Now, a couple of outsiders had spotted something he'd missed. Something to do with his mother. That at least narrowed his focus, but it still took a second close reading before he spotted it.

'Sebastian. What can I do for you?' Marius Fennel asked when the young man knocked on his door.

'The Araton file, sir. It appears some of the text messages are missing.'

'Missing?'

'The metadata doesn't match with the message texts.'

'Doesn't it?' Fennel didn't sound terribly surprised.

'I thought we could requisition the full content from GCHQ. They'll have it on file, but I'll need your signature on the—'

'Have the Bluebelle people asked for it?'

Harroway hesitated. 'No, sir.'

'I understand your interest, Sebastian, but you are only liaison.

This is not your case.'

'I thought—'

'Let's leave it until such time as they do ask then. If they ever do. No point wasting GCHQ's time, eh? And please, leave that file with me for the time being. Thank you. If Healy and Child do have any queries, direct them my way, will you, please?'

*

Susan Burdon considered Rosten's report.

Red Jag, 2 occs left B'mth 11:49. Proceed to 14 Plover Pl. Stratford-sub-Castle, approx 55 mins. Loc. did not permit surv. Confirm 2 occs depart, heading nth-wst A338. Continuing pursuit.

She threw the burner phone onto the bed. So they'd visited his sister *and* the missing man's home. Being thorough; fair enough. But what were they doing in Araton's house for almost an hour?

Rosten was right to keep out of the way. Especially as he was working on his own. There'd been no word from Reaves, and the tracker signal was still roaming all over Hampshire.

They were supposed to be professionals! Reliable, her controller assured her. Local people with local knowledge who'd blend in. Reaves had blended in all right. So well that he'd vanished! And Rosten appeared to have placed the tracker so inexpertly that the targets spotted it the first time they stopped for gas.

Burdon fumed quietly and paced to the sliding door, cursing the CIA surveillance. It was tempting to take matters into her own hands, but doing so too early would expose her and attract unwanted attention. Barty needed to be assured she really was just another harmless tourist.

*

'Not possible,' Matt was told, the words so clearly enunciated that they might have been separate sentences.

'We can meet with a couple of their security team in the village,' he told Jane as she pulled up beside a postbox at the top of Plover Place, 'but there's no way they'll let us into Porton Down itself.'

'I can't say I'm disappointed,' she replied, handing him the padded envelope containing Jean Harroway's keys and Araton's mail. Matt leaned out and posted it, and she drove on, thinking about the NBC suit hanging on Araton's wardrobe door.

Not just that, the whole house made her uneasy. Childhood memories, perhaps. But also the vague idea they had missed something.

Porton, an unassuming village five miles northeast of Salisbury, was best known for its secretive neighbour, Porton Down, a 7,000-acre science park and military camp. Established in 1916 in response to German gas attacks during World War One, its scientists and staff quickly developed anti-gas respirators and weapons of their own. Chlorine, phosgene and mustard gas killed and crippled hundreds of thousands of troops on both sides in such a horrific and devastating manner that the Geneva Protocol of 1925 banned the use of chemical weapons – but not their development, or their deployment in retaliation for an enemy's chemical attack. So research, production and stockpiling continued.

In the late 1930s, the Germans developed a new form of chemical weapon. Instead of arriving in choking, blinding, burning clouds, Sarin gas was a colourless, odourless agent that disrupted the body's neural pathways. The overall effect was the same, death – in this case by suffocation due to lung muscle paralysis – but Sarin was vastly more toxic.

In response, Porton Down developed Venomous Agent X, more commonly known by the abbreviation VX, an amber-coloured, oily liquid that kills by direct contact. A pinhead-sized drop on the skin rapidly leads to convulsions, paralysis, and death.

But there was more to Porton Down than chemical weapons. With a staff of three thousand and an annual budget of half-a-billion pounds, it formed an epicentre for Britain's defence, research and security industries. Home to the Defence Science and Technology Laboratory, Public Health England, and a number of privately-owned research and pharmaceutical companies, there was nothing to suggest that Terence James Araton was anything other than an ordinary scientist. Except for that suit.

The Two Knights pub off Winterslow Road looked as uninviting as the village itself. A modern, two-storey brick edifice with a car park in front and an off-licence at the far end. A wooden sign hung above the door showing two armour-clad figures charging at each other on horseback, lances at the ready. A steady breeze animated it, making it squeak and groan as it swung back and forth.

The interior of dark, wood-grained laminate was brightened only by the rattle and glare of slot machines along one wall. The air seemed smokey without actually being so, the result of sunlight angling through grimy windows.

They ordered coffees and took a seat as far from the noisy machines as possible. Jane went to sit in a shaft of sunlight, but Matt waved her back. 'This side. Let's keep the spotlight on our visitors.'

'Is this an interrogation?'

'Never ignore a natural advantage, no matter how slight.'

Their coffees arrived, lukewarm and bitter, and shortly after, two figures stepped from a black Range Rover in the car park.

The woman introduced herself as Margery Tumbrull, a Capability Advisor for DSTL. The man, Reginald Wyatt, as Head of Security.'

'Thank you for meeting with us,' Matt said. 'Can I get you anything?'

They both declined.

'Wise choice.' Jane made a face as she set down her cup.

The woman smiled and seemed on the verge of replying, but a glare from her companion shut her down.

Wyatt was mid-fifties, balding with close-cropped, steel-grey hair and steel-framed glasses to match. He had a weathered face, a stocky body beneath his dark suit, and an expression that suggested he got little pleasure from life.

'Let's keep this short, shall we? Dr Araton is a valuable member of the DSTL community, as are all our staff, and his disappearance is as unsettling to us as the disappearance of any of our staff would be, regardless of their status or rank.'

'What *is* Mr Araton's status or rank?' Matt asked.

'I thought you already knew that.' Wyatt nodded at the file in front of Jane. 'He's a senior research chemist.'

'In what division?'

'I can't tell you that.'

'Can't or won't?'

'It's classified.'

'I don't suppose you can tell me what he was researching?'

'That is hardly germane to your investigation. The man went missing while on holiday.'

'We're trying to determine why he went missing. What his state of mind might have been. Did he have any problems at work?'

'He was in the middle of a three-week holiday. His disappearance hardly seems to be work-related.'

'And that hardly seems like an answer.'

Wyatt blinked. Jane saw Matt was right about the lighting. It wasn't an interrogation spotlight, but it did show every twitch of the security man's expression – including the fine beading of sweat on his forehead.

Matt lightened his tone. 'He went missing partway through his holiday, as you say. We're trying to get a picture of the man, trying to determine his state of mind. Most disappearances aren't the result of foul play or accident. Sometimes people just get fed up and walk away.'

'Dr Araton has been with us for more than twenty years. I would have thought if he found the work distasteful, he'd have sought other opportunities by now.'

'Distasteful? That's an unusual word to use about one's work.'

Wyatt's lips compressed slightly, but he said nothing.

'So you're not aware of any problems then? General dissatisfaction with the job, disputes with colleagues, being passed over for promotion, personal grievances or ... security problems?'

After his previous slip, Wyatt's face was a mask. 'No.'

'When were you first alerted to Dr Araton's disappearance?'

'That too must be in your file, Mr Healy. Have you considered reading it?'

'I have read it, Mr Wyatt, and there's no mention of DSTL Security being informed at all, yet Araton's sister, Mrs Jean Harroway, received a call from your office shortly after filing the Missing Person's report at the Stratford Road police station. I have a copy of it here.' Matt passed it to him. 'As you can see, it asks for details about the person – a physical description, distinguishing marks, any medical conditions. It asks for a photograph, a mobile phone number, and details of the circumstances in which the person went missing. But nowhere does it ask about the missing person's employer. And nowhere did Mrs Harroway supply that information.'

Wyatt said nothing.

'So I'm curious about when DSTL became involved. And how.'

'I don't see—'

'One-hundred-and-eighty-thousand people are reported missing in Britain each year, Mr Wyatt. That's a lot of filing, a lot of reports.

'The drive from Stratford Road police station to Mrs Harroway's home in Bournemouth is approximately one hour. Halfway through that drive, within half an hour of filing a Missing

Person's report about her brother, she had a call from DSTL Security asking for more details.'

Wyatt closed his mouth.

Matt continued. 'You know what I think? I think DSTL – probably through its Ministry of Defence connections – can tag people as Persons of Interest. If a POI comes up on another government computer system – like, say, the police – your office is informed automatically. I think the moment Mrs Harroway's report was entered into the Missing Persons system, your office received an alert.'

'Even if there were such a system, and I'm not saying there is one, what possible relevance could that have to this case?'

'There's what, three thousand staff at Porton Down? I don't imagine they're all tagged as POIs. In fact, I imagine only a handful are. Important people, senior people, security-of-the-realm type people. People like Dr Araton.'

Wyatt breathed heavily. 'I fail to see how this is relevant to locating a man missing for more than a week now, Mr Healy.'

'And I fail to see why MI5 should be so intent on us finding a man still technically on holiday. Or at least I did until now. Either Araton himself, or what he was working on, is of national importance. And I think that is *very* relevant to the case.'

Wyatt shifted in his seat and glanced at his companion. 'As I said earlier, Mr Healy, the well-being of *all* our staff is important to us at DSTL.'

A politician's answer. Not a real one.

Matt tried a more direct approach. 'Is Terence Araton a threat to national security?'

'I could not and do not comment on idle speculation. I'm a security man. I deal in facts. I suggest you two do the same.

'Now, if there are no more questions ...?' Wyatt got to his feet. 'I'm a busy man, Mr Healy. I have more important things to do than nurture tabloid-newspaper conspiracy theories put about by a pair of amateur detectives. Good day to you.'

Tumbrull made an apologetic face and trotted out after her boss.

'You were right about that Persons of Interest thing,' Jane said. 'He's a cold fish, but I saw your comment register with her.'

'Odds-on he's ex-police, or military, or both. Old School, too. That's why they sent him out with a minder to watch his Ps and Qs, but he couldn't quite resist that crack about amateurs.'

'I just thought of something. Quick, pass me that file.'

Outside, the Range Rover's hazard lights flashed as Wyatt unlocked it with his key fob.

Jane flicked to the back, pulled out her phone and dialled.

Through the window, they saw Wyatt pause and take out his phone as he was about to get into the vehicle. He studied the unknown number then answered cautiously.

'Mr Wyatt?' Jane said cheerfully.

'Who is this?'

'We just met. Perhaps you'd like to tell us why you called Dr Araton five times within a two-hour period on the morning of Friday the fourteenth?'

Wyatt looked up, glaring at the window of the pub before stabbing his phone to silence. Jane smiled and waved. The Range Rover sped off in the direction of Porton Down, tearing two channels in the loose gravel of the car park as it left.

15

'We need a dead-end road, but not an obvious one,' Matt said. 'Two or three miles long would be ideal.'

'Is Blue-Audi-Man still there?'

'Hard to tell with these winding lanes, but let's assume the worst.'

Jane studied the GPS, zooming and tracking. 'Take a right at the next intersection, then the second left. The road looks like it ends up at a farm overlooking the down.

'Perfect,' Matt increased speed.

They'd been driving for some minutes when Matt's phone rang. Jane took the call.

'Oh, Ms Child. It's Margery Tumbrull here from DSTL. We just met at the Two Knights.'

'Hello,' Jane replied, switching on the phone's speaker so Matt could hear. 'Sorry we didn't get a chance to talk properly.'

'Yes, well, Mr Wyatt's under a lot of pressure at the moment. There's something you should know that he didn't get a chance to tell you. Something that may or may not have a bearing on your enquiries. We had a new auditor start the week Dr Araton went away. Because of the vacancy, she started in his department first. I don't know any more. All I do know is there was some sort of discrepancy that caused a bit of a fuss.'

'What sort of discrepancy?'

'I have no idea. Just that figures didn't add up or something. Several other people were called in, including Mr Wyatt, and since then the shutters have come down.'

'I see.'

'It's probably not relevant. I mean, Dr Araton was away at the time so he wouldn't have known, but I thought I'd let you know, just in case.'

Jane thanked her and hung up. 'Well, well, well. That wouldn't be the first time someone's been caught on the fiddle while they're on their hols.' Jane knew from her banking days that that was when many frauds came to light.

She turned to the file and flicked to the back where she'd written Wyatt's name above the legend "Caller excluded from enquiries". 'Tumbrull's right, Araton wouldn't have known – *except* that Wyatt called him on the evening of the fourteenth and left a message. To which Araton never responded. And two days later, he went AWOL. If Wyatt mentioned the audit in his voicemail, it makes an interesting connection.'

'Agreed,' Matt said, then, 'Here we go. Hold onto your hat ...'

The paved road ran out, and the surface turned to gravel. As they hit it, Matt eased up on the accelerator, pulled on the handbrake, turned the wheel and executed a neat hundred-and-eighty degree turn in not much more than a car length. He released the brake, tapped the gas, and the Jag gave a little wheel-spin before heading back the way they'd come, zipping back between the narrow hedgerows and the occasional farm building. Half a mile on, slowing for a tight, right-hand bend, they met the Blue Audi coming the other way.

'Gotcha!' Matt muttered, giving no outward sign of recognition as the two vehicles slowed, edged left, and squeezed past each other. Jane kept her eyes fixed straight ahead.

'This *has* been a useful side trip,' Matt said. 'We've learned Araton was important enough to be on some sort of national-watch database, that Wyatt made several attempts to contact him while he was on holiday – most likely because of problems with a surprise audit.' He glanced in the rearview mirror. 'And whoever is in that Audi appears to share our interest in his whereabouts.'

They rounded another corner and met another car coming in

the opposite direction. There was more room here, and the two vehicles passed each other smoothly and continued on.

'Did you see that?'

'A bit hard to miss,' Jane said, looking over her shoulder at the departing vehicle. 'A green BMW. *My* green BMW.'

*

Following the path of the sun, they headed west, pausing at Bath for a late afternoon tea, then swapping drivers and joining the M4. Jane kept a weather eye on the rearview mirror, but it was almost impossible to tell if the blue Audi and green BMW were still following them. Motorway driving; motorway traffic. Besides, they may have changed vehicles by now, and as Matt said, 'If they're after Araton, they know where we're heading.'

Sunlight reflecting off the Audi's windscreen obscured any view of its driver, but Jane had got a fleeting glimpse of the BMW's occupant: a young woman with short auburn hair.

A woman! Was that who'd pursued her from the phone box near her house? If it had been, it was somehow more outrageous that a woman should try to intimidate another woman like that.

A black ute raced past in the outside lane, its nearside windows down to reveal a group of young men yelling and jeering and making arm gestures as they passed the little red sports car with its female driver. Any one of them might have chased her through the rain and laughed about it later to his mates, but a woman ...?

'The black ranger,' Matt said quietly, fishing for his notebook as the vehicle disappeared. 'Araton's neighbour said a big black Range Rover visited his house after his sister left on the Thursday.'

'Like the one Wyatt drives?'

'And probably the rest of DSTL Security. It parked up Araton's drive. She was worried about it backing out as the schools were coming out, which makes it a couple of hours after Jean Harroway went to the police.'

He checked his notes. 'Two men got out and disappeared around the back. Ten minutes later, they came out the front door, locking the door behind them.'

'They didn't try the front door first? Knock?'

'No, because they already knew he was missing. They went round the back so they could pick the lock without being seen.

'Porton Down is only fifteen miles away, so it's no great stretch, but Araton was important enough to warrant some sort of trigger warning on police files *and* to warrant a search of his house.'

'But his sister beat them to it. She'd already been in and tidied up.'

'Did she just tidy up? Remember the heavy bag she carried in and the empty one she carried out?'

'Could she have planted something to throw them off the scent? Or left something they'd expect to find there?'

'Whatever it was, they didn't take it with them. The nosy neighbour said they left empty-handed.'

'But it does suggest Jean Harroway knew what would happen when her brother's workplace discovered he was missing.'

'It's more than that, Jane. There were two previous visits. One on the Tuesday and one on the Sunday morning, not too many hours after Wyatt first called Araton on his mobile and got no reply.'

They reached the start of the Prince of Wales Bridge with the Severn Estuary below them and Wales shimmering in the distance.

'I'm starting to think we're heading in the wrong direction. I'm starting to think the truth is back there somewhere.'

*

Mick Rosten swapped cars at Bristol. He'd taken a call from Reaves while he was trying to execute a U-turn in a country lane so narrow you'd have had to back up a horse.

'Where the hell have you been?' Rosten said.

'Never mind. What's your status?'

Rosten told him about the Jag doubling back.

'Didn't you check where they were going on your satnav?' The rebuke was mild, especially coming from Reaves.

'I've been doing a solo act all day, remember? These lanes are narrow. And windy.'

'Yeah, yeah, all right. Get yourself to Bristol. I'll arrange a change of vehicles.'

'What about the targets?'

'Forget 'em for now. We know where they're heading.'

Rosten paused a beat. 'Are you all right?'

'Why wouldn't I be? What's it to you anyway? Get your fat arse to Bristol. I'll text you the details. And be sure to keep your fucking phone charged!'

That sounded more like the Reaves he knew and loathed.

Rosten left the Audi in a multi-storey car park at the edge of the city centre. Ticket stub in the glove compartment, keys on the left rear wheel. There were four wheels on the car. Why pick the one he'd got the puncture in? Was Reaves having a dig?

The other directions said he was to purchase certain items in town then proceed to Yippee Cars 'n' Campers where he'd find a pre-arranged rental. The hiding place for the keys may have been chance – a one-in-four – but he was certain the choice of rental agency wasn't. What the hell kind of place was it with a name like that?

The yard contained a line-up of ten-year-old sedans, three four-wheel drives, and a couple of pop-top vans, evidently the "campers" in the company name. The office was a converted shipping container at the back of the yard. Its exterior walls were brightly graffitied with phrases like "Yippee!", "Yah-hoo!" and "Yee-hah!". Intentional, apparently.

Rosten went in and was met by the duty manager, a tall, skinny guy in his forties, wearing a rumpled, misbuttoned paisley shirt, droopy moustache, and hair halfway to his waist.

'Hey dude! You got to be Bennett, right?' The duty manager swayed and flexed his knees as if moving to some inaudible beat. His look and manner said 60's hippy, California, but his accent was pure West Country.

'That's right.' Rosten set down his overnight bag.

'Saw you checking our wheels. Said to myself, you the man! Got your booking right here, dude, courtesy of the ol' triple-dub.' He hit a key on the keyboard, and a nearby printer began grinding out a contract the size of a modest novel. 'Booked and paid for a whole week. Cool!'

Rosten took out his wallet and dropped a driver's licence in the name of Allan Michael Bennett on the counter. The duty manager bopped and swayed to the rhythm of the printer, then gathered up the sheaf of papers and stapled them in one corner. He took up the licence, checked its details against that on his paperwork and handed it back. 'Slough, huh? Friendly bombs and all that, eh?'

Rosten gave him a blank look, wondering if the guy was on drugs.

The hippy shook his head. 'Heavy, man.'

The guy rattled through a list of waivers and exclusions before asking for signatures in three separate places. Then he took a set of keys off a pegboard and led Rosten back out into the yard. They passed the campers and the four-wheel drives and the ten-year-old sedans and kept going. Three shoeboxes stood under a graffitied sign of Day-Glo colours peppered with arrows and exclamation marks.

'There ya go, man. Yours is the Hi-Ho-Silver one. Our Yippee Special. Unlimited mileage at just £20 a day.'

'What the fuck ...?' Rosten muttered. Reaves had to be taking the piss.

It was hardly silver, more an oxidised grey, and the only thing special about it was the wildly optimistic design team who'd given it four doors. It might just about seat four kids, but not four adults.

Certainly not ones of Rosten's size.

'I can see what you're thinkin', man. You booked a Suzuki, but the badge says Mazda, am I right?' Rosten wasn't quite thinking that. 'They're the same, man. Suzuki Kei, Mazda Laputa. Suzi make 'em for the Maz, just put on different badges, you know? Engine's the same.'

'Engine?' Rosten half-expected it to be propelled by a wound-up rubber band.

'Straight-three, double overhead cam, 658cc of raw power. Most economical motor on the planet. You'll get sixty MPGs out of this baby, plus save a forest.' The keys dropped into Rosten's nerveless hand. 'It's a great way of getting from A to B.'

'Yeah, so is walking.'

The phone in the container office rang. The duty manager sprang away to answer it with a 'Happy travels, dude!' leaving Rosten staring at the badge on the back of the car. Laputa. *La puta.* He knew enough holiday Spanish to know what *that* meant. Reaves was definitely taking the piss.

16

It was after nine o'clock when Jane and Matt reached the village of Wysbech on the south coast of Wales. They'd spent the evening in Cardiff, dining at a traditional Welsh restaurant and doing a little sightseeing. After all, they were supposed to be on holiday.

'Mmm, smell that sea air and look at that view!' Jane said, stepping from the car. 'Not bad for just a car park, eh?'

The moon was high, and the tide was out. A broad band of blackness stretched away below their clifftop vantage point, turning to mild, shimmering sea where the lights of several ships could be seen on the horizon.

Gathering their things from the back seat and boot, they headed into the BB Inn, a whitewashed, stone-walled building with a thick mane of thatch, neatly trimmed in a pageboy haircut. The landlady, a diminutive woman in a stripy apron, welcomed them in with cheerful *Noswaith dda* and a broad smile. 'Did you find us all right?'

'My navigator's infallible,' Matt said.

The woman, who'd identified herself as Beth, gave Jane a nod of acknowledgement.

'Not me,' Jane laughed. 'He means the satnav.'

'There, and I thought you looked a proper map reader! The atlases are shameful about this part of the country, and the road markings aren't up to much either. When my Benji and I first came here fifteen years ago, we got into a frightful row about which way was which. Up until them googly maps, many of our guests did too.

'Now, I do hope you've eaten because I'm afraid the kitchen

closed at nine.' She indicated the glass doors of the dining room where a solitary guest was finishing up. 'We're edging into off-peak, you see, and there's little point keeping it open later. Mind, if you haven't eaten, I can put together a cold collation.'

Jane assured her there was no need.

Matt, bent over, filling out the register, gave her a nudge. Jane took the hint and kept Beth talking.

'Do you get many visitors this time of year?'

'It's steady enough, but we're not turning them away at the door like in high summer.'

'Where do they go then?' She moved to the leaded window. 'Is that a campground over the road?'

'No, no, that's the village green.' Beth followed her.

Behind them both, Matt turned back several pages.

'Some of them try it as a camping ground, but Tom Thomas from The Barrow soon puts them right.' There was a faint click from Matt's phone as she indicated the pub bordering the green. 'The proper campground's half a mile further out. Past that stile there, you see?'

Matt joined them, indicating he was done with the register, and Beth showed them to their room.

Compared to the Barleycorn Loft with its warped wooden floors and low-beamed ceiling, the BB Inn was airy luxury. The corner room had a westerly aspect, looking out over the moonlit bay. In addition to the king-size bed and en suite, (all gleaming and modern, no sixteenth-century communal plumbing here!), there was a tiny kitchen area and a sofa and a huge television. The bed was covered with a gaily patterned duvet, and there was an electric heater against one wall.

'Just the one night, wasn't it?' Beth asked, handing Matt the key.

'Would it be a problem if we stayed an extra day?'

'Friday night too? I shall have to check. Weekends are still popular, but I think we might be all right for our deluxe room.

Should I pencil you in if there's a vacancy?'

'Please do.'

The door closed. Beth's footsteps sounded on the landing. Jane turned, about to say something about the view, but stopped when she saw Matt's troubled expression.

'What is it? Something in the register?' She gestured at his phone.

'I haven't looked yet. It's what I saw as we came upstairs ...'

*

When Tasha Kayne emerged from a fast food restaurant at motorway services between junction seventeen and junction eighteen on the M4, Taliq Khan was waiting in the car park. He'd just arrived from London, driving a pile of crap that clearly hadn't come from the motor pool. She sneered and made a sarcastic remark, then learned it was his own vehicle. 'A typical British office worker's car,' he said, his dark eyes flashing. 'My cover, remember?' Back home, Tasha had a purple Camaro.

Taliq didn't do sarcasm or humour, or much of anything else as far as she could tell. He was dark and intense, and also kind of dishy and exotic. But he didn't appear to do *that* either.

Still, he was good to have on-side. It was Taliq who'd suggested they check the CCTV footage of their target's collision with the couple coming out of MI5. And it had been Taliq who'd spotted the card drop, zooming the image in and slowing it down until Tasha could see the move too. But it had been Tasha who'd jubilantly reported the observation to their boss, and Tasha who'd received the fulsome praise.

'Did you want something?' She gestured with her thumb. 'I could—'

'No time. You should get rid of that car. It may have been sighted. Twice now.'

'It's miles back to London, and this is just a training exercise.'

'The training exercise was to keep a watch on Sierra Bravo.'

Sierra Bravo! That is so Taliq. Why not just use the damn woman's name?

He added, 'It appears we are now involved in something more.'

'It's *still* a training exercise, Taliq.'

'So, in the field, you would continue to risk using a potentially compromised vehicle?'

'We're not *in the field,* and it's not compromised! OK, they might have spotted it on that country road, but so what? Haven't you noticed, there are tons of BMW's around.'

'You said yourself you used it to follow the woman from her home to a public telephone. A car. Following a walking person.'

'It was bucketing down, what was I supposed to do? Anyway, there was no way she could have seen the car because it was dark and it was raining. Hard.' Tasha hadn't been quite as honest as she might have been in her report of that evening's events, but what the hell, it was only an exercise.

'Still,' Taliq said. He had a way of saying that one word that made it sound like a complete sentence. Like a whole argument.

'How come you brought your own car?'

'Traffic. I was at home when I got the call. Going back in would have added at least another hour to the trip.' Taliq flatted in Chiswick.

'Where are they now?' Tasha gestured at Taliq's phone, seeking to change the subject.

'The last plate cam recorded their vehicle leaving the M4 and taking the A48.'

'Translation?'

'They're heading for Cardiff.'

'And Araton's last known location then. Like we expected.'

'The *vehicle* appears to be heading in that direction. *We* can't be certain Target Two and Target Three are still its occupants.'

Tasha rolled her eyes. Just like Taliq to be so pointy-headed precise. 'This isn't Mission Impossible, you know. We're not tracking a couple of FSB agents intent on industrial sabotage or something. It's just a pair of home-town PIs doing a bit of legwork for MI5.'

Taliq glared. She probably shouldn't have said that out loud in a public place. She knew how his mind worked. There might be surveillance cameras, hidden microphones, lip readers with telescopic lenses, and all manner of high-tech interception equipment aimed at finding out about their rookie mission.

Still, she relented, adding, 'Well, at least we can take turns now.'

'No, Mr H wants me back in London to keep an eye on Target One.'

'Oh?'

She felt a stab of something. Disappointment? Annoyance? Envy, perhaps. Was she being farmed off with the dull job while he went back for the fun part? She'd been looking forward to a couple of days away and relaxing. Just getting out of the office would be good, and getting to know her new partner might prove worthwhile too. Who knew what he'd be like stripped down to his shorts in a straw hat with a dirty martini in one hand?

'Well, watch out for stairwells,' she said.

It was hard to tell in the low light of this part of the car park, but she had the impression his dark eyes darkened more. The story of Taliq tripping over his own laces in the stairwell of the British Library had brought him some ribbing at London Station, but she now sensed he hadn't been quite so truthful in his report either.

He changed the subject. 'We should swap cars. You take mine, I'll take yours back with me.'

'Is that why you trailed me all the way out here, so you can cruise around town in something more comfortable? No way, mister. If I'm heading off the beaten track, I'm not going in a ... what is that thing anyway ... a Toyota Corroder?'

'I did not follow you to just—'

'You could have texted me where they were heading, you

know. Or called my cell.'

'I did not follow you to merely deliver information.' He picked up the rumpled rucksack at his feet and took out a small bubble-wrapped envelope. 'I brought you this.'

The envelope wasn't sealed. It contained a cellphone and charger.

'The phone's loaded with an ANPR app.'

Tasha looked at him blankly.

'The Automatic Number Plate Recognition system?'

'Yeah, yeah, I know.'

'I've pre-loaded it with the Jaguar's plate. Whenever it's spotted, you'll be notified of its location.'

'Oh. OK. You know they're moving into a part of the country that doesn't have many traffic cams? But thanks.'

He reached in again and took out a larger padded envelope. 'Also this.'

She could tell what it was the moment she felt its weight. The only real question was, what type of gun was it? She reached in and grasped the handgrip of a Glock 17.

'Yes, yes, why don't you bring it out and wave it about? You can show everyone.'

Perhaps Taliq did do sarcasm after all.

'Are you serious? You know possession of a handgun's a criminal offence in this country?'

'So don't get caught with it.'

'But ... what do I need it for?'

'Contingencies.'

'What contingencies?' Taliq said nothing. 'You mean Mr H gave you this?'

'Not personally. But he authorised it.'

'Shit!' Tasha closed the top of the packet, folding it over on itself before looking up to find him staring at her.

He said, 'Still think this is a training exercise?'

Tasha bit her lip.

'One more thing.' Taliq reached into his pocket, took out his car keys, and held them up. 'Swapsies. Mr H's orders. You may also need camping gear. You'll find some in what the British call the boot.'

*

'Did you notice the dining room?' Matt asked.

'The dining room?' Jane replied. 'Is this another of your little tests?'

Matt had been an undercover cop for years, surviving on his quick wits and extraordinary observational skills. Banking required neither, but Jane was well equipped with the first and a keen student of the latter, to the extent it had become something of a game with them. Over a quiet meal out, one might ask the other the colour of the waitress's eyes or whether they'd noticed she was a heavy smoker. A walk in the park might result in a quizzing about the occupants of the bench they'd just passed. At first, it proved difficult. The brain didn't usually take in a lot of incidental details, but Jane soon discovered it was something you could learn, like playing the piano or a new dance step. She might never be as good as a maestro like Matt – it was hard to beat experience and natural talent – but damned if she wasn't going to try!

'The dining room ...' she said, fixing the image in her mind. 'The doors are wooden, painted a pale peach with ten ... no, twelve glass panes in each. Two rows of six. Bevelled glass, so they're probably quite old. There's a sign in the fourth panel up of the right-hand door saying it's closed and directing enquiries to Reception.

'The dining room itself faces south. I could only see half a dozen tables from Reception, but it looked like there were more around the corner to the right. Servery is on the left. Visible tables were all small and round. Two-person jobs with gingham tablecloths. Chairs are plain wood with padded bases. Half the lights were off when we arrived, and there looked to be only one customer in there, presumably finishing up.'

Matt nodded, but said nothing, suggesting he wanted more.

'The customer was seated halfway between the doors and the windows. I only got profile because of the lights.' Jane closed her eyes to picture the scene more clearly. 'It was a man, I'm sure of that. Either bald or with close-cropped hair. A big nose too. Jowls. Slightly overweight. Someone stocky and solid. Oh, and he's right-handed. Or at least, he picked up his glass with his right hand.'

'Very good,' Matt said. 'In fact, very, *very* good. Star pupil. You picked up a couple of things I missed: the gingham tablecloths and the guy's right-handedness. My guess is that that is Mr A M Bennett who arrived an hour or so before us.' He zoomed in on the photograph of the register he'd taken on his phone and pointed out the name.

'And ...?' Jane said, sensing there was more.

'I'm not a hundred percent certain, but I think I've seen that profile before. Sitting in a blue Audi in an underground car park.'

'What, you mean he beat us here?'

'While we were in Cardiff.'

'I didn't notice any Audi's outside. He must have swapped vehicles.'

'Or parked further away.'

'Hold on, you said he was here before us. That means he knew where we were going. So why bother following us?'

'To see where we stopped and who we spoke to along the way. Once we spotted him, he gave up and came straight here.'

'Which implies it's a one-man operation, not a team.'

'I still think he's working for Burdon.'

'And the CIA woman is following him, or us, or both. What a muddle!'

Matt pointed to the photo on his phone. 'Bennett's booked in for one night, like us. So I thought we'd stay an extra day and see how he reacts.

'We won't do the coastal path tomorrow. We'll wander around

the village instead. Chat with locals, see if anyone remembers Araton. Following people in London is one thing. It's quite another in a quiet village. Let's see how he manages that.'

Jane scrolled back through the photographs Matt had taken of the inn's register. 'Araton was here all right. Two weeks ago on Saturday.' She zoomed in on his name. 'Odd to think that might be the last thing he ever wrote.'

'Provided you exclude smutty texts to his sister.'

Jane did a double-take then said, '*Eeewww!*'

17

Matt woke briefly, uncertain where he was for a time, the voices of his former colleagues filling his mind. He'd been back in the Counting House sharing banter with Rudyard, Yvette, and Con as they emptied out the first of the morning's bags. A wad of cash spilled out over the edge of the sorting table and onto the floor.

'Jesus fuck, not again! I mean, what the hell does this guy do with the stuff? Look at it. How can you run a business like this?' Con, never at his best in the morning, shook out the last of the crumpled bills and scooped the overflow off the floor, some of the notes screwed up so tight you could have used them for a game of table soccer.

Rudyard laughed and gave Yvette and Matt low fives. 'He got Brighton Billy again! That's three times in a row, man. You done the hat trick. Tomorrow, the cat trick.'

'What the hell's a cat trick?' Yvette said.

'Four times, man.'

'What's that got to do with cats?'

'What's three got to do wid hats?'

'Silly arse.' She chuckled.

'What's five times?' Matt asked. 'Bats?'

'Bats? Where you from, bruv? Don't get no bats down Streatham. But we do get plenty of ...' he made a brief drum roll with his fingertips on the tabletop '... rats.'

'So hat trick, cat trick, rat trick then. What's next?'

'Never got to no next, man. Most old Wobbles ever scored in a game was a rat trick. Away game too. Five-nil. You shoulda seen the other teams' faces. Man, but that was some after-match party!'

Con turned to the courier-guard standing behind him. 'I'm going to need gloves for this lot.'

There were four courier-guards, one stationed behind each counter. It was their job to deliver the locked bags and keep an eye on proceedings, verifying the contents matched the slips of paper inside and that nothing went astray. Normally, it was bare forearms work – "nothing up my sleeves", less chance for sleight of hand – but there were exceptions.

Most of the money came in loose or roughly bundled, sometimes even rubber banded, but Brighton Billy seemed to revel in making their job as difficult as possible, screwing up his day's takings, pounding them into a corner of the bag and sometimes adding extras. Dog shit on occasion, dry and not so dry, or slimy fast-food wrappers and pizza crusts. Once even a needle. Matt imagined a bitter, disgruntled addict forced to hand over a small fortune every day in return for a tiny commission in the form of enough white powder to see him through another twenty-four hours. Whoever he was, whatever his situation, he did good business and his count was always accurate – the only two things that mattered.

Jay handed Con a pair of thick rubberised gardening gloves. It was one-size-fits-all and they swam on his grizzled hands as he began flattening and arranging the banknotes into countable piles.

'Your Wobbles sounds like he could've been a player,' Yvette said to Rudyard.

'Hell, yeah. That boy coulda been big time. Word got round to the scouts, you know? The FA boys? Least, that's what we reckon 'cos we started getting strangers turning up at our games and practice sessions. Guys with notebooks. Nobody says nothing like, but we all knew.

'Then some fucker hits old Wobbles with a bit of blow and a bit of smack. He's the man, bro. Club champ, hero, on his way to the bright lights and the big times. He can handle anything, man. 'cept he can't. Ends up getting knifed over some deal gone wrong.'

'Dead?'

'Worse, man. Crippled. Waist down.' Rudyard shook his head. 'Livin' hell for a man so light on his feet.'

Matt looked down at the takings spread on the sorting table in front of him. He'd struck it lucky with his first bag. Bundled notes and a neatly written total slip: £1,650. Someone who drew a diagonal line through their zeros to differentiate them from the letter O. A money market dealer or a stockbroker, perhaps. Definitely somewhere upmarket: the West End or Docklands. Funny how you could tell so much from a bag of banknotes.

Con let out a sigh and took off the gloves. 'All right. All set.'

'No surprises today, man? You look disappointed.'

'Fuck off, Rudyard.'

Rudyard laughed.

'All right, people. Heads down,' Jay said.

The other couriers stepped forward to watch as Matt and his team counted and checked the first round of bags. They bundled the notes in folds of ten, confirmed the dealers' slips, then passed the money on to Matt, who, as well as checking his own bag, acted as banker, gathering the folds of bills into bundles of ten. Ten fivers in a fold made fifty, ten folds made five hundred.

Slips and totals from the first round confirmed, Matt locked the money away in a cash drawer, rapped on the tabletop and called, 'Next!'

One of the couriers tossed out four more bags, they took one each, upended them, and the process began again.

They'd been like a family, Matt thought, drifting back to sleep, recalling their banter and their jokes. Grumpy old Conrad who turned out to have a voice like an angel and sang in a choir, Rudyard with his endless yarns, and Yvette, bawdy and coarse one minute, caring for an endless variety of waifs and strays in her council flat the next. As close as he'd ever come to having a real family undercover.

They were just ordinary working people – despite their

employer. The sort you'd find in any office. That was the way the business was run. From the Counting House up, it was a web of offices and small businesses, all secretly interlinked to form the equivalent of a criminal corporation. How many of those further up the chain questioned where the money came from or even cared?

That's what Matt was there to find out. SOCA weren't interested in the little people like Con, Yvette, and Rudyard. They were after the big fish, the ones at the top, the ones who organised the shipments and lived the high life on the profits.

But Matt had betrayed them. His co-workers. His mates. His family. He shuddered at the thought of what had happened to them. What they believed he'd done to them. It was all his fault. It was all down to him.

Seconds, minutes, hours later – it was hard to tell in dreamland – he saw them again, transformed now, overlayed with that sinister, smiling face.

Please, Penny. No!

He jerked awake and lay gasping in the darkness.

*

'It's happened again,' Jane told Sally, one eye on the bathroom door, one ear on the sound of the shower. 'I don't know what to do.'

'Is it that woman again, Penny?'

'It's getting to be every night.'

'Have you asked him?'

'Obliquely.'

'What does that mean?'

'You know, "Sleep all right?" "Yeah, fine." "Only you seemed a little restless." "Was I? Sorry if I disturbed you. Dreaming, I suppose."

'He says he never remembers his dreams. Envies people that do because it feels like he's missing out on something. But is that even possible with a dream that recurs night after night?

Something that jerks you awake, calling out to ... to some floozy?'

'Stop it, Jane. You don't know that. You're just going to have to ask him, simple and direct.'

'I can't do that now. I keep pretending he hasn't woken me.'

'What about that "no secrets" deal of yours?'

'What about it?'

'Didn't last long, did it?'

'What do you mean?'

'He's not telling you about his nightmares, and you're not telling him how he keeps waking you up.'

She was right. They'd been lying to each other.

'Next time, Sal. Next time it happens, I'll confront him. Oops, better go. The shower's stopped. He'll be out in a minute.'

She hung up, put the phone aside, and went back to her book as the bathroom door opened. Matt stood wrapped in a hotel towel, his long hair wet and steaming. 'Come, woman. Man want breakfast,' he said in a caveman voice.

'Oh yeah? Well woman want read.'

He grunted, surveyed the scene for a moment then lunged, diving his hands beneath the covers and catching her by the ankles.

'Get off me, you oaf!' she cried in mock alarm.

'Man want woman.'

'What about breakfast?'

He grunted again. 'You. Breakfast. Yum-yum.'

Jane laughed as he dragged her down the bed towards him. There was no doubt about his desire. The bath towel had come undone. Still, a part of her remained aloof in their lovemaking, watching out in case he slipped up and whispered someone else's name.

*

Mr A M Bennett sat with his back to the window reading from a folded newspaper and sipping a cup of tea when Jane and Matt breezed into the inn's dining room shortly before nine o'clock.

They giggled and whispered and nudged each other like a couple of newly-weds, having already decided that since this was to be their first proper appearance in front of the man who'd followed them from London, they'd present the least possible professional image they could manage. After all, they were supposed to be on holiday.

Jane had already been for a run, spiralling out from the BB Inn, checking every road and track and parking spot for signs of the blue Audi. She'd even made a circuit of the campground. Nothing. Which was disappointing. Proof would have been nice since Matt wasn't a hundred percent certain this was the man whose tyre he'd let down. But there were other ways of obtaining proof.

Matt returned to their table with a handful of tourist brochures about the local segment of the Wales Coast Path and began talking about which way they'd go, when they'd leave, and which bus they'd need to get back.

Bennett set down his cup, folded his newspaper, nodded to the waitress and returned to his room. Five minutes later, Jane spotted him in walking gear and backpack, buying a bottle of water from the reception desk.

'Looks like he's planning to get a head start on us. That should keep him busy for a few hours,' Matt said. 'Come on, eat up. We've got work to do.'

There was no local policeman. The nearest station was at Barry, twenty minutes drive away, but there was a local go-to man, Beth told them. Head of the village's volunteer fire brigade and civil defence. A lifeguard and on-call member of the lifeboat crew, Old Llew was the man you went to for everything from a clifftop rescue to a kitten stuck up a tree.

He was something of a giant. Six-six, at least. A good four inches taller than Matt, and broad and sinewy to boot. And not old at all.

They found him behind a briar hedge, working at an enormous

and vigorous vegetable garden beside a picturesque stone cottage.

'It's a sort of village nickname,' he told them. 'My predecessor on the lifeboats was New Llew, right up to the day he retired. There was Llew before him, see? Then the Lovages from the general store called their boy Llewellyn, so he got Young Llew, which didn't leave much for me when I moved here. I did suggest Newer Llew, but they didn't take to that. So I'm Old Llew compared to Young Llew, but I'm not so old as New Llew.' He smiled amiably and added, 'How can I help you?'

Once they'd identified themselves as private investigators hired by the family of Terence Araton to look into his disappearance, Old Llew dusted his hands on his dungarees and beckoned them into the cottage. The interior was as quaint as its exterior. Wooden beams, whitewashed walls, lead-lighted windows, and furniture that might have come from a BBC drama set in the 1950s.

They followed him through to a lean-to kitchen at the back. Still a work in progress, it smelled of linseed oil and wood shavings.

'One of my projects,' he said, filling the kettle, setting it on the hob, and taking three mismatched mugs from a shelf. 'We've only had the house a year, but the wife insists on her comforts.'

'Beth Tyrell at the BB Inn said you're the go-to guy for any problems around town,' Matt said.

'I get the lot. Everything from sorting out pub fights to chasing campers off the village green. I can't imagine why they always ask me.' He smiled. 'Apart-height, the wife calls it.'

He poured the tea. They made small talk. Then he said, 'So this Araton chap is still missing then? Odd case, that.'

'In what way?'

'We've only had the cottage a year, but we've been in town for seven. In all that time, we've never had a proper missing person. There's the occasional enquiry about someone overdue from the coastal walk. Nine times out of ten they're in the pub or the cafe after a change of plan, though I did find a young German girl with a badly sprained ankle back in May. Taking selfies out on Pace Rock. Got caught by a tidal surge and stepped into a hole. Hard to say if she was more upset about her injury, being late back, or getting seawater in her phone.

'There's a sort of step by step procedure with these things normally. Check the bar and cafes, check the hotel and campground, then check the track. But with Mr Araton, no one called for me to check the pub or ask around the village or anything like that. The police came straight here. Mind you, he had been missing a few days by then.'

'You didn't notice any unusual happenings in the village in the intervening time?' Matt asked

Old Llew shook his head.

'But they did find his car here.'

'They did, yes, and that was a little odd. Seems he spent the night at the BB Inn – had a booking and everything – and signed in shortly after the afternoon bus came through. There was no mention of using the car park, and no car in the car park either. If there had been, Beth and Benji would have noticed straight away that he hadn't been back to collect it.

'The police found it up at the campground behind some of the summer cabins, tucked away out of sight. The cabins hadn't been used all week. Why park there? It's a half-mile from the BB Inn.'

'What happened when the police arrived?'

'That was odd too. They didn't look like police. Plain clothes, plain car, but I suppose the ties were a bit of a giveaway. A sergeant and an inspector. From Cardiff, too. We usually just get a squad car from Barry.

'They asked around the village then came to me. Asked the same questions you did. Any odd happenings in the last few days, anyone hanging round or unusual activity?

'They wanted to check the coastal path. Get the lie of the land, they said, though we'd had a dozen or more people through in the meantime, and no one had reported anything untoward.'

'You mean they were looking for a body?'

Old Llew nodded. 'The sergeant came along with me. Taciturn chap, didn't have much to say for himself, but took a lot of notes and photos on his phone. Asked me about the tides. You know about our tides?'

Jane and Matt shook their heads.

'The Severn has the biggest tidal range in Britain. Up to fifty feet in places. There's a bit of up and down on this part of the coastal track; beaches and clifftops and side tracks to sheltered bays. We checked them all.

'By the time we got back, it was all over. The other chap had found Araton's car up at the campground. We got back in time to see them taking it away on the back of a lorry. All wrapped in plastic, it was. For proper examination, apparently.

'Forensics?'

'Whole team of them, they had. I talked with Eirene Thomas, who lives across from the campground. She looks after the place for the owner.

'After he found the car, that inspector chap asked her a lot of questions and borrowed the keys. No one had used the cabins for a week, but it didn't stop him calling in reinforcements. Eirene reckons there were ten or twelve of them. Two white vans plus the lorry. Went all through the cabins, fingerprinting and photographing and such. All through the undergrowth around the car too. Then they wrapped it up like a Christmas present, winched it onto the lorry, got in their vans and drove away.'

'Have you heard anything since?'

'Not a dickey-bird. Until you two, of course.'

'Do you have a theory about what became of Araton?' Jane asked.

Old Llew sighed and sipped his tea. 'Accident or suicide would be my guess. It was nice weather. Perhaps he fancied a dip. Go out too far, get caught in a rip, and before you know it you're halfway to the North Atlantic. I've seen it before with an untethered dinghy.'

'There'd be evidence of that, surely? Clothes, a backpack, possessions left behind.'

'I did mention the tides, didn't I? They soon sweep a beach clean. In fact,' he turned to a nautical calendar pinned to the wall, 'there was a spring tide two days after he set off. The Wednesday. Two days before the police arrived.

'A spring tide is like spring cleaning around here. Reaches all the corners you usually miss, you know?'

'So if he'd left his shoes and backpack on low rocks ...?'

Old Llew made a sweeping gesture with one of his massive hands accompanied by a wooshing sound.

*

The path to the campground ran behind the village school, where a gaggle of noisy children were on their mid-morning break. It rejoined the road, ran parallel to it for a hundred yards, then angled across a scrubby field before rejoining it again on the other side of a lazy curve.

'So, half a mile by road, a little less than that on foot,' Matt said.

'Still, why park out here?' Jane looked around at the broad, grassy circle bounded by trees and gorse. A single tent sat in a sunny space beside an old Toyota. A number of caravans, most closed up, occupied an adjoining field, and three weathered cabins sat along the south side, their windows shuttered.

'Good question. I have some more pressing ones, though.' Jane glanced at him. Matt's face was stony. 'Why doesn't the report Harroway gave us say exactly where the car was parked? Half a mile from the inn is a suspicious circumstance. And why the immediate police interest in a misper? Old Llew said he finds nine out of ten overdue walkers down the pub or at the cafe, yet Cardiff – that's Cardiff Central, not the nearest nick at Barry – sent out a

DI and a DS without even checking with their local man beforehand. They clearly suspected something was up.'

'Then they summoned a forensics team,' Jane said.

'Another point not mentioned in the report. I would expect to see *something*, even a negative result.

'They got here double-quick too. My guess is they were on standby. And they worked bloody quickly. A proper scene examination can take days. It's like they wanted to get in and out with the minimum of fuss.'

Jane nodded. 'Avoiding publicity, as Harroway said.'

'He used the phrase "initial over-enthusiasm", remember? That must've been it.'

Jane turned to examine the cabins. 'According to Old Llew, the police searched and fingerprinted them. Did they think he'd been hiding out there?'

'A logical assumption if his car's nearby. But we may be able to get an answer to that.'

To their left, a middle-aged woman advanced towards them across a neighbouring field, homing in like a guided missile. Her head was wrapped in a crimson scarf, and her figure and features resembled those of a matryoska doll, but she climbed the intervening fence nimbly and strode towards them in Wellington boots, calling out a greeting.

'You'll be the detectives then.'

'Small towns, eh?' Jane whispered.

'Old Llew said to expect you. I'm Eirene Thomas.' She held out a ruddy hand, they introduced themselves, then she gestured at the cabins. 'I heard you're staying at the BB Inn. I don't expect you'll be wanting one of these.'

'Do they get much use?' Jane asked.

'They're booked months ahead in the summer, but it's really only the weekends at this time of year. Friday and Saturday mostly.'

'Were they booked last weekend?'

'Oh yes, that's why I told your colleagues to get a move on if they wanted to look them over. First arrivals were due in at seven, same as tonight.'

'They obviously asked you about Terence Araton,' Matt said. 'Did you know the man?'

'They did, yes, and no, I'd never heard of him before.'

'Where was his car parked?'

'Out of sight there behind Number 1, half backed into the gorse. I thought it must belong to someone from the campground.'

'Can you remember when you first noticed it?'

'Sunday evening when I went over to tidy and lock up. Weekend guests have to check out by four o'clock, you see. I went over about five and saw it parked up there. Not in one of the cabin spots, a bit behind them, but not in the campground either. I had no more bookings that week and never gave it a second thought. Not till your lot turned up on the Friday.'

'So it sat there from Sunday to Friday?' She nodded. 'You said it was backed into some bushes. Did it look like someone tried to hide it?'

'No, it wasn't hidden. More like a bit of bad parking.'

'Can you show us where, exactly?'

They crossed to the cabins, and she did so, pointing out the faint yellow patch on the grass where the front half of the car had blocked the sunlight.

'They took it away in a big plastic bag on the back of a lorry, you know.'

'But you didn't see it arrive?'

'No, there's always a bit of coming and going at the weekends, especially at the campground. I don't pay much mind to it.'

'Is there someone there we can talk to? A manager, perhaps?'

Eirene Thomas laughed. 'That'll be me then. There's no call for a proper manager. The place isn't big enough. People book and pay on the internet mostly. Sort themselves out. If there's any ruckus, anything I can't handle, I call Old Llew. One look at that man-mountain usually quietens them down.

'The campground and cabins are owned by a company based in Pwllheli. They have several of them around the coast. They pay me a small retainer to look after the place plus a commission on fees and rentals. I can give you their number if you like. They'll have details of who came and went that week.'

'But you'd have noticed if anyone was using one of the cabins without permission?'

'They'd have to have light and heat and something to eat, wouldn't they? My place is on the hill back there. Front room looks right over the cabins. I'd have spotted them all right. Besides, they're shuttered up and padlocked. Even your colleagues could find no sign of forced entry.'

They took the campground company's number, thanked her and headed back to the village.

'So why did Araton park his car out there in the first place?' Matt said. 'Despite what Eirene Thomas says, I think he did try to hide it. Did you see the bruising and scraped bark on that tree at the back? I wouldn't mind betting there's a sizeable dent in his rear bumper.'

'Why not do a proper job then, move it somewhere else?'

'I think he was in a hurry. The cabin guests had to be out by four, the caretaker went over at five. I suspect Araton ditched the car somewhere in between those times.'

'What makes you think that?' Jane asked.

'According to Beth at the BB Inn, he arrived in town by bus. There's only one bus on a Sunday afternoon, and it swings past the campground about 4:30. He knows the area, remember? He's walked the coast path before, and he probably knew those cabins would be unoccupied during the week.

'You saw where he parked. Halfway between the cabins and the campers. The sort of spot that could have belonged to either group, even if he didn't manage to hide the car completely. So he left it there, ran for the bus and flagged it down.'

'But why?'

'I don't know yet. But I do know one thing.' Matt's face hardened. 'We've only been told half the story. The fact his car was found half a mile from his hotel is a relevant detail, but there's no mention of it in the file. Nor is there any mention of the intense police interest, or that the car was taken away for forensic examination – which should have been done by now, by the way. Add in the missing text messages to and from his sister, multiple calls from DSTL's head of security that were never returned, and you start getting a very different picture of a man supposedly missing on a holiday walk.'

'Perhaps he was being followed,' Jane said, thinking of green BMWs and blue Audis. 'Like we are.'

18

Sally was thinking of Matt when she opened the front door of Jane's townhouse and left the morning mail on the breakfast bar. She wasn't as old fashioned as to think that his nightmares might be the sign of a guilty conscience, but she was worried for her friend. Paul had never called out a woman's name in his sleep – she'd soon have it out of him if he did – but Jane was less robust and less forthright than she was when it came to relationships.

'Puss, puss, puss.'

She picked up the cat bowl, but it felt like another wasted visit. Yesterday's kibble had hardly been touched. What did this cat live on, air?

She topped up Bluebelle's water bowl then checked her watch. She was catching up with former colleagues for lunch and could get a bit of shopping in beforehand. It was Friday. It would be a boozy lunch for them, but not for Sally, not in her condition. Water was something she and Bluebelle had in common at the moment.

*

Tasha Kayne almost unzipped herself into trouble. A good operative should be prepared for anything, but after an uncomfortable night on a leaky air mattress, finally dropping off as the sky outside was lightening, then waking inside a sweltering tent in the middle of the morning, she wasn't at her best. The draft of cool air on her face and sweat-soaked T-shirt was intoxicating, but just as she was about to clamber out, Target Two and Target Three walked straight towards her in the company of the woman who managed the campground.

Stifling a cry of alarm, she reeled back, reaching under the sagging air mattress for the bubble-wrapped packet containing the Glock. There was no cover in here if it came to a shoot-out. She was cornered. A solid wooden wall or door might slow a bullet. A steel door would be better. But tent fabric? She might as well try hiding behind a sheet of paper.

Thrusting a shaking hand into the packet, she held it out before her, not even bothering to remove the bag, but as she eased towards the open flap, she caught the sound of casual conversation, casual footsteps, and a light laugh. The three long shadows advanced up the side of her tent and continued on.

She sat back on her heels and let out a sigh, suddenly picturing herself in the clammy tent, one hand jammed inside a white, bubble-wrap envelope like a postal worker on the take.

'Jeez, girl, get a grip,' she told herself, blowing out her cheeks and tucking the bag back under the air mattress, suddenly glad Taliq had returned to London and that there'd been no one to witness her momentary panic.

*

Mick Rosten didn't rate scenery, or walking, or fresh air. He couldn't understand the obsession with nature trails, fen hikes, or mountain tracks. Why go to Africa to look at lions when you could get a brilliant view of them on the telly with your feet up, a cold lager in one hand and a packet of crisps in the other?

Nature documentaries: yes. Nature: no.

He'd once read of a film crew spending weeks trekking through jungles to track down a rare flower, then more weeks filming its growth and development, all for about ten seconds of telly. And after all that expenditure of time and effort, it turned out the damned thing smelt of rotting meat!

Rosten paused and stretched, begrudgingly acknowledging the walk was at least doing something for his aching back.

Poxy little car! La Puta, all right. Fancy booking me that. I'm a professional! Bloody Reaves. Just wait till I get my hands on that punk ...

'Morning, Michael.'

'Jesus Christ!'

'Close, but no cigar. Though I can understand your confusion.' Reaves stretched out his arms and hung his head like a crucified man, then giggled.

'Where did you come from?'

'Other end of the trail. Been jogging.' He was wearing a nylon tracksuit and baseball cap. 'And watching you approach for about half-a-bloody-hour.'

'What the hell are you doing out here, Reaves?'

'Your job, as usual.'

'Piss off.'

'Where are the targets?'

'About twenty minutes behind me. They were finishing breakfast when I left the hotel.'

'So you scuttled on ahead? Worried you wouldn't be able to keep up?'

Reaves prodded Rosten's belly. He was shorter than Rosten, wiry with a taut face. All bony angles and tightly stretched skin. What he lacked in height and breadth, he made up for in attitude.

'I came on ahead so they could overtake me. Looks less suspicious that way. I also plan to strike up a conversation, find out about their movements so we can plan ahead.'

'And get yourself fucking noticed?'

'I've already been noticed at the hotel. The hotel *you* booked me into happens to be the same place *they* are staying.'

'Yeah, well, bit of a rush, weren't it? You can poodle on back and put your feet up. I'll take over sentry duty from here.'

'What the hell's going on, Reaves? What are we watching these two for anyway?' Rosten studied the younger man's face. They might not be bosom buddies, but they had worked together before. Enough to learn each other's quirks and tells. Reaves' was his right eyebrow. Despite his all-knowing attitude, it twitched in times of uncertainty. It was twitching now.

'You've seen the brief, pal. Discreet surveillance, report all movements, and hit the red button if you see 'em with the tall geezer.'

The tall geezer was Terence James Araton. They'd both been required to memorise his details and appearance from photos and a shaky phone-cam recording. He was their principal target. Healy and Child were secondaries who might just lead them to him. There was a healthy bonus for Rosten and Reaves if they did so.

'We're mushrooms,' Rosten snorted. 'Kept in the dark and fed shit.'

'Well paid mushrooms,' Reaves reminded him. 'Go on, sod off. Go back to the hotel and stay put. Take a break. You did all right yesterday.' That was about the nearest Reaves ever got to a compliment.

'Where were you, anyway?'

'You know me, Rosten. Everywhere and nowhere. Man of mystery, me.'

'Tosser.'

No need to mention yesterday's humiliation, Reaves thought. He had a reputation to protect. He was already weaving a fantasy about how he'd bamboozled Hampshire police with his smooth talk and quick thinking. No need to mention being caught out without a fake ID and his embarrassing climb-down at the station.

Of course there'd been no cat, neutered or otherwise. But he wasn't interfering with a motor vehicle. Some bloke in a pub had given him twenty quid to stick a tracker on a rival company's courier van. They'd find it wedged between the fuel tank and the floor. (Which they did.)

Could he describe the man who'd made him the offer?

Reaves could. He described Rosten.

After a long wait in a locked room and a number of warnings about his behaviour, he'd been let off with a caution.

He told Rosten, 'I'll call you later with instructions.'

'What are you going to do?'

'What you were s'posed to do. Keep an eye on 'em. But I'm going to keep my distance.' He took a pair of compact binoculars from his backpack and grinned. 'Nice day, quiet beaches. Who knows, maybe that bird'll fancy a bit of skinny dipping.'

Rosten made his way back, not ungrateful for the interruption of his walk. He rehearsed a cheery 'Good morning' for when he passed the targets heading the other way, but he didn't see them on the coast path at all or at the hotel. He tried calling Reaves to say he'd been mistaken, but Reaves was out of range. There was no cell signal on that remote portion of the coastal path, so all he could do was leave a message.

*

Matt licked his ice cream and said, 'We're being used.'

'Isn't that the nature of our business?' The ice creams had been Jane's idea on their walk back through the village.

'There's a difference between hiring our services and treating us like mugs. MI5 sent us to look for a missing man *after* a crack police team and forensics unit had had a go. Seriously, what do they expect us to find? What was it Wyatt called us: a pair of amateur detectives with tabloid-newspaper theories?'

Jane choked on a bite of her cone. 'We bloody well are not!'

'I know, I know. I'm just trying to look at it from their perspective. I'm trying to work out what they might gain in having us go over ground they've already covered in considerably more depth.'

'You mean the missing data in that file and the stuff we've had to work out for ourselves?' She sighed, thinking about the green BMW and the blue Audi and the man in the dining room at the hotel. 'You're right. About the only thing we have achieved so far is to draw attention to ourselves.'

Matt stopped licking his ice cream and said thoughtfully,

'*That* is a very good point.'

Jane knew that look. 'Oh, you're kidding! You don't really think they're using us as decoys so they can look out for whoever comes after us? That's ... that's creepy!'

'It does have a kind of sick, Security Service logic to it though. It also underscores what we've learned about Araton in the last couple of days: that he's both more important and more desperate than we were led to believe.'

'So what do we do about it?'

Matt grinned. 'Something unexpected, I think.'

19

'You said twenty minutes, you tosser. I've been out here fucking hours!'

Rosten held the phone away from his ear, then jammed it back again in case the lunchtime guests in the BB Inn's dining room heard Reaves' invective.

'I left you a message,' he said quietly, trying to remember which button lowered the volume on his phone.

'Which I've only just got because there's no fucking signal out there! You could've come out and told me, you wanker.'

'You sent me back and told me to stay put,' Rosten said reasonably.

There was a spluttering sound on the end of the line, so he added quickly, 'There's been a development. We need to talk. Where are you?'

They arranged to meet at a lookout near the eastern end of town.

'See you there in ten minutes.' Rosten ended the call without waiting for a reply, and hurriedly finished his dessert.

The lookout was only a short hike from the BB Inn, but Reaves was there ahead of him, pacing.

'Well?' Reaves snapped. 'What's this fucking development?'

'They've split up.'

'What?'

'Healy and Child. They had a row right outside the window of the hotel bar. Something about money, I think. Anyway, she grabbed the keys and took off in the Jag, driving fit to bust. I'll be surprised if there's any rubber left on those tyres.'

'And you just sat there nursing your drink and let her get away?'

'What the hell was I supposed to do? That piece of shit you booked me does nought to sixty in about four days. She's driving an F-type, man, and driving it bloody hard!' Someone famous once reckoned that revenge was best served cold. Well, Rosten delivered that lukewarm, but he had more for afters. 'Anyway, you got your tracker back yesterday, didn't you? We can sit back and watch where she goes.'

Had he guessed right? Reaves hadn't mentioned his precious tracker since he'd gone AWOL trying to retrieve it. His scowl and his deepening colour told Rosten he had.

'Don't tell me you haven't put it on the Jag yet.'

Reaves snorted and turned away. Rosten was fairly certain he wasn't admiring the view.

He let him stew for a bit then tossed him a lifeline. 'I reckon she'll be back. I reckon she's just gone to blow off steam. They're booked in for another night.'

'How do you know that?'

'He told me.' Reaves turned to face him. 'He came into the bar, ordered a pint. I used the opportunity to offer a little bloke-to-bloke sympathy. He reckons she'll go into Cardiff, spend the afternoon putting a dent in the credit cards and come back this evening all sheepish and ready for a bit of make-up wotsit.'

Reaves chewed his lip. 'You call it in yet?'

'Not yet. Do you want me to?'

'Nah. Nah, I'll do it. You better get back and book yourself another night.'

*

Jane was in love with the car all over again. The made-up row with Matt gave her an excuse to gun it from the inn's car park, and the surge of power and the responsive handling were intoxicating. 'Steady girl,' she told herself, glancing at the speedo and easing up on the accelerator. 'You're still on B roads.'

A long, steady climb took her up a steep hill five miles from the village. The lead-up was wooded on either side, but the road was dead straight. Jane slowed as she neared the apex and checked her rearview mirror. Not another vehicle in sight. If she was being followed, they were a long way back.

A hundred yards further on, she came to a T-junction. The signpost said Cardiff was a left turn. Jane went the other way.

If Matt was right about the guest who'd signed in as A M Bennett, the guest they'd spotted seated by the inn's bar window when they returned from the village, and to whom their pantomime argument had been directed, he would do one of two things: try to follow her – which he clearly hadn't – or listen to Matt's tale of woe and have his contacts keep an eye out for the distinctive car heading for Cardiff. There was a third possibility. He might accept Matt's assurance that Jane would be back this evening after a little retail therapy, but there was no point in taking chances.

'And that's why you have to go, Precious. You're just too gorgeous,' Jane said, patting the car's dashboard. 'But not right away, eh? We can have a little fun first.'

*

Tasha Kayne returned to her tent, not sure what she should do next. The BB Inn was booked out for the weekend, though the kind woman in reception had taken her mobile number in case of a late cancellation. The two AirBNB's nearby were also full. How was she supposed to keep watch on the targets from half a mile away?

Simple answer: she couldn't. The nifty red sports car was still in the car park, so they were obviously exploring the Wales Coast Path – exactly as she thought they would. If they were energetic – and they looked it – they might go all the way to St Donat's. Whatever. There were buses back on a Friday afternoon, at 2:30 and 4:30 pm, and they came right past the campground. All she'd have to do was keep an eye out then amble in after them.

With the air vents open and shade coming from a nearby larch, the temperature inside the tent was now bearable. Her restless night, combined with the walk to and from town, had left her weary, so she settled in for a brief siesta.

She woke an hour later, bleary-eyed and briefly wondering where she was. An insistent buzzing came from beneath the air mattress. It took several more seconds to realise it was the other phone. The one Taliq had given her.

She hauled it out, stared at the screen, then sat bolt upright. *What the fuck?* The traffic cam app showed the red Jag had just passed junction 33 on the M4 heading east.

'Shit, shit, shit!' She had no chance of catching it now. All she could do was call Taliq and ask for advice.

*

Jane maintained a steady pace heading for Bristol, not over-confident she'd shaken off her mysterious pursuers. They'd been remarkably persistent. Which was why the next stage of the plan was essential, and why she kept a weather eye on the rearview mirror.

Traffic was moderate with more coming west than going east, and she made good time. The rental agency was expecting her. She'd called ahead. Prestige cars suggested prestige customers, and Jane was given the red carpet treatment. No, there was nothing wrong with the vehicle, it was magnificent and she'd be sure to recommend the agency to her friends, but a family emergency had curtailed their holiday. She accepted the manager's hand-wringing sympathy, declined his offer of a ride to the airport or railway station and abandoned Precious without a backward glance.

The rental agency lay in an area occupied by a number of other rental yards. Jane wondered whether the manager's offer of free transport wasn't at least, in part, motivated by the idea of whisking her away from potential rivals. If so, he was about to be disappointed.

At first she wasn't sure what drew her to Yippee Cars 'n' Campers. Then she realised she'd seen its Day-Glo graffiti-like logo on a car in the BB Inn's car park. A bright circular sticker inside the rear window of a rather tawdry looking shoebox. There had already been enough odd happenings and coincidences in this case. Was it possible Blue-Audi-Man had swapped vehicles for one of these?

There were two similar vehicles parked at the front of the lot beneath a flapping banner that read *Try our Yippee Special. Unlimited mileage for just £20 a day!*

'Great deal for cheap wheels,' a voice called.

Jane turned to see herself addressed by a man who had either slipped through a time-warp from the sixties or who was en route to a fancy dress party. He wore a faded paisley shirt, baggy cords, love beads, a wispy goatee, and long, wavy hair secured by a brightly patterned headband. He also wore a badge that said he was Marc and that his role was Duty Manager.

'The paperwork's a breeze. You can be cruisin' for the weekend.'

The voice didn't quite fit the image. It was pure West Country.

'Do you rent many of these?' Jane asked.

'A few. Mostly to students and backpackers. A cool lady like yourself should be in something more stylish.' He gestured to the larger, newer vehicles further up the lot.

'I think I know someone who hired one of these a day or two ago. An older man, a little chunky. Name of Bennett ...'

It was worth a shot. She didn't really expect a result.

'Yo! I remember the dude.' Marc, the duty manager, rocked back on his heels. 'Didn't look like a Kei-car man to me, more of a business dude, but I s'pose he was on a budget.'

'*Was* he on a budget?'

'I don't know. But he was on a poetry budget, I can tell you that. A Slough man, right? I gave him that line about friendly bombs, and he looked at me like I was trippin'.'

'You mean, "Come, friendly bombs, and fall on Slough! It isn't fit for humans now"*?*' Jane said.

'"There isn't grass to graze a cow."'

They combined voices for the next line: "Swarm over, Death!"

The duty manager laughed and offered her a high-five. 'Yeah, you're the man! I mean, ma'am. Imagine a Slough man not knowing that!'

Imagine.

'You wouldn't have his number, would you? My mobile was stolen, and I've lost all my contacts.'

'Oh man, that's heavy! But no problemo, seeing as you already know the dude.' Then he added, 'And your Betjeman.'

Five minutes later, Jane left Yippee Cars 'n' Campers giving the duty manager a cheery wave. In her pocket was a piece of paper containing Bennett's mobile phone number. She also had – thanks to a simple distraction – a photographic copy of the front page of his rental agreement on her very-much-not-stolen mobile phone.

Around the corner and out of sight, she stopped at another agency and hired another car, an ordinary, unobtrusive family estate. She'd been tempted to give Yippee the business, but a stray word when Bennett returned his vehicle might tip him off that they were onto him. As it was, she'd strongly suggested Bennett was a rather tedious business contact, so the duty manager was unlikely to ask if his friend had called him.

After texting Matt her status and a copy of the rental agreement, she had some time to kill. Along with the car's papers, the glovebox contained a bundle of sightseeing brochures. She leafed through them; the Clifton Suspension Bridge, *SS Great Britain*, Cabot Tower, and Brandon Hill sounded interesting, but she didn't fancy playing the tourist on her own. The Bristol Museum had a special exhibition about life in the trenches during World War I. It was advertised with a grainy photograph of gas mask clad troops huddled in a ditch.

Jane shuddered, recalling the NBC suit hanging in Araton's closet. She thought of his house, much older than the ones around it, with its neglected garden and grimy exterior underscoring the difference. It was bigger too than the newer houses, more solidly built, and she guessed it had once been an old farmhouse, the centrepiece of a patch of land since swallowed up by housing estates.

Bigger and more solidly built ...

She recalled her aunt's place from her childhood, a similar solid old house, almost identical in design and construction, but far better kept. Still, to a child – and she couldn't have been more than five or six – it seemed a dark, foreboding place, an impression emphasised by the teasing stories of her older cousins.

What was it about that place?

She thought of Araton's sister's visit. Of the heavy bag she'd carried in and the empty bag she'd carried out.

And then she had it. The pieces clicked into place. Or some of them.

Was it possible?

It was an idea, at least. Something to do. She had some time to kill before heading back to the BB Inn. Besides, it was Friday. If she didn't act now, the only source of the information she required wouldn't be available till after the weekend.

Following signs back to the M4, she joined it and continued heading east.

20

Matt zoomed the image on his phone, studying the rental agreement of the man in the hotel bar who'd identified himself as Al. According to the paperwork, he was Allan Michael Bennett, a resident of Slough. A glance out the window confirmed the make and registration of the car in the BB Inn's car park.

'How the hell did you manage that, Janey?' he chuckled to himself. She was a remarkable woman. He must remember to tell her that when she got back.

With a free afternoon and the added incentive of doing something to rival his partner's investigatory prowess, he decided to indulge in a little old-fashioned police work. After a call to friend and former colleague DI Colin Avery to see if Allan Michael Bennett's licence tripped any bells on the Police National Computer, Matt took one of the photographs of Terence James Araton from the file, tucked it into his pocket and headed out for a bit of door-knocking.

*

Tasha Kayne gave a sigh of relief as the traffic cam app showed the red Jaguar leaving the M4 at junction 19 and turning onto the M32.

'They're going to Bristol,' she told Taliq on her other phone. She was halfway there herself now, having ripped up stakes and rammed all the camping gear onto the Toyota's back seat. The damned air mattress, which refused to stay up all night, now partially blocked the rear window because it wouldn't go down.

'I see that.' He had a copy of the app on his own phone. 'I'll keep an eye on the local council's traffic cams to pinpoint its location once you get there.'

'Thanks. How's it going with Sierra Bravo?' she asked, trying to sound casual.

Taliq sighed. 'Hotel, coffee shop, sightseeing then back to the hotel. So far, so boring.'

Tasha grinned. So she was seeing a bit more action after all.

'I'll call you when I reach Bristol.' She hung up and reached behind her as she drove, trying to find the valve on that damned air mattress.

*

Jane swung into a park near Salisbury Cathedral and walked the short distance to the council's information centre on Fish Row. From there, she was directed to Wiltshire Council on Bourne Hill, where a kindly clerk, taken in by her sweet smile and professed hopelessness with technology, quickly located the original plans to Araton's house in Stratford-sub-Castle. For the princely sum of £2.50, he even printed her out a copy.

Returning to the car, she was glad she was no longer driving the Jag. She couldn't wait to show Matt what she'd discovered, and the temptation to do so as quickly as possible would have resulted in a large number of speeding tickets.

*

'That Jag's all done, chief. Where d'you want her?'

The agency manager arched an eyebrow at his car cleaner. 'Already?'

'Sod all to do. Interior was fine, so I just ran her through the wash. She's gleaming like a new penny.'

'You've done the full checklist? The *full* checklist?'

'Yeah.'

'Show me.'

The cleaner sighed, retrieved his clipboard and returned to the office with it; every item ticked off, the form signed, dated, and timestamped.

The agency manager grunted.

'So where d'you want her? Out the front?''

'No ... er ... leave it back there for the time being. I'll ... sort something out on the lot. Move some cars around. Show it off properly.'

The cleaner put the keys on the board, grinning to himself. Everyone knew the manager fancied himself behind the wheel of the fancier motors. Bristol branch didn't see too many, and any vehicle that wasn't rented by closing time could be his for the evening.

One of the agents called out to him as he headed back across the lot. 'Oh, Terry, do you know if that F-type's available? It's not up on the system yet, but Mr Faraji here has an XJ booked for the weekend and was wondering about an upgrade.'

The customer regarded him hopefully.

'I was just about to RTS it, Jan. All yours, sir. Lovely motor, sir. You'll have fun with that.'

Terry saw the manager glaring at him from his office window and gave him a cheery wave. Wasn't he always saying the customer came first? And hadn't he just saved him from having to rearrange the front of the lot?

The agency manager didn't wave back.

*

Susan Burdon picked at the snack tray left by room service as she paced to and fro. A collection of mobile phones lay on the bed, cheap handsets, identical, colour coded with bits of tape, her only real connection to what was going on since the tracker had died.

Reaves still hadn't fully explained that. Some sort of signal problem, he said in his report. Which was true to a degree. Shut up in a police evidence locker, the device was struggling to send any sort of a signal.

Still, hadn't it always been like this? In her time as an operative, days, weeks, and sometimes months would go by with nothing but a word here or a suggestion there. The infinitely careful shuffling of pieces on political and diplomatic chessboards often felt like the slow drip of Chinese water torture, but back then there had always been colleagues to share it with, superiors to report to, and sometimes the cathartic release of action. This time she was on her own.

She blew out her cheeks and tried to focus on Reaves' last report. What the devil were the Bluebelle people playing at? They were supposed to be professionals. Having what amounted to a lover's tiff in public, right in front of one of her agents, sounded suspicious. Or was she reading too much into it? They were a couple, after all, and couples sometimes fought and fell out. She knew that well enough.

What if it was a ruse? What if Jane Child really was up to something other than a bit of retail therapy? Neither of the people Burdon had on the ground – supposedly her eyes and ears – would have a clue.

Operations invariably had hiccups. The only thing you could really expect was the unexpected. Still, Jane Child had impressed her with her quick thinking and initiative. The way she'd had that burner phone delivered was clever, and their meeting in the British Library had shown she was an astute woman, smart and intuitive.

Remind you of someone?

It did. And that was the problem. If Susan Burdon had somehow been able to meet up with her younger self, she wouldn't have trusted her for an instant.

21

A cat ran out between parked cars as Sally neared the top of Jane's road. She didn't need to brake, there was plenty of room, but she had a sudden, sickening premonition. There had been no sign of Bluebelle again, and her food looked untouched since this morning. Had something happened to her? Was she sick, perhaps? Or ...?

No, no, not that, surely. Not a day or two after Jane and Matt had gone on holiday ...

She was just being wary, that was all. And who could blame her after Dylan yesterday, chasing her and pulling her tail? There was no way of explaining to a cat that she'd deliberately come early to prevent a repeat of that.

Thinking of Dylan, she checked her watch. She'd better get a move on. The play centre fined parents for late pick-ups.

*

Matt sat alone in the dining room of the BB Inn, aware of the casual scrutiny of his new friend at the bar. Except that Al – Allan Michael Bennett – wasn't really who he said he was. A call back from Avery confirmed the licence was cloned and that the real Allan Michael Bennett had been spoken to by officers in Slough, completely unaware of his alter ego.

A pair of headlights swung into the car park beyond the bar and went out. The unreal Allan Michael Bennett swivelled in his seat, peered into the evening gloom, then swivelled back, giving Matt a thumbs-up and a wink. But Matt already knew who it was. Jane had been back an hour, waiting up at the campground in her inconspicuous car for it to get sufficiently dark. As a double precaution, she'd stopped at the far end and parked behind an SUV.

She stepped into the inn's reception area, her lips pursed, looking contrite, a pair of brand-name shopping bags in one hand. Matt stood and went out to meet her, rolling his eyes to indicate they were being watched.

'Hi,' he said.

'Hi.' Her gaze dropped to the floor.

'You OK?'

'Yeah.'

'Been shopping?'

She looked up wanly. Nodded.

He held out his arms. She hesitated a moment then fell into them.

After a long embrace, she said, 'I'll just ...' Gesturing to the stairs and to her bags.

'Can I come too?'

She nodded.

'Have you eaten?'

A shake.

'I'll get them to send something up.'

They parted, their hands lingering, then Matt returned to the dining room to speak with the waitress. His last glimpse of the unreal Al was of the man giving him a satisfied grin and a double thumbs-up.

*

Tasha Kayne was nearing Bristol when the phone with the traffic cam app bleeped. It had been silent for more than an hour, and Taliq had narrowed down the Jag's location to a few blocks slightly west of the city centre. Ten seconds later, her own phone rang, and she hit the hands-free.

Taliq's voice. 'It's on the move again.'

'I see that. Where are they heading?'

'Out of town.' The cam phone bleeped again. 'M32, heading north.'

'What? I've just hit the M32 heading south!'

'Then you'll have to find an interchange.'

'Fuck, fuck, fuck,' she muttered, craning around, looking to escape the solid knot of Friday traffic heading for the city centre.

*

'I'm worried about Bluebelle,' Sally said. 'I haven't seen her since Dylan chased her and pulled her tail yesterday. She wasn't there this morning, or when I popped in this afternoon.'

'You didn't take the mobile monster in with you, did you?' Paul asked.

'No, I left him in the car.'

'Still, you two are bound to be associated now. She'll be wary.'

Sally picked up a fried wonton and crunched into it, unconvinced. It was Friday night, takeaway night, and Paul had brought home a Chinese banquet for two. The food was delicious, but she couldn't help thinking about Jane's cat.

'She seems to be off her food too,' Sally added. 'Her dish had hardly been touched. She might be poorly, Paul. I might pop over after dinner and double-check she's all right.'

'No, you will not,' Paul said firmly. 'Friday night's about the only night we get to spend together these days, what with my job, your course, and him upstairs. You know what cats are like, Sal. Jane's only been gone a couple of days. I doubt Bluebelle's suddenly come down with something like catarrh, or ... catalepsy, or ... or ...'

'Or what?' Sally grinned. 'Come on, one more. You can do it.'

'Shut up, woman, you're putting me off. I was going to say cataloguing, but that's not right.'

'Cataloguing?' She laughed.

'Cataracts! Ha! There, gotcha! Point to me.'

'Conceded. You got there in the end, but it was a bit of a stretch.' Sally sat back and sipped her low-alcohol wine. She was allowing herself one glass a week, which, frankly was enough. The taste was so bland she wasn't tempted to try more.

'But you agree with me?' Paul said.

'I'm sure you're right.'

'And Jane did say "cat feeder" not "twenty-four-a-day kitty companion".'

'Yes, she did. But I will pop over there first thing if you keep an eye on Dylan.'

'Deal. She'll be fine, trust me. Now, what about this stir-fried pork ...?'

*

'Room service is on its way,' Matt told Jane, closing the door behind him. 'What did you buy me?'

Jane set the bulging shopping bags on the bed and pulled off an upper layer of tissue. Inside each was a thin, summer-weight duvet.

'Oxfam. Two quid each.'

'I hope you kept the receipt. This is on expenses, you know.' He grinned. 'All the way to Bristol for a couple of old duvets.'

'Oh, I didn't get them in Bristol. I've been to Salisbury. I've got some news.'

'Me too.' He took her in his arms. 'About Araton and our friend downstairs.'

'Who's first?'

'*We're* first. You and me.' He kissed her. 'The news can wait.' He kissed her again. 'The kitchen's got a rush on. Dinner could be twenty minutes yet.' Another kiss. 'Great performance down there, by the way. And stunning work tracking down that rental car.'

Jane giggled. 'What is this, a performance appraisal?'

'You can appraise my performance later if you like.' He slipped his hands under her T-shirt and peeled it off in one smooth movement.

'Is this still part of the routine?'

'What routine?' He paused unbuttoning her jeans.

'In case your friend downstairs puts his ear to the door.' Jane grinned. 'It's just that I've never had made-up make-up sex before.'

*

Bluebelle was puzzled and confused. The thing didn't work the way it was supposed to work. Despite all the pawing and nudging, it wouldn't budge. Most frustratingly, she could see the world outside through it. It was getting dark. Her people would be home soon. There'd be ear rubs and warm laps and toys to play with.

She tried again. No, stuck fast. All she could do was settle down and wait. Someone would be along soon and let her out, surely.

*

Room service provided a brief respite from their activities, and they lay side by side feeding each other morsels. Matt proved particularly imaginative when it came to the consumption of dessert. Jane doubted she'd ever be able to think of crème brûlée again without a rueful smile.

After another round of lovemaking, they lay together in a tangle of sheets and spent dishes, toasting each other with the last of the champagne. Jane sighed and clinked Matt's glass. 'I could really get used to expense account living.'

'Don't get too comfortable. We've only got another couple of hours.'

'It's all work, work, work with you, isn't it, Healy?'

'Not quite all.' He bent and kissed her breast. 'And you haven't given me my performance appraisal yet.'

'Oh, you get a ten for extracurricular activities, but what did

149

you get up to while I was away?'

'Apart from thinking about you?'

'You know, I might even raise that to an eleven.'

'Eleven out of ten, eh?'

'Who said the mark was out of ten?'

'What?'

'You just assumed ...'

'My male ego is shattered!'

Jane reached beneath the sheets. 'It doesn't feel too shattered to me.'

'I'll give you twenty minutes to stop doing that,' Matt said.

Jane laughed and reached for her glass. 'So what did you discover while I was away?'

'Well, thanks to your brilliant detective work, I learned that our Mr A M Bennett is the clone of a real Slough-dwelling A M Bennett. So it seems I was right about his profile. He *was* the guy in the blue Audi, and he's followed us from London.

'I also did a bit of door-knocking, something the DI and the DS from Cardiff wouldn't have had time for, and happened to run into a local bus driver on her day off.'

'Don't tell me she remembers picking Araton up outside the campground after he'd dumped his car?'

'No, quite the opposite. She remembers him running for the bus as it reached town. Saw him in her rearview mirror and waited, thinking he was running to catch it, but he slowed when he reached the bus stop and turned off towards the BB Inn.'

Jane considered. 'So ... he ran from the campground to time his arrival in town with that of the bus.'

'Exactly. The last bus of the day.'

'Which explains why he didn't have time to properly conceal his car.'

'Got it again. Now get this. The reason she remembers him in particular is that she did pick him up the following morning.

'Remember how Old Llew mentioned a place called Pace

Rock? It's about three miles from town along the coastal path. But there's another way to reach it. A half-mile hike along a regular track from the road. That was where Araton flagged her down. He stayed on the bus all the way to Bridgend, then got off at the railway station.'

Jane pictured the scene: Araton leaving the BB Inn with a cheery wave and a casual mention of that day's destination, then heading for the coast path. Another of the thousands of walkers who did that segment every year. But partway in, he slipped away and caught a bus.

Matt continued. 'She also remembered that he didn't have any gear. Day-walkers carry backpacks and water bottles and sun hats and walking poles. Not Araton. All he had was what he stood up in. Yet when I checked with Beth, she's certain he left with all the gear he'd arrived with.'

'Which means he ditched it somewhere. Like Pace Rock.'

'A place subject to tidal surges. Remember what Old Llew said about that German girl?

'I think Araton planned his disappearance. He left his gear at Pace Rock, but he couldn't be too obvious. He didn't want other walkers finding it too soon and asking questions. Ideally, it was tucked away well enough to get overlooked by passers-by, but not so well hidden that a police search four days later wouldn't find it. From which they'd draw the obvious conclusion.

'Except there was a spring tide in the interim that either washed away the evidence, or buried it.'

Matt took a breath. 'We know there was some sort of trouble at work. Something to do with an audit and the head of security. Something he seems to have been avoiding after that first message from Wyatt. Now we know he was last seen heading for Bridgend railway station. The question is, where did he go from there?'

'I think I know,' Jane said. 'I think he went back home.'

22

'Darling, this *is* unexpected!' Jean Harroway gave her son a peck on the cheek and steered him away from the railway station crowd. 'Can I take anything? The car's around the corner.'

'All good, thanks.' Sebastian Harroway shouldered his laptop and overnight bag.

'How's Samantha? Everything all right?' Her words were casual, but their import wasn't. His mother had come up to London a couple of months earlier when he and Sam were going through a rough patch.

'Splendid. She sends her love.' His reply sounded unusually bright. 'She took a half-day to head up to her sister's for the hen party. No men allowed. I was at a loose end, so I thought I'd pop over. Get out of the hurly-burly for a couple of days.'

'When's the wedding?'

'Middle of next month.'

'Lovely. There's nothing like a good wedding.' Sebastian kept his eyes fixed on the middle distance. 'Your father's still in Riyadh, so it'll just be the two us.'

'Aren't you forgetting a couple of chaps?'

A furious barking began as they swung into sight of the car, and Jean Harroway was obliged to open the hatch so that Claudio and Cosworth could greet their master properly.

Once order was restored, the excited dogs rehoused, and Sebastian's bags stowed away, he settled beside his mother as she slotted her phone into its dashboard dock and backed out of the car park. He glanced at the phone briefly then turned his eyes back to the road ahead.

*

Even though it came via the protected VPN, the message still took fifteen seconds to decode. Susan Burdon studied it:

Target has failed to make contact. Status?

But there was no status to report. Rosten and Reaves were still in Wales, the happy couple were reconciled, and all was right with the world. Except it wasn't. Her mission was to watch the opposition and ensure a clean retrieval, but their man was overdue.

Unless ... unless there really had been more to Jane Child's afternoon absence. She'd been missing for eight hours, the equivalent of a day's work. You could get a lot done in eight hours ...

Burdon stopped pacing. She was sick of being cooped up here, sick of Barty's team of watchers, and sick of waiting for reports from the half-assed halfwits she'd been assigned. It was time to take matters into her own hands.

She knew that watching and waiting was the worst part of any surveillance operation, and that shift changeovers were the best time to move. There was always momentary confusion if the target did something unexpected. Is it the going-off-shift guy's job to handle it, or the guy coming on shift? If the agency still kept to its regular hours – four on, four off – the next changeover would take place in a couple of minutes time, at 8:00 pm. Burdon waited in the stairwell, one eye on her watch and one on the narrow glass panel in the door that overlooked the lobby of the Pimlico Heights Hotel.

The new guy was early. She watched Mr Soon-to-be-off-shift toss his news magazine onto the table in front of him, rise and stretch, one eye on the wall clock behind the check-in desk. It was the same guy who, two hours earlier, had followed her out to a restaurant.

The new guy was a gal. She entered the hotel's revolving door, looked around the lobby, made eye contact with the man she was relieving, and loosened her overcoat. As she took a seat, Burdon moved.

She pushed through the stairwell door, not glancing left or right, not pausing to drop her keycard at reception. Just straight out into the street and the semicircular driveway outside.

A black cab started its engine the moment she emerged, the driver spotting her commanding look and raised finger. 'Liverpool Street Station,' she said. 'Can we go via the South Bank, please. Lambeth Bridge.'

'Be quicker via the Embankment this time of night,' the driver said.

'I'm in no hurry.'

She didn't attempt to disguise her interest in the scene outside the cab's rear window. The off-shift guy and on-shift gal emerged together, one watching her departure – presumably noting the vehicle's registration plate – the other hailing another cab.

Burdon turned back in her seat and said conversationally, 'I'm being followed.'

'Oh yeah?' The driver's eyes met hers briefly in the rearview mirror.

'That's why I asked you to go via the South Bank. I really want to go to Waterloo Station, but I don't want my husband back there to know. If you could find somewhere near Waterloo where I can slip out without being seen from behind, I'm quite happy to pay you for the full trip. And all your time and effort, of course.' She leaned forward through the sliding glass window and placed two fifty-pound notes on the seat beside the driver.

'Lights at the corner of Cab Road'll be your best bet,' he replied as if this sort of request was all part of his daily grind. 'There's a bit of a curve, bit of road works going on. I'll time the light, you slip out to the left, and you'll find Waterloo station across the street to your right.'

It was just as he suggested. A single lane, the road coned off to protect an open manhole cover and a line of Thames Water vehicles. Flashing lights; the beep-beep-beep of a reversing truck; milling men in high-vis vests. Burdon slipped into their midst and watched her taxi drive away, followed by the second cab. She waited till they were out of sight, crossed the road to the station, then checked the time to see she still had ten minutes before the departure of the 8:20 to Salisbury.

*

A little after midnight, Matt woke Jane from a light doze. She sat up, instantly alert. 'All set?'

'All packed and ready to go. Phones off, batteries out.' He held his up, showing her the dead screen. She did the same.

Slipping on a pair of soft-soled shoes, she took one of the bags and followed him to the door. The hallway beyond was silent and softly lit by evenly spaced up-lighters, their dim glow adding to the whispering silence. Matt closed the door behind them with a faint click and hung a Do Not Disturb sign on the handle. They tiptoed to the stairs and down to reception.

'I settled up with Beth last night,' he whispered. 'Said I wasn't sure, but that we might make an early start.'

The front door of the inn was locked. There was a night bell.

'This way.' He gestured to the dining room. 'Out through the kitchen.'

They stuck to the grassy perimeter around the gravel car park and didn't speak again until they reached the shadow of a hulking SUV.

'What did you get us?' Matt whispered.

Jane introduced him to Precious II, a beige Vauxhall Astra estate.

'Bit of a comedown,' he sighed, 'but ten out of ten for anonymity.'

Jane switched on the ignition. 'I'll leave the lights off till we reach the main road.'

'Good idea. Oh, I nearly forgot. Give me a minute.' Matt rummaged in his overnight bag, ducked beneath the line of cars and followed the grassy perimeter strip back towards the hotel. Jane peered over the parked cars but couldn't see him. She did, however, hear a faint spurting hiss. Ten seconds later, once the sound had faded, it was followed by another.

Matt returned waving his Swiss Army knife. 'A little going-away present for the unreal Mr Bennett. Call it my calling card.'

'*Two* tyres?' Jane started the engine and eased the car onto a side street. 'That really is mean.'

'I know.' Matt grinned happily. 'Sometimes I can be an utter bastard.'

*

Tasha tapped the green button on her mobile. Taliq's voice. No greetings or small talk, just, 'What's your current location?'

'Oh, hi Taliq. Nice to hear from you. Long time, no see. How's your Friday evening going?'

'What is your current—?'

'Yeah, yeah, I heard you the first time. I'm on the M5 heading for the junction with the M6.'

'You're about twenty miles behind.'

'Thanks for the update, but I do know that.' The traffic cam app on the other phone continued its regular updates, so regular now she'd switched off the warning tone. 'I'm going as fast as I can.'

As fast as I dare with a damn gun under my seat.

'You're in luck. The Jag just pulled into Hilton Park services between junctions 10A and 11.'

'Good. I'm going to need to gas too.'

And a pee.

'They've been going for a couple of hours so they'll probably take a break. Give you a chance to catch up. I'm just trying to tap into the forecourt cams to confirm visuals.'

'Are you still at the office?'

'Where else would I be?'

Jesus. Friday night in London and he's still at his desk!

'So what have you got?'

'Forecourt feed quality is shit. Black and white, no zoom. Hold on. The vehicle's heading for a takeaway ... parking up ... driver emerging ...' There was a clacking of keys then a faint, '*Shit!*'

'What is it? What happened?'

'Abort, abort. It's not them. Vehicle has a single occupant. Driver is a black middle-aged male, definitely *not* Target Two or Target Three. Turn around, Tasha. They've given us the slip!'

23

Araton's house in Stratford-sub-Castle lay swaddled in darkness. A sodium street lamp three doors up lit only the front fence. Jane and Matt parked two streets away and walked slowly down the footpath, arm in arm like a pair of late-night lovers. They went right past the house, not giving it a second glance. In reality, they were studying the street, the parked cars, the neighbouring houses and the lay of the land.

They continued on, around the block to the street behind. Matt counted footsteps from the corner.

'Looks like it backs onto 14 Plover Place.'

'You're right. I recognise those plane trees.'

Unlike its rearward neighbour, this house was surrounded by manicured lawns, trimmed privet hedges, and rectangular cut-outs of crisply turned earth for flowers and vegetables. It also had a dog. Something small and yappy that gave two rasping barks as they eased around the side of the house before it fell silent again.

The rear fence was high. Wooden, with railings on Araton's side, but a compost bin provided a leg-up while a plane tree provided leverage and support. They dropped side by side into the unkempt garden beyond.

Jane reached into her shoulder bag and handed Matt a head torch, taking a small, powerful hand torch for herself. She switched it on, masking the beam with her left hand and keeping it directed at the ground as they made their way to the back of the house.

Matt adjusted the head torch till the beam was on its lowest setting then aimed it at the door lock. 'Borrow your credit card, ma'am?' he whispered.

Jane had her wallet out already and slid a white Visa card from one of the slots near the back.

'Unless you want to do it?'

'Have we got all night?' she whispered back.

'You need the practice, but I take your point.'

He slid back the top of the credit card to reveal a selection of lockpicks in the lower section. 'Torsion wrench and snake rake, I think,' he said to himself, taking out two of the tiny metal tools. Jane watched carefully.

The end of the torsion wrench was not much fatter than a sewing needle. After inserting it into the lower portion of the lock and applying pressure, he slid the other tool in with its S-shaped end and began the delicate task of working it along the lock's pins. The process took several minutes.

'Sorry, I haven't done this for a while.'

'No rush,' Jane whispered back, keeping an eye on the back garden where a cat prowled the fence they'd just climbed, its iridescent eyes watching their every move.

'Ah!' Matt's sigh was louder than the faint click from the lock. He straightened, tucked away his tiny toolkit and pushed open the door.

They moved silently through the laundry and into the kitchen where a shaft of moonlight glancing off a benchtop provided some unexpected illumination. Jane gestured to the stairs, playing her torch over the cupboard below them before opening the door to reveal a vacuum cleaner, a broom, and a dustpan and brush beside a square bucket containing cleaning materials. It wasn't what she'd been expecting.

'Sorry, I think I got this wrong.'

He shook his head. 'It's not going to be obvious, or the DSTL boys would have found it.'

Undaunted, he began lifting things out and placing them in the hall.

The base of the cupboard was carpeted, a single piece running from the hallway – another reason why her idea must be wrong, Jane thought – but when Matt knelt to examine it he discovered its edge and sides hadn't been tacked down. Folding it back, he played his torch over a neat rectangular hatch cut in the far corner of the floor. The lid of the hatch included a smaller hatch on one side that opened from underneath.

'Looks like a recent addition,' he whispered, running a finger over the roughly-cut edge of the smaller hatch.

'But what's it for?' Jane whispered back.

'Once the main hatch is closed, he opens the little one, reaches through and drags the cupboard stuff and carpet back over the top.'

'That's clever!' Jane pointed her torch at a flush-fitting circular brass catch in the middle of the larger hatch. Matt hooked a finger through it and raised the lid.

A smell of damp earth and dirty laundry wafted up. The rungs of an aluminium ladder angled away from the opening, disappearing into darkness.

Lying flat on the floor, Matt took off his torch and hung over the edge, playing the beam around the hidden room below. Then he pushed himself back, nodded, and gestured for Jane to take a look.

The old coal cellar looked as grim as it smelled. The walls were unlined brick, the floor bare earth. Plumbing, drainage, and electrical fittings ran around the sides and between the floor joists. A single, overloaded socket provided power to the place. Multiple adapters crowded in on each other, and crudely tacked-up leads led to lights, a heater, an ancient music centre, and a laptop quietly charging on an old apple box.

An alcove in one side was stacked with wire-mesh cages, a few larger ones on the bottom – rabbits, perhaps? – with ten or so smaller ones on top. All were empty. Beside them, on a hangar, was a modern hazmat suit, its reflective bands glowing eerily in the torchlight.

Opposite the alcove, a crudely hung shower curtain partially masked a chemical toilet, and a single tap stood dripping slowly into a porcelain handbasin streaked green with age and algae.

There were a few concessions to comfort. A couple of scatter rugs on the floor, a lumpy looking sofa shrouded in a blanket, a reading lamp and headphones on a workbench by the wall, and a collection of books and DVDs with which to pass the time.

The single bar of the electric heater glowed in the darkness. An LED light on the charger blinked on-off, on-off.

Aiming her torch to the far side of the room, she picked out a slumbering figure on a camp stretcher covered with an unzipped sleeping bag. The figure was turned away, moving slightly as its breath rose and fell. All that was visible was the back of a head, but the straight, silvery hair was unmistakable: Araton.

She switched off her torch and sat up, faintly embarrassed, as if she'd been caught peering through an uncurtained window. 'It's him all right,' she whispered. 'What now?'

'Let sleeping dogs lie, I think.'

Matt carefully lowered the hatch, closing it with the faintest bump. Then he replaced the carpet and moved the cleaning things back to where they'd been.

'Nice work, Janey. Technically, we've just solved this case.'

'But?' she said.

'Only three of us know where Araton is right now, and one of them's the man himself. Since it doesn't look like he's going anywhere, I'd like to know what he's doing down there, who else is after him, and why.'

*

The police car came out of nowhere, and Tasha Haynes had no time to rectify her mistake. Then she was trapped, left making feeble excuses, breathing into a breathalyser and trying to explain what she thought she was doing.

'The crash barrier was down because of the roadworks. I remembered I'd left something in Bristol and thought I'd take a shortcut ...'

It had looked like a good plan in the light of her headlights and the orange roadworks signs: cut across the broad grass median strip to the southbound lane and cut at least twenty miles off the round trip to the next interchange. But she hadn't banked on the culvert in the middle of the median strip. The Toyota's front wheels had gone straight into it and got stuck. It was all Taliq's fault. If she'd still had the beemer she could've engaged four-wheel drive and hauled herself out again.

The harridan of a policewoman inspected the breathalyser's nil reading with a disappointed scowl. She'd already checked Tasha's licence, the vehicle's registration disc, and called in its index number in case it was stolen.

'You couldn't give me a tow, could you? Just to get me out of the drain? It wouldn't take much, and I am in a bit of a hurry.' Tasha gave the harridan's dishy young colleague an appealing look.

'We are not a towing service, madam,' the harridan said. 'Besides, I've already summoned a recovery vehicle.'

'Can I ... um ... stay with the car?' Tasha was thinking of the bubble-wrapped packet under the front seat. They hadn't arrested her, but what if they wanted to take her back to the station? Should she take it with her or leave it and hope the towie didn't spot it? If they hoisted up the front of the car, it would slide out into the rear footwell. 'Only, it's my boyfriend's car, and he'll be really mad.'

'Nor are we a baby-sitting service, madam. We can't leave you wandering about on a motorway, especially at this time of the morning, so I think it's best if you come with us to the nearest drop-off point. The recovery driver will have a card. You can organise transport from there.'

'This might be him now.' The dishy one gestured to a pair of flashing yellow lights approaching in the distance.

The three of them stared. Tasha said a little prayer.

The vehicle slowed as it reached the start of the coned-off roadworks. It was the truck!

Finding a gap large enough to weave inside the cones, the

truck rumbled to a stop beside them, and the driver leaned from the open window. 'So, which one of you lot's stuck in a drain then?'

24

Before they left Araton's house, Matt tore a small piece of paper from his notebook, sidled around to the front, and wedged it in the gap between the door and the jamb, low down where it wouldn't be noticed, leaving only a tiny white triangle visible.

'What's that for?'

'A flag,' he whispered back as they slipped through Araton's front gate and into Plover Place, where they resumed their late-night lovers routine, walking away arm in arm. 'If anyone comes or goes, we'll be able to see from the street.'

Jane glanced back. He was right.

It was close to 4:00 am by the time they got back to the car.

'I suppose we could find a motel for a few hours.'

'Hardly seems worth it,' Jane replied, 'especially as we've got those duvets in the back.'

They returned to Goose Green Grove, following the narrow, one-way road to its apex. There, just before it curved back downhill again to pass the other ends of Lapwing Lane, Dotterel Drive, and Plover Place, they found an unkempt park and a parking spot below a line of yews being hustled by the wind. Moonlight flickered on a distant pond, and the swings of a nearby playground creaked in the breeze.

With a bit of internal rearrangement – the front seats flattened and pushed forward, the rear seat folded down – they were able to make space for themselves in the back. As they snuggled in side by side, using one duvet as a mattress, the other as a blanket, Matt whispered, 'I knew I'd get you out camping one day. In a white van too.'

'It's an estate car, not a van,' Jane said sleepily. 'And it's beige.'

Two hours later, Matt woke with a jolt, sweating, staring at the trim on the rear passenger door three inches from his face, trying to get his breathing in check.

That damned dream! More vivid than ever. Flashes of the old desperation around the edges. Why did the mind torture itself like that, reliving and repeating the same events time after time. Was it seeking some sort of resolution? Finding its own way out of the moral maze?

Good luck with that!

He listened. The trees and the playground swings creaked in the wind. A dusting of rain glanced off the roof of the car, as light as falling leaves. He could feel Jane behind him, but couldn't catch the rise and fall of her breath. He turned and found her on her side, resting on one elbow, studying him, her hair fringed with shafts of early morning light coming in through the trees. She looked ethereal, an angel of the morning, but her expression was grave.

He said nothing, swallowed, then croaked, 'Again?'

She nodded. 'Who's Penny?'

He cleared his throat. His mouth was dry. 'Jane, there's something I need to tell you.'

*

Burly men with loud voices and plates of fried eggs, bacon, and hash browns filled the cafe. Formica tables, plastic chairs, condensation on the inside windows. But the coffee was good.

Jane and Matt took a table near the back, sipping from thick-rimmed cups and picking at a pair of day-old Chelsea buns.

'Remember our deal? No secrets?'

'It's not a secret, it's just ... something I haven't mentioned before.'

Jane said nothing, steeling herself, fixing her eyes on his.

He saw her expression and put down his cup. 'I'm sorry, Jane.

I'm such an idiot. It's that name, isn't it? Penny? But it's not what you think. Penny was a man.'

*

The public imagined the police and intelligence communities to be one big happy family, working side by side in their specialist areas, arresting villains and saving the world, but the truth was a far cry from that. All the agencies – GCHQ, MI5, MI6, NCA, NFIB, OSCT – were fraught with rivalries and turf wars, disputes over jurisdiction, petty jealousies, and personality clashes. Operational priorities differed. Careers depended on results. Egos and personal vendettas influenced objectives.

But in his early days, Matt knew nothing of that.

He graduated from Hendon, not just top of his class but also top of his year, and was snapped up by what was then known as SOCA – the Serious Organised Crime Agency. After a specialised induction course, more training, and a couple of small operations, he was sent undercover to investigate a gang importing and distributing cocaine and heroin.

The term "gang" suggested a group of thugs in leather jackets hanging around street corners and intimidating passers-by – another popular misconception. There were certainly lowlifes in back alleys and on council estates dealing the stuff, but they were more like freelancers or contractors – the corner store distributors of a corporation's products. You might as well describe a tobacco manufacturer, a supermarket chain or an oil company as a "gang". Beyond street level, the real gangs, especially those involved in drugs, were managed like the businesses they were, with internal hierarchies, department heads, executives and assistants. And, of course, a cash flow.

Like any corporation, large criminal groups operated behind respectable fronts, with teams of accountants and lawyers and bankers, their principal investors armour-plated and impregnable. *That* was the real interface between the underworld and the everyday world. What was the point of making millions if you couldn't spend it?

Just as police executives in their glass-walled offices wouldn't sully themselves in a street-corner brawl, so drug executives never handled and rarely even saw the products their underlings dealt with daily.

'My cover name was Donald Churchman. SOCA created a full background and profile. Former stockbroker forced to resign for insider trading. Circumstances hushed-up to protect the brokerage, so no charges laid, but word went round the finance houses that I wasn't to be trusted.

'Meanwhile, Churchman had a Docklands apartment and a fancy car to maintain. Drug-wise, he was a strictly recreational user – something he'd had to curtail because of his circumstances. SOCA built him up as an East End boy made good. Someone who'd pushed his way through the class hierarchy by sheer talent and balls, but who was now teetering on the brink. Desperate to find something – anything – and not too choosy about what that might be.

'The first approach was to do a re-up for a dealer in one of the swankier pubs in Islington. I treated it like a business meeting. Turned up in a good suit and briefcase, shook the guy's hand, bought him a drink, then slipped him the package under the table.

'It was a setup of course – a test. But I passed with flying colours. They liked my approach. No nudges and winks or clumsy exchanges in the men's room. No skimming a few grams for myself and cutting the stuff. I got more work. Real work. I was in.'

The group Matt worked for didn't handle the back alley, street-level stuff cut with everything from talcum powder to rat poison. This was top gear for top people, and his job was to deliver fresh supplies to dealers in London's more exclusive pubs, clubs and restaurants.

'I used to get backdoor passes to theatres and music venues, knew the doormen on all the clubs by name, and once even made a delivery to the House of Lords.'

But those weren't the people SOCA were after. Many were already on their database, and arresting them would only cause a temporary hiccup. They were after the source. 'Prune a shoot and another one grows in its place. Tear up the roots and the whole plant dies.' Matt's brief was to infiltrate the organisation, build trust and work his way up the corporate ladder.

'I did all right, they liked my style, and the thing about the underworld is that it's no different from anywhere else: smart, capable people are hard to find.'

There were plenty of opportunities, and Matt soon worked his way into what might have been called lower-middle management. He took on oversight of what was known as the Counting House, the place where the cash from the dealers ended up. The money, great wads of it, couldn't simply be deposited in the firm's building society account. It had to be split up and funnelled through a bewildering array of personal and business accounts – some fake, some legitimate – the first step in its path towards the offshore banks from which it could then be legitimately repatriated.

'First, it had to be checked and counted. Honestly, you wouldn't believe the state of some of the stuff that came in. Then again, considering it came from some of the poorest and most desperate parts of the city, it was hardly surprising.'

Matt had a team of three helpers, part-timers who came in for a few hours every morning and went home at lunchtime with fifty quid in their back pockets. Any discrepancies were dealt with by the enforcers who collected the bags, while the neatly bundled banknotes moved on to the accounts team responsible for filtering them into the banking system. The whole collection and redistribution operation was overseen by a man named Toby Penhaligon. 'Not his real name, obviously,' Matt observerd. 'No more than mine was really Churchman. Whoever he really was, Penhaligon was known as Penny, for short.'

Matt had been running the Counting House for almost six

months when Penny called him into his office. He was American, a big man with grizzled features and the bearing of an ex-Marine. Rumour had it he was a key player in the organisation. He was certainly someone to keep on side because he knew where the money went.

'We've got a problem, Don. We've got a mole. Friends in high places tell me SOCA's got a source inside the Counting House. I want you to find out who it is. Once you've done so, let me know.'

Matt did his best to hide his consternation. 'Are you sure? Where did the information come from?'

By way of reply, Penhaligon merely tapped the side of his nose.

Matt was in a dilemma. What could he do? *He* was the mole. The rest of his team, who by now had become workmates and friends, were innocent. Or was this simply another test of his loyalty and ingenuity, like that first re-up?

He had to determine whether Penhaligon was telling the truth. Was there any possible way there could have been a leak? Matt contacted his superiors and was assured his operation was watertight. Relieved, he went through the motions of having his colleagues' backgrounds checked, having them watched, bugging their houses and phones, and monitoring their online activities. Then he reported back to Penhaligon with his findings: nothing.

Penny merely nodded and accepted the result.

'When I got in the following day, there was no one there. My workmates, Con, Rudyard and Yvette, weren't about, but Penny was waiting for me. He said, 'They're in the basement,' and led the way.

Matt paused and took a long, slow breath. 'They were there all right. Dead. But they hadn't died easy. They'd been tortured. Mutilated.

'Penhaligon seemed to find it amusing. He said, "Funny, you torture a man enough, and he'll tell you anything you want to hear. Anything at all. According to this lot, they were all moles. So were their mums and dads and sisters and brothers, and the whole damn planet besides. Still, we had a bit of fun and reckon we've solved your problem for you. But it looks like you're in for a busy day till we find some replacements."'

Matt looked away through the hazy interior of the cafe. 'That was down to me, Jane. Three innocent people. And don't give me that about working for gangs. Those people weren't pushers or dealers or even users. It was the only work they could get. And they died ... horribly ... because of me.'

Jane pushed her cup aside. Suddenly the coffee tasted foul. 'Did you get them in the end, the gang?'

Matt said, 'I'm not finished yet.'

SOCA and the other agencies shared information on a regular basis, and that included their undercover operations, especially where there was a danger of overlap. But often, the sharing was one-sided. Troops on the ground didn't matter when careers were at stake in head office.

Penhaligon knew who the real mole was right from the start. He told Matt as much the night when he visited him at his apartment.

When Matt opened the door and found Penhaligon standing in the passage, he was surprised, but not half as much as at Penhaligon's greeting.

'Good evening, Don. Or should I say, Matthew? Sorry, old man. I'm afraid your cover's blown. But I have brought you a parting gift.'

He drew out the gun and put two bullets in Matt's chest.

'I staggered backwards, fell, and found myself looking up at him as he lined up a head shot. He was smiling. "I knew it was you all along. I just wanted to see how you'd play it. You did well, I must say. If it's any consolation, your pals in the Counting House would've had to go anyway. Clean slate and all that. You get that, right?

"'And as for me and my little operation ..." He shook his head.

"You Brits, messing with things you shouldn't. The whole set-up's a CIA gig. Of course, now I've told you that, I'm gonna have to kill you."'

As he raised and aimed the pistol, the lift doors opposite the apartment pinged open. A woman saw the blood, the outstretched arm, the gun, and screamed.

Matt twisted his head as Penhaligon fired once then ran for the stairs.

The bullet scored a line across the side of Matt's scalp. 'Always have had a thick head,' he said.

Prompt action by the couple in the lift saved his life, though they were never told.

'One of the bullets passed between my heart and spine. The other punctured a lung. I was in hospital for almost two months.'

But long before then, Don Churchman had officially been declared dead. Murdered by an unknown assailant.

'Penny was telling the truth. The whole thing was a CIA dirty tricks op to allow them to funnel funds to whatever tinpot dictator or covert crook they wanted. The drugs were being flown into US airbases disguised as ration packs. Our Foreign Office had a word; this really wasn't cricket, old boy, and the whole operation was moved to Europe.'

Jane said, 'And it's still going?'

'I have no idea.'

Jane leaned across and took his hands in hers. 'What became of Penhaligon?'

Matt shook his head. 'Where he went afterwards and what he did, I have no idea. But he never faced justice for what he did. Those sort of people rarely do.' He sat back and sighed.

'I can't believe you didn't tell me earlier.'

'Hardly my proudest moment, Jane. Not the way I bungled things.'

'I don't see what else you could have done.'

'Ah, well. it's ancient history now anyway.'

'But the nightmares. You never had them when we first met. Why have they suddenly made a comeback?'

'A combination of things, I think. Getting shot again a couple of months ago didn't help, and now this MI5 business, to say nothing of Susan Burdon and her CIA mates.'

'If you'd told me, if you'd said, we could've turned the job down.'

'What, and miss all this?' He forced a grin. 'At heart, I'm still a copper, Jane. Still curious. Still want to do the right thing. It's just that intelligence agencies ... well, I don't trust *any* of those treacherous bastards.'

25

Reaves called at 6:00 am, waking Rosten from a very pleasant dream involving one of the waitresses in the inn's bar.

'What, now? It's the crack of bloody dawn ... All right, all right. Give me ten minutes, will ya?'

The lookout was deserted, except for Reaves in running gear doing calf and hamstring stretches. The wind was picking up, and the sky looked ominous. So did Reaves. His lip curled as he turned towards Rosten. 'Christ, the state of you! You might have got dressed first.'

'I did get dressed first.' Rosten was wearing baggy track pants, a grubby T-shirt, and open-toed slip-ons.

'Don't tell me you sleep in the all-together?' Reaves scowled at the image and shook his head. 'No, don't tell me. I don't want to know.'

'So what's going on, *Roger?*' A slight emphasis to needle the prick.

'That's what I was going to ask you, *Michael.*'

'What do you mean? I gave you my report last night after the bird came back from her shopping trip. Tete-a-tete in reception, quiet word with the waitress, dinner switched to room service, Do Not Disturb sign on the door. They're probably still at.'

'Are they now? And where are they *still at it*, precisely?' Seeing Rosten's bafflement, Reaves added, 'I just came past your hotel on my morning constitutional. Did a circuit of the car park. Actually, I did two because I couldn't believe my fucking eyes. Have you checked the car park lately? Because there is no red Jag in it. In fact, no Jag's at all.'

'What?'

Reaves turned his face skywards as if seeking guidance. 'I really don't know how I can make this any clearer.' He turned back and bellowed in Rosten's face. '*There is no fucking Jag!*'

Rosten scowled and wiped the flecks of spittle from his face, not absolutely certain he was actually awake.

'What is your sole function in this little caper, Rosten? To keep an eye on that bloody couple, to note where they go, who they meet with, and what they do. That's all. It's not bloody rocket science. And what did you do last night? Got pissed out of your tree on expenses and tried chatting up some waitress half your age and a quarter your girth, you sad old fuck.'

'How d'you know—'

'Cos I keep *my* bloody eyes open! Like you're supposed to do.'

'So it was there last night then, was it?'

'What?'

'The Jag. It was in the car park last night?'

Reaves, wrong-footed, hesitated. 'I ... Yeah, I s'pose ...'

'So they must've taken off earlier today then. There's only one road out of town, which means they must've gone right past your digs. Get much traffic out your way this time of the morning, do you? Jag-sounding traffic?'

Reaves said nothing.

'If not, it means they must have gone past while you were out on your morning constitutional.'

'*You* were s'posed to keep a watch on them.'

'I'm not a fucking machine, Roger. What d'you expect me to do, prop my eyelids open with matchsticks and stare out at the car park all night? We're supposed to be a team, work together. All you do is ponce around in your tracksuit, shoot your mouth off and look for excuses. If you hadn't lost that tracker—'

'It was faulty. I told you.'

'So why didn't you get another one? What the fuck were you

doing the day before yesterday anyway? You still haven't explained yourself.'

'Who do you think you are, my mother? I don't have to explain anything to you, you fat fuck.'

Rosten grabbed him by the scruff of the neck and dragged him off his feet. 'You've got a mouth on you, boy, and I'm not past planting my fist in it.'

The movement was surprisingly quick, and the grip surprisingly strong. There was hard skin on the knuckles of the raised fist, and Reaves recalled something of the big man's reputation: slow to boil and slow to cool.

'All right, all right, Mick. We're a team like you said. Working together, yeah? The targets have scarpered, so what do we do now?'

'I'll tell you what *you* do.' Rosten relaxed his grip, but only slightly. '*You* take that fancy car of yours and try to catch them up. Meanwhile, I'll go back to the hotel, find out what time they checked out and see if they said where they're going.'

'Right. Right. Good plan.'

'Well get a move on then!'

Rosten flicked him off like flicking off an insect and marched back to the BB Inn with considerable dignity, especially for a large man in track pants and grubby T-shirt.

*

'You're up early.'

The words took Sebastian Harroway by surprise because his mother, never an early riser, was up before him. Yet there she was, sitting in the kitchen in her dressing gown, nursing a cup of tea.

'It's the quiet countryside, I think.' He went to the window and looked out over the garden. 'You get used to the background hum of the city. The silence seems almost unnatural.'

'Your father called,' Jean Harroway said by way of explanation for her own early appearance. 'He always forgets the time difference. He'll be back Monday afternoon. You'll miss him.'

'Is everything well, between you two?'

She gave him a so-so nod and sipped her tea, her cellphone on the sideboard beside her. 'The kettle's just boiled if you want a cup.'

'Thanks, but I think I'll take the dogs out for a walk first. Something else I don't get to do in London.'

'Splendid idea. They'll love that.'

Before she could call them in, a pair of red setter heads appeared at the French doors, their eyes alight with expectation. Somehow, their keen hearing had picked out the words *dogs* and *walk* in proximity to each other, and they'd already made the connection.

Jean Harroway watched her son disappear up the lane with the romping dogs, envying the animals their boundless energy and carefree lives. She'd guessed what Sebastian's unexpected visit was really all about, and would have done so even without the courtesy call from Marius Fennel. The fact that Sebastian hadn't yet mentioned his missing uncle was all the more telling.

She wouldn't go for a shower until she saw him returning, she thought. Her phone could stay where it was. Let him get that bit over with at least. His secret agent subterfuge. Not that there was anything to find. Not any more. She'd deleted her entire call history.

She sighed. He would have to be told. And this weekend was as good a time as any to do so.

*

Sally arrived early, noting the signs of absence. No cat on the front doorstep or sofa; the food bowl barely touched; a scatter of ping-pong balls in the lounge unmolested. She checked the house from top to bottom; underneath beds, inside cupboards (imagining a wind-blown door), the front garden, the back garden, calling,

'Puss, puss, puss,' all the while.

Nothing.

She clambered up for a look over the back fence into the school playground behind the house but found just an empty field in the misty, early morning light.

Finally, steeling herself, she went out the front and began checking the street, thinking of thundering wheels and the way cats could dart out. A grim business: checking gutters and verges and squatting awkwardly to peer beneath parked cars, wondering what she would do if her worst fears were realised.

Nothing but a few fallen leaves and the usual London street litter.

She got to her feet and rested against a neighbour's fence. Well, that was one thing, but in a sense it was only the beginning. She took out her phone and told Paul.

'Do you want me to come over and help?' he asked.

'No, but thanks.' He'd have to bring Dylan, and a wary cat wouldn't appreciate her prime tormentor charging around the place. 'I've got my laptop with me so I'll stick around for a bit, see if she shows up. Once the local vets and RSPCA open up I'll give them a ring. She may have strayed. Someone might have turned her in.'

'That was how Jane got her in the first place, wasn't it? As a stray?'

'That's right,' Sally replied a little too brightly. 'She does have a history, doesn't she? And cats are opportunists.'

'What about Jane? Should you let her know, you know, just in case?'

'Oh no, not yet, Paul. They're on holiday. Besides, it's barely eight o'clock. Let's just ... let's just see what happens, eh?'

*

Susan Burdon's hotel room had a view of Salisbury Cathedral. What was more important, though, was what it *didn't* have, namely, oversight by Bartram Horovitz and his school for spies. She knew the CIA commanded immense resources and that he'd soon catch up. All she had to do was keep one step ahead of him.

It felt good to be out of London. The whole damn United Kingdom might be one-third the size of Texas, but the place felt bigger on the ground. In London, Wales seemed more distant and more remote than Brussels, Berlin, or Rome.

It was the right move, and just in time too. Neither of the freelancers her employer had foisted on her inspired much confidence – especially now after an early morning call to say their targets had "temporarily" slipped the net.

'Left early,' Reaves told her. 'I'm trying to catch 'em.'

The background sound was of a racing engine and a car taking corners too fast. Even if he didn't kill himself in the process, Susan Burdon doubted he'd succeed.

Call it instinct, call it intuition, but *that* was the main reason she was here: Jane Child. Yesterday's lovers' tiff had struck her as phony from the outset. A convenient excuse for Child to slip the lead and do ... what? A whole afternoon to herself, unobserved. Where had she gone? What had she done? What had she discovered?

Whatever it was, it led them to steal away just hours after Burdon received the message from her employer about the target failing to make contact. Was there a connection? There had to be. She looked again at Rosten's text from Thursday afternoon:

14 Plover Pl. Stratford-sub-Castle, approx 55 mins. Loc. did not permit surv.

Fifty-five minutes at Araton's house. He obviously wasn't there, so what the hell had they been doing all that time?

It was a place to start, at least.

Burdon surprised the reception desk by checking out early and asking for directions to the nearest car rental agency.

26

Jane made a face at her red-eyed reflection in the rearview mirror and followed Matt to the door of Jean Harroway's house, their arrival forewarned by a pair of deep bass barks. But it was Sebastian Harroway who opened his mother's front door.

'What are you two doing here?' He was ashen-faced, his frame rigid. The air in the house crackled with tension that even seemed to restrain the dogs' greetings. 'I thought you were checking the coastal track.'

'We were. Now we have some more questions for your mother.'

'What sort of questions?'

'One's we'd like to put to her, please.'

'Not right now. She's not in any—'

Jean Harroway's tear-streaked face appeared in the hallway behind him. 'It's all right, Sebastian. Let them in. They might as well know too.'

'Mother! This is family business.'

'It's all right, Sebastian,' she repeated more firmly. 'Anyway, aren't these the people who provoked your interest in the first place? Marius told me about his slip-up with the phone data, or whatever it's called.' She touched her son's shoulder. 'That's really why you're here, isn't it? To look at my phone and see what those redacted messages were all about?'

'Mother, that's an outrageous suggestion!'

'Oh, I don't blame you. Who wouldn't be curious, especially given the circumstances. But if you could find them, anyone could. So I wiped the lot. As you may have already discovered.' He spluttered. 'I didn't want you finding out that way.' She dabbed her cheek. 'Hence our little talk.'

With pursed lips and deepening colour, the younger Harroway turned away as his mother beckoned the visitors in.

The same paved patio and long back garden, but no Maria today to provide refreshments. None were offered. Sebastian, to his mother's evident relief, excused himself, beckoned the dogs, and continued on to the stream at the bottom of the property.

Whatever upset preceded them, it had softened Jean Harroway's features. The woman who settled in the wicker chair opposite seemed more herself and more at her ease than on their previous visit.

'I should start by telling you that Sebastian's boss, Marius Fennel, and I are old friends from Cambridge. That my son ended up in his department is pure chance, but I suspect it is one of the reasons you were engaged to investigate my brother's disappearance.

'My brother and I have always been close. Always,' she added significantly. 'After our parents died, we grew closer. Terence was fourteen, I was thirteen and ... we comforted each other and continued to do so for several years. No one knew. We were careful. Discreet. It's supposed to be wrong, but ... it was the purest form of love I'd ever known. Accepting, unquestioning, undemanding.

'The recriminations came later, mostly self-inflicted, and we never spoke of it, except once in our mid-twenties. I was recently married to Philip, and we were going through a rough patch. Terence had just broken-up with an old girlfriend. We comforted each other again, just for one night ...' She took a breath before continuing. 'And Sebastian was the result.

'Neither of us knew, not until a month ago. I did wonder, of course, but ... nature and nurture ... you can never be sure, can you? At least, you couldn't, not in those days. DNA testing wasn't available thirty years ago.

'My husband, Philip, the man Sebastian always thought of as his father, recently developed an interest in genealogy. He spends his free time trawling through online records and making contact with long-lost relatives around the globe. And of course he insisted we all have our DNA tested.

'It turns out that Philip's lineage is a melange. English, Irish, Spanish, Swedish, and Italian with dashes of Indian and Ashkenazi Jewish too. Mine and my brother's are almost entirely English. You see the problem?

'Sebastian's results came back while Philip was on one of his trips. I opened the letter and saw ... well ... Sebastian has a younger sister, Ellen, and only her profile shows the expected mix.

'I kept the letter hidden from my husband while I tried to work out what to do. Philip thinks there's been a slip-up at the lab and wants the test redone. I consulted with my brother. Terence was shocked at first, then overjoyed. He and his late wife never had any children, and as he said, this gives him and Philip one each.

'I wanted to get Ellen's test repeated and pass hers off as Sebastian's, but Terence disagreed. He wanted it all out in the open. Or at least, for Sebastian to be told. We argued, out there in the garden, shortly before Terence went off on his holiday, and we argued again in our text messages. The messages Marius redacted because they involved an old friend who happened to be the mother of a member of his staff. He too urged me to tell Sebastian ... and now it's done.' She looked down the garden to where her son, half-hidden in the undergrowth, squatted staring at the stream while the dogs romped and frolicked nearby.

Matt said, 'Is that all you have to tell us, Mrs Harroway?'

'What do you mean, *all*? Is that not enough? The shame of my life—'

'I meant in relation to your brother's disappearance.'

She looked at him, the flash of anger giving way to something else. Her reply, when it came, was muted, almost confessional. 'I don't know what you mean.'

'Before you reported him missing, you told us you checked his house and consulted with his neighbours, but none of the neighbours we spoke to have any recollection of you doing so.

'Oh. Well. They're an odd lot around there.'

'What did you take into the house, Mrs Harroway? You were seen entering with what has been described to us as a heavy gym bag, yet when you left the bag was empty.'

'Who told you——?'

'Does that really matter? You were carrying supplies in for him, weren't you?'

'Supplies? No. No, just a few things he asked me to pick up for him. Camping-type food, some books and DVDs – some of which I noticed he already had – and a power lead for his computer. He said to leave them on the kitchen bench, and he'd arrange for someone to collect them and forward them on to him.'

'Forward them on?'

'Yes.'

'Who? How?'

'I have no idea.'

'You didn't query him?'

'I couldn't very well, could I? He sent me a note.'

'A note?'

'A letter. By post. To the place I work. I help out at a local charity shop two afternoons a week. As I was about to leave the Wednesday before last, the postman arrived with a letter addressed to me from Terence. No return address, no stamp; I had to pay postage.'

'Did he often communicate that way?'

'Never.'

'And you didn't think to mention it when we spoke to you before.'

'He said not to. He said I shouldn't mention it to anyone, and especially not to Sebastian or Marius.'

'Do you still have the letter?'

'I destroyed it. Burned it. Like he said.'

'So you took him the supplies he requested and kept the note secret. What else did it say?'

'Not much. Just that ... he was in a spot of bother at work.'

'A spot of bother?'

'He didn't elaborate. He's never talked about what he actually does at that place. "OSA!" he'd say and put a finger to his lips: Official Secrets Act. He took it very seriously.

'Whatever it was, he said it would soon blow over, and he just needed to keep a low profile for a week or two.'

'So why did you call the police and report him missing?'

She lowered her head. 'He asked me to do that too.'

Jane and Matt exchanged a glance. Jean Harroway continued.

'He didn't say what had happened at work, just that he was sick of the whole business and needed a fresh start. There was no way he'd get one with the way the system was, so he was planning another way out. He wanted me to report him missing and warned me not to be alarmed about what the police would eventually conclude.'

'Meaning what?'

'I'm not a hundred percent certain, but I think he was planning to stage his own suicide.' She drew a breath and looked up plaintively. 'But he didn't, did he? No one's found anything. You. The police. He really has just vanished.'

Matt said, 'What then? If the police did confirm he'd committed suicide, what was he planning to do afterwards? Return like Lazarus?'

'He had friends helping him, he said. Friends who would sort things out. A new identity, a new life. Somewhere safe, somewhere warm ...' She hesitated before adding, 'Somewhere I could join him if I wished.'

'Join him, as in ...?'

'I ... suppose ... With a new identity, there'd be nothing to connect us ...'

'And that's what you planned to do?'

'Oh, God, I don't know! How can I give up all this? It's all been such a shock. One thing after the other. The DNA business, then Terence, then the police, then dealing with Marius and Sebastian.

'I had no idea he still felt that way about me, not after all these years.' Tears started in the corners of her eyes. 'Things haven't been good between my husband and I for some time. Terence knows that. And when I look in a mirror these days, I suddenly see an old woman staring back at me. What right does she have to expect ... well, anything now but old age and declining health.' She pressed her hands to her face, took a long, shuddering breath.

Matt waited then said, 'One last question, Mrs Harroway. Do you have you any idea who these friends helping your brother are?'

She answered with a firm shake of her head.

Seeing his mother in tears again, Sebastian Harroway hurried back. 'That's enough,' he told Jane and Matt. 'I think you'd better go.'

Jean roused herself enough to ask anxiously, 'What will you do now?'

'Continue our investigations,' Matt said.

27

Mick Rosten had no luck at the BB Inn. All Beth was able to tell him was that the nice young man had settled up the night before, saying he and his lovely partner might have to leave early the following morning. Quite how early or where they were heading, she had no idea. All she could tell him was that the keys were in the returns box when she came in just after seven.

After relaying the information to his partner, Rosten settled down to the inn's generous Big Breakfast before finally checking out himself. Whistling tunelessly, he strolled out to the car park, swinging his overnight bag in one hand. Nothing further from Reaves suggested the young punk was getting precisely nowhere, a prospect he found oddly satisfying.

Halfway to his car, Rosten stopped dead, the bag still swinging slightly from his frozen arm. The whistle stopped too, but his lips remained puckered as he took in the back view of the little Laputa, sitting in the gravel car park on its wheel rims. A moment later, his mouth began forming the first words in a string of uncharacteristically colourful language that, along with kicks and swings of the overnight bag, went on for some time.

*

'Can I just say one thing right now to clear the air?' Jane asked when they got back to the car.

Matt nodded.

'*Eeewww!* Running off into the sunset to shack up with your brother? Seriously? What the hell ...?'

'She hasn't actually done it yet.'

'No, but she's thinking about it!'

'Human beings, eh? Call me jaded, but after years in this game, there's not much that surprises me any more.'

'*Eeewww!*' she said again.

'Seriously, Jane, do you think she knows about the cellar?'

'I have a feeling that if she did she'd be down there with him.'

'OK, so that leaves a couple of unanswered questions.'

'Like?'

'How did Araton know there was a problem at work if he didn't respond to the security chief's calls? They were all short. The longest was just over forty seconds which can't have amounted to much more than *Got a bit of a problem here, old chap. Please call me back.* I can't imagine a head of security like Reginald Wyatt discussing DSTL's secrets over an unencrypted phone line.'

'Which suggests Araton knew what he was talking about.'

'Exactly. Whatever it was, it shouldn't have been discovered so soon. Araton wasn't expecting it to be picked up until some time after his holiday.'

'By which time he'd be gone for good, according to his sister.'

'Except that a new auditor started the first week he was away. You can imagine the scene, can't you: "Oh, that office is empty. Why not start there?" Then the auditor strikes gold on her first dig, informs Wyatt who calls our man. "Ah, Araton. Got a bit of a problem with your petty cash receipts ... "'

'Except it's something more serious than petty cash,' Jane said.

Matt nodded, then continued. 'Hearing the news, Araton hastily improvises a Plan B: Suicide. He leaves his backpack and cellphone on the beach, concealed just enough for a police search team to find it. Maybe there's even a "Farewell, cruel world" note attached.'

'But he stuffs it up. Or rather, the spring tide stuffs it up for him a couple of days later.'

'So he gets home on the Monday, late, after dark. It must've been late because none of the neighbours saw him.

'He clears out the kitchen cupboards, grabs what he can and dives for his bolt hole. But there's not enough food for a fortnight, and there are other things he's forgotten. Like the power lead for his laptop. Also, something to do down there. Like reading or watching DVDs.'

'Why not just go back up and get them?'

'He can't go out for food. Too much risk of being seen. And he doesn't have a car any more. Easier to get his sister to deliver it.'

'What about the laptop lead? He could have grabbed that. And Jean Harroway said he asked for books and DVDs, some of which he already had. Why not grab those too?'

Matt shrugged. 'You've got me there.'

'Hold on a sec,' Jane said, pulling out the file and rifling through it, pausing at the pictures of the interior of Araton's house. 'I don't think he wanted to leave gaps in the shelves. That would make it obvious he'd been back.'

Matt frowned, leaning against her shoulder, studying the photographs. 'They have these things called bookends, you know. You could just move them up.'

'You don't see it, do you.' Jane tapped the photocopied page. 'When did you say that black Range Rover first visited?'

'A couple of hours after Jean Harroway reported him missing.'

'No, before that. You said the neighbour saw it on the Sunday and the Tuesday of that week.'

'That's right. She thought they were keeping an eye on the place for him.'

'They were doing more than that. Look.' Jane pointed to the tiny digits in the bottom corners of each photograph. 'They all say the same thing: 10/18. I thought it was a job number or something, but it's not. It's the date. In American format. Month followed by day. October the eighteenth. The Tuesday. They photographed his house two days *before* his sister even reported him missing!'

It took Matt a moment to register the importance of what she was suggesting. 'So whatever that audit uncovered, it was deeply serious shit. Serious enough for DSTL to suspect he'd already done a runner.'

'They photographed his house on the Tuesday and the Thursday, and probably several times since. That way, they can quickly see if anything's been disturbed because that would indicate he's been back.

'Think about it. Araton, in his hideaway. hears them clumping about up above. They probably took dozens of photos. This will just be a subset. If he goes up later and even so much as grabs his laptop lead, there's a chance they'll spot it's gone missing.'

'So he pens a note to his sister asking for more supplies. Food, no doubt dried or tinned – the sort of stuff you might use on a camping holiday – along with books and DVDs to keep him entertained. Some of which he already owned.'

'There's a postbox at the bottom of the street by the bus stop. He must have sneaked out late to send it. Remember what Jean Harroway said? It wasn't even stamped. She had to pay the postman.'

Matt smiled. 'That has a satisfying ring to it. Which just leaves one more question. Who are these friends that are supposedly helping him? Friends that will find him a new identity and a new life somewhere safe and somewhere warm?'

'Government agencies can do that easily enough.'

'Except we know it's not one of ours. At least, not MI5 or the police.'

'Which leaves some other country's.'

'That's my thinking too. But whose, and why? The only reason they'd do that for a man like Araton is if he provided them with something in return. Something valuable. State secrets or intelligence.'

'If he'd done that already, surely they'd just whisk him away. Why is he still hiding in his cellar?'

'Because whatever he offered them requires verification. Two to three weeks' worth. Hence the holiday.'

'If that's the case, then his time is up this weekend. Araton's due back at work on Monday. If all this hadn't blown up when it did, it would do so in a couple of day's time when he no-showed.'

'You're right. We'd better get back to his house. He may be getting ready to move.'

'Shouldn't we let MI5 know?' Jane pointed back at the house. 'We do have a man on the spot.'

'Not him. Not his own father. This needs to go through Fennel.'

Jane took out her phone and found the battery. Matt stopped her from connecting it.

'Not that way either. As soon as you turn that on, it'll tell whoever was following us exactly where we are.' He started the car. 'I'll contact Fennel through Avery. All I need is a phone box or a police station. But we have to get back to Araton's double-quick and keep a watch on his house. We don't know what stage he's at with his negotiations. He could leg it at any time.'

28

'Just heard from my contact at GCHQ,' Taliq told Tasha. 'T2 and T3's cellphones went off the grid within minutes of each other in the early hours of this morning. They're still dark.'

'The question is, are they just giving us the slip, or have they been taken?' Tasha replied.

She was back in Bristol, on foot, and hadn't yet mentioned her brush with the local constabulary on the M5 median strip. Given the agency's considerable data collection facilities it was bound to be on file somewhere, but for now, she preferred to save her off-road experience for the post-op drinks.

Or maybe for her memoir.

'Impossible to say,' Taliq's voice was as businesslike as usual, 'but I've alerted the chief.'

The tow truck driver had been very obliging – people often were when you offered to pay them in cash – and all he'd had to do was drag the Toyota's front wheels out of the culvert. There was no damage to the bodywork, the steering was fine, and she hadn't even got a flat. By that time, the police had been called away to another incident, so, apart from a cursory torchlight inspection of the car's interior, she'd walked – or rather, driven – away scot free. And two hundred pounds lighter.

She hadn't even minded going twenty miles in the wrong direction before being able to double-back. The rental agencies didn't open till eight o'clock, so there was no rush. But now, after a few hours sleep in the back seat, she was doing a good old fashioned door to door.

Taliq added, 'Any luck at your end?'

'The rental was checked back in just after one o'clock yesterday afternoon. By the woman alone, no guy. She said something about a family emergency and having to head home immediately, but declined the manager's offer of a lift to the airport or railway station and headed off on foot.'

'Which suggests she used another rental agency, probably one close by.'

'Which I am currently checking.'

Tasha struggled to keep the exasperation from her voice. He was always like this, giving orders by way of suggestions. Suggestions she'd already picked up on herself.

'And?' he asked.

'So far there's zilch at Hertz, Europcar, and Enterprise, so I'm checking the smaller fry. Of course, they may really have gone by train or plane.'

'Negative so far. We've got eyes on the south London house. There's been no movement except for visits from the cat feeder.'

Eyes on the house ...? We ...? Okay, so this was no longer a training exercise, but how big was it?

'Other news,' Taliq continued. 'Target One is AWOL.'

'What? Su—?' She almost said the name, checked herself. 'Sierra Bravo? Who was on that?'

'She gave Meg the slip at Liverpool Street station last night and hasn't been back to her room.'

'Liverpool Street? But isn't that for trains going north and east?'

'It's also a major Underground station. We've got a team going through surveillance footage, but nothing yet. She could be anywhere.'

Tasha drew a breath. They'd lost all their leads. *No pressure then!*

'I gotta go, Taliq. It looks like I'm about to be mugged by one of the Fabulous Furry Freak Brothers.'

'What? Who? Repeat, please.'

'I'll call you back.' Tasha hung up and smiled at the man from Yippee Cars 'n' Campers.

Ten minutes later, she was back on the phone. 'Game on, baby. Have I just saved your ass or what?'

'Details?' he demanded.

'The Furry Freak remembered Target Two. She didn't rent from him, just asked about a friend who did, then carried on up the street. So I went the same way. Right around the corner is a crowd called Devon Rentals. Jane Child hired a two-year-old beige Vauxhall Astra from them about two o'clock yesterday afternoon.'

'Just give me the index number. Now!'

*

They hit the rain again when they returned to Stratford-sub-Castle, an insistent, persistent drizzle that left a misty veil over the suburban streets. Hunkered against it, the hood of her lightweight running jacket pulled up, Jane passed Araton's house and gave Matt the signal. He'd dropped her off at the start of Goose Green Grove, continued around the one-way street, and now waited at the far end of Plover Place. She raised her arm and waved to indicate his 'flag' – the little piece of paper he'd wedged in the front door – was undisturbed, meaning Araton was still in his cellar lair.

Matt raced off to raise the alarm as Jane continued on to the bus stop at the end of the street. She wiped the rain-smeared glass of the shelter so she could keep an eye on any comings and goings. It wasn't a great view, the rain wasn't helping, but it was good enough to see if Araton had any visitors.

'Don't do anything,' Matt had warned her. 'Just watch and note down the make, model, and index number of any visitors. I'll only be an hour, tops.'

The street was quiet. The rain kept people in. A solitary silver hatchback cruised towards her along Plover Place, keeping to a steady speed before swinging right onto Goose Green Grove and passing the bus shelter. It wasn't moving fast, but there was a pothole right outside that sent a sloosh of rainwater across the pavement and over Jane's feet.

'Oh great. Thanks!' She shook out her sodden shoes.

Jane took out her notebook and scribbled down the number of the silver hatchback in case it later proved relevant.

That was, of course, assuming Araton got picked up. He'd made it home on public transport and might make his escape the same way.

Maybe we'll end up sharing a bus.

She was still half-tempted to charge into Araton's house, kick open the door and pound on the hideaway hatch, yelling that the game was up, but as Matt pointed out, they had no powers of arrest. Besides, they didn't know if anyone else was watching the house or in what strength. Securing Araton safely for MI5 would require a proper operation.

A solitary postman in a yellow raincoat made his way along the street. Should I note down his badge number too? Jane wondered.

Jane considered what a "proper operation" would involve. Screaming police cars and blocked-off streets, or a quiet security detail from DSTL? Whatever, the case was almost over. With a bit of luck, they might even be back in London late this evening. That would mean a lazy Sunday. And her own bed! No more car camping, and a whole day of lounging around the house with Matt and Bluebelle and a good book. Who needed holidays when you had all that at home?

The silver hatchback was back, coming towards the bus stop from Goose Green Grove this time, which meant they'd done a complete circuit of the one-way system. Perhaps they were lost. Perhaps they wanted to apologise for splashing her.

Indeed, it looked like they might because the car slowed and stopped as it reached the bus stop. The passenger-side electric window came down, and the driver leaned across. Someone looking for directions, Jane guessed as she stepped forward.

She stopped.

The driver was pointing a gun at her. Straight-armed. Straight in her face.

'Get in!' A half-familiar voice snapped.

29

The collision happened as Matt was about to turn into Greencroft Street across from Wiltshire Police on Bourne Hill. He'd indicated a left turn and slowed to give way to traffic on his right, but the van behind him didn't slow quickly enough, and the result was a bumper-crunching crash.

Matt applied the handbrake, put on his hazard lights, and got out to inspect the damage. The van driver, a large man in a leather jacket, sunglasses and jeans, did the same. Scratching the back of his closely cropped head, he said, 'Sorry, fella. My bad.' An American accent.

Saturday morning traffic was backing up behind them. The van driver indicated a loading bay further up, so they eased into it, parking one behind the other. Matt and the American got out again to swap details, but this time the van driver had a gun.

'You know, I really only need your name and insurance details,' Matt said.

'Shut it!' The driver stood side-on, keeping the pistol concealed behind his crossed arms with the barrel pointed at Matt's chest while two more equally big men emerged from the van's nearside sliding door.

'In,' one of them said.

The trio accompanied him, covering all escape routes.

The back of the van was kitted out like a minibus, with rows of seats for at least a dozen people. They shoved him into the first row, handcuffed his left ankle to one of the seat supports then slid the door shut.

The driver, gun now tucked away, returned to the driver's seat.

One of the others climbed into the passenger seat, while the third man took Matt's car, switched off the hazard lights, and drove away. The van followed it, this time keeping to a safe following distance.

The whole operation, Matt reckoned, from accident to kidnap to departure, hadn't taken much more than two minutes.

*

Since childhood, Jane had been told never to get into a stranger's car. But no one had told her what to do if that stranger was aiming a gun at her. Besides, Susan Burdon wasn't a complete stranger.

Jane got in.

Burdon kept the pistol aimed at her chest. 'On your own, Ms Child? Not another lovers' tiff, I hope.'

'So the tubby guy *is* your man? We thought so.' Jane said, struggling to keep her voice level and her tone casual.

'Where's your partner?'

'Around and about. Keeping an eye on things.'

'Like Araton's house, for example?'

'Who?'

Burdon smiled. 'Nice try, but no cigar. From the way you're staking the place out, it looks like you're expecting some movement down there.'

Quite a lot of movement, actually. In about fifteen minutes time.

'Down where?'

'Don't play dumb with me. I know what you're working on. What I want to know is what you're doing here, now? Are you expecting the missing man to make a miraculous reappearance? Because that's what it looks like to me.'

Jane shrugged. 'I'm just waiting for a bus.'

Burdon lowered the gun, stabbing it into the side of Jane's right leg. 'I won't kill you, Ms Child. At least, not intentionally. Murder complicates things enormously. But I do need to know

196

what you're up to, and I need to know now, so here's the deal. Answer my questions, and I won't shoot you through the knee.'

Jane looked at the gun and Burdon's pale, determined face but said nothing.

'Angle is everything when it comes to gunshot wounds, you know. This way, I'll just shatter your kneecap. You'll probably walk again. Stiff-legged, but at least two-legged. But here,' she moved the gun half an inch, 'you're looking at major damage. Amputation of the lower leg.'

Jane swallowed. Her mouth was dry. 'How do I know I can trust you? Even if I do answer your questions, you might shoot me anyway.'

'That's a chance you're going to have to take.'

'And afterwards? Once I've told you everything? Do you seriously expect me to believe you'll just let me walk away?'

Most people under threat of their lives or serious injury didn't think about the future since the present was all-consuming. It was clearly a question Burdon hadn't considered either. Jane saw a flicker of uncertainty in her face. She also glimpsed something in the car's wing mirror.

Her first thought had been to keep Burdon talking, but she didn't know when Matt would return, or in what strength. With the cavalry and a full accompaniment of flashing red-and-blues, or in stealth mode with a couple of black-glassed Range Rovers.

Her second thought was of this meeting. It *had* to be a chance encounter. She and Matt had swapped vehicles, shaken off their tail, and changed plans on the fly, so there was no way it could be anything else. Which meant that pulling a gun and demanding information had been a spur of the moment decision on Burdon's part. Something she hadn't thought through. That meant Jane would have to do her thinking for her.

'And how will you know I'm telling the truth?' she added. 'I could make up a pack of lies. Say Araton's due any minute now, or tell you he won't be here for hours.'

'Cut the crap! Just tell me what you fucking know!' Burdon snapped as a deep-throated bellow sounded from behind them.

Burdon's glance back at the approaching bus was automatic, but Jane had seen it coming in the wing mirror and was ready. She raised her legs and simultaneously seized Burdon's wrist, forcing her hand down towards the floor. The gun fired. A single barking cough. The retort sounded shocking in the confined space. Then Jane brought her legs down again, trapping Burdon's arm against the seat.

The bus horn sounded again. Two blasts. More insistent. It was a one-lane, one-way street and the bus couldn't get past the illegally parked car.

Burdon, right-handed, had twisted in her seat to confront Jane. Now her arm was trapped, and she was perched at an awkward angle.

Jane didn't hesitate. Using the full swing of her upper body, she slammed the back of her bent arm into Burdon's face, her elbow striking the bridge of the other woman's nose. Something gave. Burdon grunted but didn't relinquish her hold on the gun. She tugged it harder, trying to free it, but the end of the grip was hooked beneath Jane's seat, and the pressure of Jane's leg kept it there. Burdon fired again in reflex or frustration, the bullet passing through the car floor an inch from Jane's foot.

The second shot gave Jane an extra burst of adrenaline – as if any more were needed – and she swung again. This time Burdon blocked her with her left. A half-hearted, self-defensive feint, but Jane had anticipated that. As her elbow connected with Burdon's raised arm, she rolled her weight with it, shoving the other woman sideways, freeing her trapped arm for a second then catching it again with her left hand.

They were all of a tangle now. Jane was half out of her own seat, half in Burdon's. The other woman still had the gun, but the wrist holding it was clamped in Jane's left hand, and her arm was hooked beneath Jane's hip.

'Let it go!' They were face to face, as close as lovers. A thin stream of blood ran from Burdon's left nostril and her nose looked bent. 'I said—'

Burdon snarled, caught a handful of Jane's hair in her free hand, and wrenched her head back, hard.

That was it. An all-consuming rage came over Jane. She shoved backwards, freeing Burdon's gun arm completely, then seized it in both hands and brought it down hard against the plastic T of the gear-shift. Burdon gasped. Jane slammed it again and again. The wrist was at a funny angle now, bent back more than it should, but the gun was still tangled in Burdon's fingers.

Jane switched attack again. Another sharp elbow blow to Burdon's broken nose, and she was off, scrambling out the car and sprinting up the road, past the angry driver and her bus full of puzzled passengers.

30

Calls to local vets and the RSPCA turned up nothing. No female tortoiseshell cats with white patches on the neck and paws had been handed in, injured, or otherwise. Sally tried to see that in a positive light. It was a relief, certainly, but it also added to her unease. *What the devil had happened to Bluebelle?* The simple fact was that barely a day after she'd been charged with looking after her best friend's cat, she'd lost it.

Paul turned up mid-morning, dressed in his handyman clothes: paint-spattered jeans and a hooded sweater so faded and worn that the homeless would have declined it. For once, Sally wasn't ashamed to be seen in public with him dressed like that. She was glad of the moral support. Dylan, who'd been briefed on the seriousness of the situation, was on his best behaviour.

They began door-knocking. The neighbours either side and across the street knew Jane and Bluebelle, but only one could recall seeing the cat recently. 'With that new ginger one from up the street. Tangelo, I think they call him. Belongs to the Wests. They only moved in a couple of weeks ago.'

She pointed out the house. Sally thanked her and said they'd try there.

Tangelo was sunning himself on the front step. The large ginger tom had a blue collar and stretched luxuriously at their approach, and even allowed Dylan to stroke his belly. But there was no sign of Bluebelle, and no response to the doorbell either.

'What now?' Paul asked.

Sally sighed. 'Widen the search, I suppose. Just keep trying.'

'I think you should let Jane know, Sal. Prepare her.'

'Not yet. Let's try a few more houses.'

*

The van and car travelled at a steady pace through the streets of Salisbury, not wishing to attract attention. Neither passenger nor driver spoke to Matt, although he was aware of an occasional glance in the rearview mirror. The streets were unfamiliar, so it was hard to tell exactly where they were heading, but despite the low cloud and drizzly rain, his inbuilt compass suggested they were heading northeast.

All three of his abductors were big guys, but they weren't just hired thugs. It was a smooth operation, and they had the cohesiveness of a well-organised team. Special Forces, perhaps?

No one spoke. Matt included. No point asking where they were taking him or what this was about. If his kidnappers wanted that known, they'd have said. Clearly, they were on a mission. Following orders.

On the positive side, he wasn't gagged or bound or blindfolded. Handcuffed by one ankle, yes, but otherwise unharmed. He could even move around a little. He was certainly free enough to see where they were going, to note passing landmarks and street names. Which meant they didn't care what he saw. Either because there was a reasonable explanation for him being apprehended ... or this was a one-way trip.

*

Jane ran, sticking to the one-lane street at first because there was no way Burdon could come after her in the car with a Salisbury Reds bus blocking the road. Besides, she was injured. A possibly broken wrist and a definitely broken nose. Could she even drive in such a state?

The answer came in an angry burst of diesel as the bus accelerated away. Jane ducked into a driveway and looked back.

Burdon had driven the silver hatchback up onto the footpath and was now half out the driver's door, her right arm cradled in her left and casting about, looking to see where she'd gone. She got back in, executed an awkward U-turn, and came back towards Jane, travelling the wrong way up the one-way street.

Jane pressed herself into the gap between a low wall and a leafy hydrangea, dislodging a torrent of raindrops. Several ran down her back and made her shiver.

She kept low, backing out of sight as the car passed.

All she needed to do was stay hidden. Matt would be back soon with reinforcements.

Except he didn't know about Burdon: that she had a gun; that she was injured and desperate and many shades of pissed off.

Still, she had her phone. Did it matter now if the various parties knew where she was? The endgame was fast approaching. She couldn't call Matt. His phone was still off. But she could call Avery or Fennel or even Sebastian Harroway.

She reached into her jacket pocket, but all she could find was the battery, no phone. Where was it? It had been there. She checked the other pockets.

The silver hatchback returned, travelling the right way down the one-way street this time. Moving slowly, its wipers on full, the driver's and passenger's windows down and its sole occupant craning left and right.

Jane waited.

Burdon swung down Araton's road, executed a U-turn, and parked so that both his house and the bus shelter were in her line of sight. Every few seconds, the wipers cleared her windscreen.

Keeping low, Jane eased out of her hiding place to get a better view. She spotted her phone. It must have fallen from her pocket after her fight with Burdon. She could see it clearly, lying in a patch of damp grass right beside the bus shelter.

*

A concrete bunker loomed out of the misty rain as the van turned off a country lane and bumped its way across a field. Up ahead, another shape resolved as they approached: the arch of an old, dilapidated aircraft hangar now filled with farm machinery. The car – Matt's car – stopped in its lee, and the van drew in behind it. The two drivers and the van's front seat passenger stood around the sliding door as one of them leaned in and released the handcuff on Matt's ankle. Then they stepped back, standing away from the van, and looked out at the grey drizzle and the open field.

Matt got out cautiously and stretched. One of the men glanced back at him but said nothing. All three wore leather jackets, jeans, and sunglasses. All three heads were closely cropped.

Definitely Special Forces, Matt thought.

The place appeared to be an old World War II airfield long since given over to more rural pursuits. The tarmac airstrip, if there ever had been one, was gone, but the long, level field remained. Matt walked to the edge of the hangar, in line with but apart from the three men, and looked out as rain pattered softly on the iron roof above and dripped in steady streams in front of him. The leather-clad man nearest looked his way and gave a faint shake of his head, as if he'd guessed what Matt was thinking: *Why not just run?*

Silly idea. There was nowhere to go. An open field in the middle of nowhere. Three against one. No vehicle. Besides, he wasn't under any immediate threat. His captors were clearly waiting for someone. Matt was curious to see who it was.

Minutes passed, then a mud brown, mud-spattered Toyota sedan emerged from the overcast and drew in behind the van. It's driver, a young woman with auburn hair, stepped out, zipping up a padded jacket. She reached back into the car, took something from beneath the front seat and slipped it inside her jacket. She nodded to the men. They nodded back. After a cursory glance at Matt, she wedged her hands into her pockets and joined their silent vigil.

More minutes passed. The steady drumming of rain on the

iron roof continued. Then a deeper sound emerged. A growing thrum that rose to a shrieking intensity. A mini-maelstrom of sound and air and rain as a helicopter settled on the grass a hundred yards from the hangar.

The churning blades slowed and stopped. A door swung back. Two men emerged, one after the other. The first out, a taller, angular man held the door for his broader, bullet-headed companion. He opened an umbrella for the other man, retrieved a slim black guitar case from the helicopter then, limping slightly, hastened after his companion who seemed careless of his efforts.

Bullet-head ignored the others lined up at the hangar's entrance and angled straight at Matt, smiling broadly and extending a hand as he approached. 'Mr Healy! I'm very glad to make your acquaintance. I'm sorry for the inconvenience. My name is Bartram Horovitz. I believe you know my ex-wife.'

31

'I'm about an hour away,' Rosten said calmly, waiting for the inevitable explosion.

'What the fuck ...?' There was spluttering on the other end of the line, then Reaves added, 'Didn't you get the client's message?'

'Of course I did. If I hadn't, I'd hardly be on my way to Salisbury, would I?'

'With all due fucking haste, you prick.'

'I have been proceeding with all due haste. Or at least, as much haste as that little piece of shit you organised for me could manage before it broke down.' No point mentioning the two flat tyres, Rosten thought. Why give the young punk more ammunition? 'It took two hours to find a garage and get it fixed.'

'Shit!' Reaves sounded like someone whose joke has just backfired, which was exactly what Rosten had intended.

'Something to do with the timing, apparently. A common fault with those toy cars. So I thought I'd better swap it for something more reliable once I reached civilisation. That meant diverting through Bristol, which meant more delays.'

'Right. Yeah, all right. Good thinking. But you're set now, yeah?'

'All set.'

'And you got the latest update?'

'The Stratford-sub-Castle address is plugged into the GPS.'

'So, about an hour then?'

Rosten checked the console of the Mercedes he'd chosen. 'Fifty-eight minutes, according to the electronics.'

'Speaking of electronics, pick up some walkie-talkies when

you come through Salisbury, will you? Client request. One for each of us. Good ones. Make sure they're charged, and get a receipt. Put 'em on expenses.'

'Like this car?'

'Yeah, yeah, like the bloody car!'

'Roger, Roger.' Rosten couldn't resist.

'Fuck off, you turd!'

Rosten smiled to himself. That was more like it.

*

Jane watched, her eyes fixed on Burdon's car, counting the seconds between each sweep of the wiper blades. She could see the woman on her phone, alert as a sparrow, her gaze swinging to and fro, from Araton's house to the bus stop at the end of the road.

She must be calling for backup. Which means she's on her own right now.

Jane checked the other vehicles in the street. No one had gone to help or speak with her. All the other windscreens were speckled with rain.

She's got a gun in a residential street, and Matt doesn't know she's there. I've got to warn him somehow.

Jane moved, but in the opposite direction. Up Goose Green Grove then left along Dotterel Drive, which ran parallel to Plover Place. She sprinted now, running as fast as she could till she reached the far end, skidding to a halt in the lower section of Goose Green Grove.

She half-expected to see a line of red-and-blues already there, but the street was deserted. She edged back down to the start of Plover Place.

Burdon had her back towards her now, but it was easy enough to spot her car. It looked like she was still on the phone.

A good sign. Also, a good time to act. Before the reinforcements arrive.

One hour, tops, Matt said. He can't be more than five minutes away now.

Keeping low, Jane began creeping along the line of parked cars, ducking between them when there was room, measuring her pace and breathing. Burdon's car was six vehicles away. Five now. Four.

She jumped as the rear windscreen wiper cycled on. A single wipe. On a timer like the front wipers.

Jane braced herself.

*

Matt didn't take the proffered hand. He remained as he was, his own hands in his pockets as he looked over the man greeting him. Bartram Horovitz was stocky, short-limbed, and round-cheeked. His business suit and tie concealed a powerful body, and he had a physical presence as strong as his voice. A pair of dark, canny eyes, fixed on Matt's, willing him to shake his hand. Matt resisted, saying instead, 'Inconvenience? You're sorry to *inconvenience* me? Is that the latest CIA euphemism for kidnapping?'

Horovitz didn't miss a beat. 'No, that would be *rendition*, ordinary or extraordinary. You only qualified for the former.' Still smiling but dropping his hand, he added, 'So far.'

All eyes were on the pair of them, Horovitz still out in the rain beneath an umbrella held by his limping assistant. Matt recognised the younger man from the British Library. After another second, he yielded and stepped back, symbolically granting Horovitz access to the hangar.

Outside, the helicopter's note went up a notch. The blades beat faster, hurling horizontal raindrops across the grass before it soared away into the gloom.

As the sound died away, Horowitz said, 'I'm a businessman, Mr Healy. I spend most of my time behind a desk, going to meetings, reading reports, and taking advice from my people in the field. People like Tasha and Taliq here.' He gestured to his assistants. 'That advice suggested you probably weren't amenable to a request for assistance, so I instigated a more direct approach. That was my decision. I'm sorry if we misjudged that or alarmed you unduly, but the responsibility is mine and mine alone.

'Now, if you'll allow me to take up a few more minutes of your valuable time, I'd like to tell you what this is all about.' He gestured, and Matt saw that while they'd been talking, the three leather-jacketed heavies had cleared a path to a small office on one side of the hangar. A bare bulb hanging from the ceiling had been turned on, and its yellow glow looked comforting in the dreary shed with the dreary day outside.

Horovitz closed the door behind them. The three heavies lined up outside, their backs to the office's narrow window. What became of the other two, Taliq and Tasha, Matt couldn't see.

'Let's not beat about the bush, Mr Healy. I know what you're working on, and you know why I'm here.'

'Do I?'

'We're after the same thing. Or should I say, the same man – Terence James Araton – and it's imperative that we find him before anyone else does.'

'Two points of clarification,' Matt said. 'Who, precisely, are *we*, and who is *anyone else*?'

'*We* are the good guys, the cavalry, the old allies. Five Eyes. Best buds from way back. The *anyone else* is whoever the hell my ex-wife is working for.'

'You mean you don't know, you of all people?'

Horovitz sized him up, considering, then relented. 'My ex-wife was a Saudi specialist. We believe she's working for the GID, Saudi Arabia's General Intelligence Directorate.'

'Aren't they good guys too?'

'There are good guys and *good* guys, if you catch my drift.'

'You're happy to sell arms to them though.'

'Hey, the Brits too. Money's money.'

'Especially oil money.'

Horovitz shrugged.

'So what's Araton got, or done, or about to do that makes him so valuable?'

'You're freelance, Mr Healy. You don't have a pay grade, but even if you did, this would be well above it. Forget about that, just help us find our man.'

'What makes you think I'm any wiser than you are?'

'You were on the trail, then you went dark. Switched cars, switched off phones, did a moonlight flit. Then you turn up back here. Salisbury, scene of the crime. Or as close as dammit. What have you got?'

'I'm still not clear where you fit in, Mr Horovitz. The CIA, I mean. I'm sure you know who my partner and I are working for. One of your *best buds*. So why the added interest?'

'Because you've been set up, Mr Healy. You and your partner don't know who you're up against. These people are dangerous. They'll stop at nothing.'

'Whereas you'll stop at ...?'

'Don't play word games with me. This is a serious matter.'

'You're the one playing word games. You still haven't answered my question. All I know about your ex-wife is that she wants to hire us when we get back to London to check on the safety and well-being of her children. *Your* children, Mr Horovitz.'

'What children? We never had children. Still don't. Either of us.' He studied Matt's face. 'Is *that* the story she spun your partner in the British Library? It's beginning to make sense now.

'Let me tell you about my ex, Mr Healy. She started out as an operative, a good one. That's where we met, in the field. Later, we moved inside. What you Brits call coming in from the cold. Sue took a job with MENA – the Office of Middle East and North Africa Analysis – learned Arabic and Farsi and God knows what else. Studied the Quran too. I think that's when her sympathies started to drift.

'She started saying stuff about how Muslims love Jesus almost as much as Christians do. How he gets over a hundred mentions in the Quran while the Prophet himself gets only five. How Muhammad said, "The dearest person to me in friendship and in love, in this world and the next is Jesus, the son of Mary.'" Horovitz shook his head. 'We're in the middle of a war on terror, and she starts coming out with shit like that.

'On and on, too, in that voice of hers. She used to quote to me – no *at* me – how Mary is the only woman mentioned by name in the whole of the Quran, and how she even has a chapter named after her. Yada-yada-yada. Thin end of the wedge. I could see where her sympathies were heading.

'In the end, I had to say something. To my employers. *Our* employers.' Seeing Matt's look, he added, 'I'm a patriotic American, first and foremost, Mr Healy. Everything else comes second.'

'So what happened?'

Horovitz made a gesture somewhere between a shrug and a sign of resignation. 'We look after our people. Take care of them.'

'They put her in a psychiatric hospital.'

Horovitz shot him a look.

'That's what she told my partner. I'm guessing that anyone suggesting détente between Christians and Muslims must be insane, right?'

It was clear the American didn't know what to make of the remark and finally decided to take it at face value. 'She was released six months ago, shortly after I was posted to London. I understand she's had a hard time since. No job, no prospects, nothing on the horizon.

'Three weeks ago she was approached by a Saudi operative, someone we keep tabs on in Washington. Two weeks later, she's in London. On my patch. Naturally, for all those reasons, professional as well as personal, I took an interest.

'At first, it really did look like a holiday. Piccadilly Circus, Tower Bridge, Parliament Square. Then one of my ops spotted a pocket drop as you and your partner exited MI5. *Bing!* Party time.'

'Hold on,' Matt said, frowning, 'when Jane and I left Thames House, we had no idea what sort of job MI5 had in mind for us. We didn't learn about Araton until the following day. You seem to be suggesting that your ex knew twenty-four hours before we did?'

'Wheels within wheels, Mr Healy.'

'So there's a leak in MI5?'

'Don't be so dramatic. Intelligence agencies keep each other apprised of their areas of interest.'

'Oh, I know all about that,' Matt said, the image of Penhaligon standing in his doorway, gun in hand, flashed through his mind. Aloud, he added, 'Are the GID also part of your information free-for-all?'

Horovitz didn't respond.

'Because that's the only way to explain how your ex-wife came to be waiting for us outside MI5.'

Bartram Horovitz made his curious half-shrug, half-resigned gesture again, and suddenly Matt glimpsed a deeper level in the chessboard of intelligence agency manoeuvring. The CIA had tipped off the GID, who in turn, alerted their operative to be on the lookout for Jane and Matt. Meanwhile, the CIA kept a god's eye view on everyone. Or tried to.

Matt checked his annoyance at their arrogance and the way he and Jane had been played. Struggling to keep his tone level, he said, 'What's exactly *is* your relationship with our employer, Mr Horovitz?'

'Like I told you, bests buds. MI5, MI6, the CIA; we're all on the same side.'

'Then why aren't I hearing this from Marius Fennel? Why did *you* take a helicopter out here?'

'Hey, your phone's off. Maybe they've been trying to call.'

'Well, I'm sorry, Mr Horovitz. It looks like you've had a wasted trip. I don't know where Araton is.' He turned to go. 'I take it the keys are still in my car?'

'We can offer you a better deal than MI5, Mr Healy. A much

better deal.'

'Which is presumably what the Saudis said to your wife.'

As Matt moved towards the exit, Horovitz stepped in front of him. 'Is that a no, Mr Healy?'

'I only work for one employer at a time, Mr Horovitz. Once I've delivered my report to MI5, I'm sure your *best bud* will apprise you of its contents.'

Horovitz continued blocking the door. 'I'm afraid it's not that easy, Mr Healy.'

32

Jane could hear Burdon talking on her phone as she hunkered down beside the rear door of her car and waited. Surprise was one thing, but there was no point alerting the other party. Then again, from the harsh, one-sided nature of the conversation, the other party might welcome the interruption.

Light rain was still falling. It drizzled down the neck of Jane's wind-breaker, but she was thoroughly soaked by now anyway. She was more concerned about drying her hands. She didn't want them to slip when she wrenched the door handle.

The phone call ended. Jane half-heard, half-felt a slight movement inside the vehicle. Burdon tossing the phone aside?

She checked her watch. *One hour, tops*. In the distance she heard the sound of an approaching car. This had to be Matt. Perfect timing.

She straightened, gripped the handle of Burdon's door and wrenched it open with her right hand. As she did so, she reached in with her left and grabbed for Burdon's damaged right wrist.

The wrist must have been broken. Burdon had splinted it crudely with cardboard and strips of sticky tape. Besides, the yell she gave when Jane seized and tugged on it was more from pain than surprise.

Good, no seatbelt.

Jane kicked away from the car, dragging Burdon with her, but Burdon was quick. She grabbed at the console between the seats with her left hand and tried to get it open. Jane guessed that's where she'd stowed the gun and tugged harder.

Burdon yelled again and came out on all fours, charging at

Jane, twisting and breaking her grip. She scrambled to her feet in a low crouch, and they glared at each other in the gloomy street.

Burdon's face was a mess. Jane's elbow had broken her nose. Wads of bloody tissue had stopped the bleeding, but the whole centre of her face was puffy and swollen and purple with bruising.

Burdon's weight shifted slightly as she prepared to kick out with her right leg. Normally, Jane would have braced or blocked or backed away. Not today. She charged straight at her, fist raised, aiming for the swollen, painful mass in the middle of Burdon's face.

The reaction was automatic. Burdon couldn't help herself. She threw up a hand and tried to pivot away, but stumbled and tangled in her own feet as she did so.

She went over, falling on her side and landing in the road. Jane went with her, landing on her chest and pinning her arms out wide as she heard a vehicle behind her come to a skidding stop in the rain-slicked street.

One hour, tops.

Perfect timing.

Jane relaxed a fraction as she heard running feet and glanced back.

But it wasn't Matt. It was a tattooed man.

Burdon screamed, 'Get her!'

*

Horovitz stood his ground. Matt didn't force the issue. He could take out the big man on his own, but there were five more people in the hangar outside, three of them Special Forces types, and at least one of them was armed.

'Where's your partner, Mr Healy? What's she doing?'

Matt said nothing.

'Let's find out, shall we?'

He took out Matt's phone, the one the Special Forces types had taken off him, and switched it on.

'No PIN. That's careless.'

'Would it have made any difference?'

Horovitz smiled. 'Not much.'

His thumbs flew across the keypad. Even upside-down, Matt could read the message: *Urgent. Call me!*

Horovitz hit send.

'At some point she's going to switch back on. When she gets your message, she'll call back, and we'll have her, so why not save us all some time and grief and maybe even prevent a little rough stuff for your partner?'

Matt said nothing.

Horovitz shrugged, turned, opened the door, and walked out of the office. He handed the phone to his umbrella man – Taliq – who had been busy setting up a couple of computers and some comms gear on a trestle table. 'Triangulate any incoming calls. I want to know the caller's location down to the nearest blade of grass.'

Over his shoulder, he said to Matt, 'I suggest you make yourself comfortable, Mr Healy, because until your partner calls, you're not going anywhere.'

*

Burdon bucked against Jane's weight and yelled again. 'Get her, damn it!'

Reaves lunged, catching a handful of Jane's wet hair as she leaned forward, readying herself to sprint away.

Jane had made up her mind at the first sight of the tattooed man. There was no point lingering. Two against one weren't good odds, even if one of them was injured. And at least one, probably both of them, were armed.

Her rain-slicked hair slipped from Reaves' grasp, and as she kicked away, she used Burdon's wrist as a makeshift starting block.

The woman screamed. The tattooed man lunged again, snagging the hood of her jacket, but the fabric ripped, and Jane sprinted away up the street. After a momentary pause, he gave chase. She could hear his footsteps following her. Pounding footsteps that, if anything, seemed to be gaining.

Jane was a runner, but so was the guy behind her. She glanced back as she rounded the top of the street and passed the bus stop on the far side. For a moment, she glimpsed her mobile phone lying in the long grass.

The tattooed man grinned back as he settled into an easy stride about three yards behind her, and she had an image of a hapless deer pursued by a powerful wolf. The predator would keep pace, take its time, and let the prey exhaust itself to make the kill easier.

Let's see how you are on hills, she thought.

Jane put on a burst of speed.

The tattooed man did likewise.

Even more so. She could sense him gaining.

Shit!

A foot kicked out, snagged hers, and sent her tumbling to the pavement. Jane grazed her knees, rolled and scrambled back to her feet, but the guy was on her in an instant, clamping her upper arm in a vicious grip. He was still grinning and only breathing slightly more than normal.

Jane thought of the wolf and deer again, then doubled over, gasping for breath, pretending to be thoroughly exhausted and far more unfit than she really was. It worked. Glowing with superiority, he relaxed his grip a fraction.

Just enough.

She swivelled and brought her foot up hard, the solid kick connecting with his balls.

Now he doubled over. But this wasn't an act. When she sprinted away this time, he didn't even attempt to follow.

33

There was no getting over it, Jane would have to be told. They'd tried all the neighbours, spoken to people tending gardens and washing cars, searched under bushes and in flower beds: anywhere an injured or sick animal might have crawled. Nothing. No hints, no clues, but that one uncertain sighting. Sally tried the Wests' doorbell again. No luck. She sighed and turned away and took out her phone.

Jane's phone went straight to voicemail, which rather threw Sally. It would be easier to deliver the news in person, provide an explanation and, if necessary, consolation. Telling her via a recorded message seemed rather harsh.

'Hi Jane, it's me,' she said, hoping to convey a hint in the gravitas of her tone. 'Can you give me a call when you get a chance?'

The end of her message was spoilt by Dylan tugging her arm and crying, 'Look, Mummy. Look!'

'What?' Sally turned, mildly annoyed, and saw Bluebelle looking back at them from the Wests' lounge window.

*

Jane's last glimpse of the tattooed man was of him sinking to his knees on the grass verge in Goose Green Grove as she darted into Dotterel Drive. Not taking any chances, she dived behind a hedge to double-check he hadn't made a miraculous recovery or that Burdon wasn't following in the car.

She really, *really* needed to contact Matt now, but there were three problems: she didn't have a phone any more, his phone was off, and she couldn't remember his mobile number anyway. That was the problem with modern technology. Using computers and phones as supplemental memory banks was fine – until you lost access to them.

Maybe the owner of the hedge could help.

It took three loud knocks to rouse anyone in the house beyond, but the cluttered porch provided some shelter from the rain, and an overgrown pot stand at least partially masked her from the street.

The door opened two inches, restrained by a length of chain, and a grey, whiskery chin said, 'Who's that? What d'you want?' She could hear a TV on in the background. A smell like boiled cabbage drifted from the house.

'My name's Jane Child. I'm a private investigator. I need to contact Salisbury's central police station urgently.

'You mean 999?'

'No, it's not an emergency. I just need to speak to someone senior at Wiltshire Police.'

The whiskery chin scowled. The face came closer to the gap, and she saw heavy glasses, a wrinkled brow and a head capped with odd tufts of white hair, like miniature icebergs.

She stepped back and held out her hands so he could get a better look at her. He was right to be suspicious given her state: soaking, sweaty, grazed knees and hands, mud-stained clothing.

'Look, I don't want to come in or anything. I'm not a robber or a burglar. I haven't got mates in the street waiting to pounce on you. Call them yourself. Give them your address and my name, then ask to speak to the desk sergeant. I can tell you what to say, or you can pass me the receiver.'

'What's wrong with 999?'

'It's not that sort of emergency. I just need to speak to someone. Confirm something. Urgently.' Given their MI5 brief and the need for discretion, the last thing she wanted was a street swarming with Armed Response officers.

'Wait there,' the man said and closed the door again.

There wasn't much else she could do.

She paced the porch, keeping a weather eye on the road. Nothing. No movement. No passing traffic. The pot stand and the hedge gave her a little protection from anyone coming past, but no one did. She waited, flexing her grazed knees through the torn fabric of her track pants.

Five minutes passed, but she could hear a muffled voice inside, a voice louder than the TV. Then the door opened again, still on the chain, and a receiver appeared in a wary hand. She took it, stretching the coiled cord to its limit.

'Good afternoon, my name's Jane Child. I'm a private investigator with Bluebelle Investigations. My partner, Matthew Healy, would have been in to see you about an hour ago.'

'What was that name again?'

Jane spelt it out for her.

'I'm sorry, Ms Child, we've had no Matthew Healys in today, and certainly not in the last couple of hours. It's been very quiet this afternoon.'

'Are you sure?' Jane said. 'Might he have seen someone else?'

'He might, but he'd have to have come through me. I've been on duty since twelve.'

'Oh.' Where the devil was he? What had happened? Perhaps he'd gone to another station.

'What was it concerning, Ms Child? Perhaps I can help.'

Jane thought quickly. If Matt was AWOL, she *had* to get back to keep an eye on Araton's house. Besides, trying to explain the situation would either take too long or get her dismissed as a loony – possibly both. Instead, she said, 'Yes, perhaps you can. Could you get an urgent message to Detective Inspector Colin Avery of the National Crime Agency in London, please? Tell him Jane Child called to say they've cracked the case, but there are at least two members of an interested party outside the target's house, and he should proceed with caution.'

The desk sergeant took a minute to write down her message

then repeated it back to her.

'Can you add that if he hasn't already heard from Matthew Healy, he may be in trouble.'

'The NCA, you say?' A quiet keyboard tapping sounded in the background. The woman was evidently checking on her contact.

'Yes, it's very important.'

The tapping stopped. The sergeant said, 'I'll make the call right away, Ms Child.'

'Thank you.' Jane handed the phone back through the gap in the door. 'And thank you,' she called to the elderly man before heading back out into the rain.

There should be enough in her message for Avery to tease out the details, even if Matt hadn't been able to get through to him. Now, certain that wheels were turning and that reinforcements were on the way, she needed somewhere safe, secure and sheltered until they arrived. Somewhere from which she could keep an eye on Araton too.

She knew the perfect spot.

*

Bartram Horovitz locked the door of the office behind him. Matt moved to the window to take in the scene outside and saw one of the heavies standing guard while his boss summoned the others. Open louvres above the window relayed every word.

'You two, back to town. Cruise around the area where you picked up Healy. Child will be somewhere in the vicinity, probably waiting for him to collect her. Take your time and stay in contact. The longer he's delayed, the more likely she is to call.'

'What about me, chief. I know what she looks like,' Tasha said.

'You go too. Travel separately. Trawl the area. I want her found.'

Taliq, seated at the trestle table, brought up a picture of Jane on one of the computers and sent it to the men's phones.

'And Ryan?' One of the heavies waved a thumb towards Matt's guard.

'He stays with me until we sight the target. I'm not sure we'll need his specialist skills yet, but if we do, we can use Healy's car.'

Matt watched the van and the Toyota drive away with a feeling of relief. Jane was miles from Salisbury city centre. She might be annoyed at being abandoned, but at least she was safe.

Taliq worked his computers. Horovitz paced, rubbing his chin.

'Mind if I check out the gear?' Matt's guard, Ryan, asked.

Horovitz glanced at the locked door and at Matt standing in the office window. 'Sure, go ahead.'

Ryan picked up the guitar case Horovitz and Taliq had brought with them, carried it to a workbench, and unlocked it. Matt moved around the office to get a better view. There was no instrument inside – at least not a musical one. The neatly partitioned interior contained what looked like the broken-down components of a sniper rifle.

The guard glanced back at the office, saw Matt watching, and snapped the lid shut.

*

Reaves headed back to Burdon's car, walking, not running, and walking with an awkward, crab-like gait. He opened the passenger door and dropped into the seat with a weary grunt. Burdon, who'd been rebinding her damaged wrist with a spool of electrical tape, said, 'Where is she? You didn't let her get away?'

He nodded vaguely.

'What the fuck's the matter with you?'

'Kicked me,' he said weakly.

'Jesus Christ, you men! Any sign of Healy?'

He shook his head.

'Where the hell's your partner?'

'Traffic. Another half-hour yet.'

'Goddam Brits. Fucking amateurs!' Burdon fumed, staring

through the rain-speckled windscreen as the wipers kicked in again.

'What was ... that all about?' Reaves asked, risking another outburst.

'The situation is that I caught that bitch keeping a watch on the target's house. On her own. No sign of her partner. My suspicion is they're waiting for Araton to return.'

'He's not in there already?'

Burdon's look was scathing. 'You think I didn't check?'

'Only, if she's on her own, maybe they're taking turns. You know, like working shifts.'

'We can find that out for certain *when* you get hold of her.'

Reaves licked his lips.

'Well, what the hell are you waiting for?'

'Right. Right, I'm on it.' He got out of the car, slowly and rather painfully.

34

Matt dusted off the cover of an ancient *Farming Quarterly* and flicked through pages advertising tractors and harvesters and muck spreaders. Outside, Ryan, the heavy on guard, stood at ease by the closed office door looking like he was used to such duty. Horovitz paced about the hangar, occasionally glancing at Taliq and his arrangement of computers and comms gear.

When Matt's phone rang, it made them all jump.

'No, Jane. No,' Matt muttered, putting down his magazine and hurrying to the window.

'What've we got?' Horovitz demanded.

'Caller display says "Colin".'

'What about the source?'

Taliq tracked a finger across one of the computer screens. 'London.'

'You sure?'

'Positive.'

Horovitz blew out a sigh. 'Let it go to voicemail.'

It didn't. The call stopped halfway through the eighth ring then immediately began again.

'Same caller, same location,' Taliq reported.

Seeing Matt watching from the office, Horovitz yelled, 'Who's Colin?'

'A mate back home.' Matt spoke casually. 'Probably calling about the football. Want me to take it?'

'Yeah, right,' Horovitz sneered.

This time there was a message. Avery's voice. 'Hi mate. Colin here. Give us a bell when you get this, will you?'

'Football!' Horovitz snorted as the phone fell silent.

What was he calling for? Matt wondered. Unless ...

Of course! Jane must have contacted Avery herself when Matt failed to reappear. Smart girl. And now Avery had called him, twice without success.

Matt returned to his magazine and kept his head down to hide his grin. Surely they realised geolocation could work both ways?

*

Jane made her way down a street of curtained windows. Evening had come early due to the heavy rain, and some primal instinct made people shutter up their lives and hunker down against the weather. She reached the house with the manicured lawns and neat privet hedges. The crisply turned earth around the flower beds and vegetable garden was sodden now, and slivers of light showed around the edges of the curtains.

The yappy dog must have been curled up by a heater because there was no sound but the continued patter of rain as she slipped down the side of the house. She made straight for the compost bin in the corner, climbed on top, swung over the high wooden fence, and landed with a dull squelch in Araton's back garden.

She might have lost her phone, but she still had her wallet. She took it out, selected a certain Visa card, and crouched by Araton's back door.

Jane was new to lock picking. She knew the tools, and she knew the theory, but she hadn't had much practice. There were only a certain number of locks back home, and finding how little time it took someone as proficient as Matt to crack them was disturbing. Still, this one had taken him a good few minutes so she might be here a while.

Less than a minute later, she felt the tiny torsion wrench move a fraction as the last tumbler clicked into place. She was in.

In record time too. Hah, In your face, Healy!

She tucked away her tools and stood on the gloomy threshold.

First priority: see if the situation's changed.

Locking the door behind her, she moved to the front room where she made out Burdon's car still parked outside.

Nodding to herself, she returned to the kitchen and used a tea towel to wipe her face and sodden hair before opening the hall cupboard. The vacuum cleaner, broom, dustpan and brush were where they'd left them, which meant Araton was still in his lair.

She settled down to wait. This was as good a hiding place as any. The authorities definitely weren't far away now. She could just hole up here until they arrived. But she still didn't know what it was all about. What had Araton done to attract such interest? Now might be her only chance to find out. Once the police and MI5 arrived, the Official Secrets cloak would be thrown over the whole affair, and she might never know.

Then there was Matt. Sitting around waiting gave her time to worry. Where was he? What had happened? Had he simply gone to another police station? If so, why hadn't he returned? What if he'd had an accident? What if the tubby guy had managed to track them after all?

Now the immediate threat was over, a thousand possibilities occurred to her, each of them equally unpleasant. Telling herself there was nothing she could do right now, that she'd have to wait, didn't help.

What would Matt do if our roles were reversed?

She didn't have to think twice about that and immediately set about uncovering the trapdoor.

Araton was sitting on the bed, his feet up, watching something on the computer. He had a pair of headphones on, but the movement by the trapdoor caught his attention, and he snatched them off and stared, his face stricken.

'Dr Araton, I presume?' Jane peered down at him, her damp hair partly obscuring her face. 'My name is Jane Child. I'm a private detective hired by your family to investigate your disappearance. May I come down?' Without waiting for an answer, she did so.

'Cosy spot you've got here.'

She reached the last rung and looked around. The square space seemed smaller and more cluttered now she was standing in it. The scatter rugs were threadbare, the furniture makeshift. What looked like a sofa by torchlight turned out to be a couple of crates and boards covered with cushions and an old curtain. Power cords snaked from a single electrical outlet behind the ladder, and the place smelt of unwashed laundry with an undertone of chemical toilet.

'How did you find me?' Araton rose to his feet. A tall man with powerful shoulders. Not the bookish type at all.

'Salisbury Council plans.'

'Very enterprising.' He looked past her. 'It is just you, I take it?'

'For now.'

'What are you doing here? How did you get into my house? You know you're trespassing.'

'Your family are very concerned, Dr Araton. Your nephew, Sebastian, hired my partner and me after you disappeared. And your sister, Jean Harroway, gave us a key to your house.'

Araton's eyes narrowed. 'Why would she do that?'

'Because you vanished without a trace. Your hasty scheme of an accident or a suicide on the Wales Coast Path failed. The police search found nothing, possibly because there was a spring tide two days after you "disappeared".'

'Ah,' he said with a sigh of resignation. 'So the police are searching for me?'

'They spent a day or two at Wysbech, found your car, and checked the coast path, but that's about all they've found so far.'

'How then did you come to be looking at council plans?'

'I had an aunt with a house much like this when I was little. Similar vintage, similar style. There was a trapdoor outside leading to a coal cellar, and my cousins used to taunt me about it. That's where the monsters and bogeymen live, they'd say. But when my partner and I looked over your place the other day, I realised there was no trapdoor. Which got me thinking.'

Araton eyed her coolly. 'So what are you doing here?' he repeated.

'To find out what you're doing here, Dr Araton.'

He arched an eyebrow.

Jane continued. 'People have many reasons for walking away from their lives. Relationship troubles, work worries, the simple desire to start again. Technically, our work is over. We've solved the case. But before we report back to your family, I thought you should have some say in the matter. After all, you engineered all this.'

'You'll be reporting back to my nephew, will you?'

'Sebastian, yes.'

'Just Sebastian?'

'I imagine he'll pass on our findings to his mother.'

'That's not what I mean. Do you know who he works for? What he does?'

Jane kept her eyes level with his. 'Why? Is that relevant?'

Araton dropped his gaze and sighed. 'No, probably not.' He glanced at the ladder and the open hatch. 'Since the game is up, perhaps I should explain myself. But let's not do it down here. I could do with a stretch and some fresh air. Perhaps even a decent cup of coffee. Would you mind passing me my jacket, please.'

He indicated a peg to Jane's left. As she turned and reached for it, Araton seized a short length of timber from his makeshift sofa and slammed it into the side of her head.

35

What Colin Avery would do next depended on what Jane had told him, Matt thought. Everything, probably, which meant his first priority would be to collect Araton. Matt would come a distant second. Perhaps a local squad car sent to check on the odd location of his phone. At which point, Horovitz would flash a badge or call a number or cite National Security and they'd go away again.

So it's up to me. And it's one against three.

He studied the computer guy and recalled his limp, how Jane had tripped him on the stairs of the British Library.

Two-and-a-half, perhaps.

Horovitz, he could handle. Computer-guy too. But Special Forces Ryan was in a different league. He had muscle and mass and reflexes and training. And he was almost certainly armed.

Matt was going to need a weapon, but offices, even farming ones, didn't usually come with gun racks or Kendo sticks or knuckledusters. The best he could find was an old umbrella and a sample packet of a fine grey powder called Pinkerton's Supa-Gro Rooting Hormone.

They would have to do.

*

The blow stunned Jane. It didn't knock her out, but it was enough to disorient her. Araton cannoned into her side, knocked her to the floor and leapt on her back. Before she knew it, he'd bound her hands with a length of electrical flex and was going through her pockets, evidently searching for a cellphone.

He threw what he found to one side then stepped away,

regarding her for a moment before hurrying to the workbench opposite and returning with a length of chain and two padlocks. He replaced the flex with a makeshift manacle, looping the chain around a water pipe running along the back wall of the cellar before securing it around her wrists.

He stepped back, gave a grunt of satisfaction, then climbed up the ladder to the open hatch.

Jane's head throbbed, her right ear rang, and she felt what must have been a trickle of blood running down the side of her head. She couldn't be certain because of her chained hands.

She was dizzy and dazed and had the impression Araton had abandoned her in the basement. Then he reappeared and climbed partway down the ladder where he spent some time replacing and arranging items in the cupboard above through the second, smaller hatch-within-a-hatch. Finally satisfied, he drew back the last segment of carpet and closed up, turning off the head torch he was wearing.

Been checking his mail, Jane thought as he descended the whole way and took a couple of advertising flyers and a bill from the back pocket of his trousers. He flicked through them, then flung them down beside her wallet and the other things he'd taken from her.

'So, you're back with us.' He spoke casually, taking off the head torch. 'It looks like we'll be spending a couple of days together. Things seem to be taking longer than I expected, so we might as well get to know each other.'

Jane closed her eyes. It felt like the room was on gimbals, and Araton's voice came and went in waves.

'If you're going to be sick, please aim for the toilet through there.' He pointed to the shower-curtained alcove where a hole had been chipped through one side of the room's brickwork. 'We both have to live with the consequences.'

Jane was about to object, saying he'd have to release her first, then discovered she was chained in such a way that she could slide sideways along the thick copper pipe – at least as far as the mounting brackets on either side permitted.

Like the chain on a dog run, she thought.

He poured water into a plastic cup then threw it in her face.

'That better? Now, tell me who you really are and who you're really working for.' He picked up the length of wood again and toyed with it. 'Cooperate, and I won't need to use this.' Then he swung it sharply, slamming it into the floor beside her foot. Jane lurched back in shock.

'Well?'

'I've already told you everything. Your nephew Sebastian hired us. We're working for your family.'

'You're lying. Do you know how I can tell?' He pointed to Jane's possessions. 'No keys. You said my sister gave you keys to the house, but you don't have any. I've checked up top. The front and back doors are still locked, and no windows have been forced. Conclusion: you're a professional. You picked the lock. Broke in. I want to know why?'

It didn't matter, Jane thought. Help was on the way. But it wouldn't do to alarm Araton, especially with Susan Burdon and the tattooed man outside. All she had to do was buy some time.

'You're right, we were hired by MI5.'

'We?'

'My partner and I.'

'Where is your partner right now?'

'Probably looking for me,' she said bitterly.

'So, am I right in assuming you were playing a hunch?'

'I had to be sure. I'm ... still on probation. I rather made a mess of my last job. I wanted to check. Make sure I was right. Then you spotted me.'

Araton smiled. 'So you thought you'd play the hero. Bring me in single-handed. After all, how dangerous can one nutty old scientist be, eh? Well, you misjudged me, young lady. I am very dangerous indeed.'

Without warning, he swung the lump of wood again, bringing it down with a splintering crash beside her. Jane lunged sideways, sliding behind the partial cover of the ladder. Araton laughed, tossed the piece of wood aside, and walked away.

'So, what's happening in the world outside, Jane Child?' He spoke conversationally, looking through her wallet, pulling out her business card. 'I'm a bit cut off down here.'

'You're missing without a trace. What I told you about the spring tide is true. That is, assuming you planted evidence for the police to find.'

'I did, and I believe you. I have a book of tide tables upstairs and just checked.' He sighed. 'One small detail. Annoying. But I don't imagine my disappearance has made the national papers. Or any papers at all for that matter.'

'Our investigation is termed critical but highly confidential. My partner and I were brought in from the outside so as not to attract attention. You're obviously an important man, Dr Araton.'

'You have no idea.'

'We really don't. Other than that you work for DSTL.'

'Not sufficiently cleared, eh? Official Secrets Act and all that.'

'We did speak with your Head of Security, but he wouldn't even tell us where you worked.'

'Reginald Wyatt, that buffoon? He wouldn't know water from dihydrogen monoxide.'

'But you would, of course. Being a chemist.'

'You know that much.'

'A good chemist. And obviously a valuable one.'

'A very valuable one. A hundred million US dollars valuable. What would you say to that, hmm?'

'Impressive.'

'Somewhat better than a British government pension, don't you think? I'm sixty-three years old, Ms Child. I have, perhaps, twenty years ahead of me. Time to live a little. Five million a year should cover it nicely. And that's just the interest on the principle.'

He perched on the edge of the bed and studied her. 'Do you know what a hundred million dollars represents in terms of our defence budget? Barely one six-hundredth of it. Britain spends sixty billion dollars a year on its military. The Americans spend ten times as much. All up, the world spends two trillion every year on armies and guns, bombs, and battleships. Meanwhile, the planet's going to hell in a handcart.'

'Is that what you worked on at Porton Down then, weapons?'

'Chemical weapons. Proper weapons, yes.'

'Proper weapons?'

'Oh, they have a bad name, but think about it for a moment. What is the real purpose of war from the aggressor's perspective? Simply to subjugate the enemy and seize his assets: land, factories, oil, minerals. Conventional weapons wreck all that. Nuclear weapons are worse. The sheer destruction involved is immense, to say nothing of ongoing radiological contamination and the fact that the enemy is liable to lob a few warheads back at you. It's mad. Literally M-A-D. Mutually Assured Destruction.

'Chemical and biological agents leave buildings standing and just kill people, but they bring with them a different set of problems, not least of which is a general abhorrence of the things. Blowing people to pieces, or leaving them hideously maimed, burned or irradiated so that they die lingering deaths over the coming days, weeks, months, or even years is considered humane. But gassing them, or infecting them with a pathogen that kills rapidly, is supposed to be barbaric.

'Of course, biological agents aren't perfect. Spores can lie dormant for decades and be stirred up again by an unwary footstep. Decontamination is a nightmare. The same with some chemicals. Sarin residues persist for weeks or months. VX gas is an area-denial weapon. It's not a vapour hazard, it just sticks to things. And it doesn't evaporate or degrade over time. Touch a droplet the size of a pinhead with your bare skin, and you're dead.

'Do you know how chemical weapons are delivered?' Jane

shook her head. She wanted to keep him talking. 'As binaries: two separate substances that are not in themselves exceedingly toxic. That makes them safer to store, transport and so on. But when these so-called precursors are combined, the result is extremely toxic indeed.

'Mixing usually occurs when the munition is fired. The old M687 artillery shell, for example, contained two compartments separated by a rupture disc. When it was fired, the shock would break the rupture disc while the spinning of the shell, induced by the rifling in the barrel of the gun, mixed the two components. On reaching its target, it would explode and release a cloud of Sarin gas. At their peak, the Americans had more than a quarter of a million M687 shells.

'Now consider a new type of chemical weapon. Another binary, but one with a harmless precursor. A water-soluble precursor that the body happily takes up and stores in muscles and fat with no apparent ill effects. It can lie dormant for years until it's exposed to the trigger compound, at which point death occurs within hours.

'Imagine the scenario. You deliver Compound One to a country's population – through its drinking water, perhaps – and do so months or years in advance. It's the ultimate peace-keeping weapon because if hostilities do break out, you simply tell them to behave. Naturally, they'll refuse to do so – until you give them a demonstration. A military base, a town, a city. You deliver Compound Two – a colourless, odourless, almost undetectable gas – and everybody dies. A chemical Hiroshima or Nagasaki, but with the infrastructure left intact.

'Compound Two in itself is relatively harmless. Not a particularly pleasant substance, but spray some around, say, the United Nations building, and only those exposed to the precursor will be affected.

'It really is the ultimate weapon. By the time you show your hand, your enemy already has Compound One deep within his bones.'

Jane stared, taking in the import of his words. 'And ... that's what you were working on?'

Araton smiled. 'No, that's what I perfected. And sold. To one of our so-called allies.

'Unfortunately, such a weapon requires a proving time. Subjects must be exposed to Compound One for at least a fortnight before the delivery of Compound Two, the formulation of which is my little secret. I made up a batch before I left work and smuggled it out in a phony Thermos flask. In the normal course of things, with a three-week holiday, no one would have noticed until the deal was done, and I was gone.

'But then bloody Wyatt brought in an auditor who went through my stock. Some of the compounds I use are rare and extremely expensive. Also, in their raw form, highly toxic. He sent me a text message requesting an explanation. I ignored him, but he persisted.

'I guessed that he or someone at DSTL had put two and two together. They knew what I was working on, and when they went through my research notes ... well, they wouldn't find anything but meaningless waffle. That's because it's all up here.' He tapped his head. 'A secret shared is no longer a secret.'

Jane recalled the shelf of improve-your-memory books in the lounge upstairs.

'I kept meticulous notes, but in the only place where no one can ever get at them without my permission.

'By that stage, my buyers were a week into the administration of Compound One. I just had to keep Wyatt and his hounds at bay for another couple of weeks, so I came up with the suicide. That would have thrown them off the scent if they'd been a bit quicker chasing after me. I went to great pains with the farewell note, too, you know. The touching story of a man disaffected with his work. Oh well.'

'So you're hiding out, waiting to hear from your buyers.'

'And expect to do so any day now.'

'It's been over a fortnight now. Maybe the stuff doesn't work.'

'Oh, but it does. Someone, somewhere is writhing and dying even as we speak. Many someones, if they're testing thoroughly.' He delivered the words with a chilling smile.

But how would his buyers contact him? Jane wondered. Without the internet and without a phone?

Araton didn't seem bothered.

'Is this where you did some of your research?' Jane asked, gesturing to the hazmat suit.

Araton laughed. 'The idea of a mad scientist in a basement laboratory is pure fantasy, you know. The equipment alone costs millions of pounds, and some of the substances I work with require constant monitoring and containment. But in the latter stages, this place did prove useful for proving the effectiveness of Compound Two.' He nodded at the empty cages. 'Wouldn't want to give my clients a dud batch, would I? Not with so much at stake.

'As for the rest of this place, whoever owned the house before my late wife and I bought it had converted this cellar into a fallout shelter. It was filled with Cold War-era stuff, including a rather comical Russian NBC suit. God knows where that came from, but I kept it. Thought it might make a fun prop at fancy-dress party. Not that I go to many parties.'

'I'd have thought a fallout shelter would be ideal for someone in your line of work,' Jane said.

'Someone in my line of work knows how ridiculous that whole concept is. Even assuming you can get to your shelter in time, what then? The Russians and Americans have more than six thousand thermonuclear warheads apiece. There aren't six thousand targets on either side. The whole basis of an attack plan is multiple redundancies. Throw ten warheads at a target and hope five get through.

'Say by some miracle you survive the blastwave, the shocks, the heat, and the fire-storms. What then? You have to come out sometime. Unless you've stockpiled enough food and water to last for decades, you're doomed to a long, slow, irradiated death.

'Shelter from armageddon?' he snorted. 'Better to be that shadow on the steps in Hiroshima than any so-called "survivor".'

Jane's blood ran cold, but not just from his words. *How would his buyers contact him when he was hidden away down here?* The question had been gnawing at her from the outset. Now, glancing at the desk containing her wallet and scattered possessions, she suddenly knew. They had already done so. They had already told him the test had been successful.

36

'What are you doing in there?' Sally said.

Bluebelle responded with a silent meow behind the plate-glass window and paced back and forth along the sill.

'Come on, there's a cat flap round here. Come on. Puss, puss, puss.'

Bluebelle kept pacing, so Paul knelt beside the step and tried to push the flap open.

'It's locked, or jammed, or something,' he said.

'Then how did Tangelo get out?' Sally replied.

The ginger tom was keeping an eye on proceedings.

'Hold on.' Paul examined the cat door more closely. 'It's not jammed. I think it's one of those self-locking ones to keep out strays. It only gets triggered when your cat goes near it.'

'Then how did Bluebelle get inside?'

'I don't know, but I think I know how to open it.' He scooped up Tangelo, carried him over to the door, and steered his head towards the entrance. 'I think it's triggered by the collar.' There was a faint click as the lock released, and he thrust his free hand inside to keep the hinged door open.

Tangelo wasn't interested in going back inside, so, holding up the flap, Paul put his mouth to the opening and called, 'Bluebelle? Puss, puss, puss?'

The front gate swung open behind them and a loud voice said, 'What the devil's going on here?'

'Ah,' Paul said, on his hands and knees on the neighbours' step, one arm halfway through their front door. He craned his head back to see a burly man and startled-looking woman regarding him from the street.

Just then, Bluebelle made her exit, pushing through the open cat flap and sprinting past them all before heading back to Jane's.

'Oh, her again!' the man said. 'That's the third time this week

He introduced himself: Josh West and his wife Caitlin. Paul and Sally made hasty explanations, and Josh laughed. 'So it's Bluebelle, is it? We've been calling her Houdini. Couldn't work out how she was getting in – at least till yesterday morning.

'She seems to have struck up a friendship with Tangelo. We guessed she was local, but couldn't work out how she was getting into the house. Tangy's got one of those magnetic cat doors. With his collar, he should be the only one able to get through it, but two days running we've come down and found old Houdini in the house with him. And once she's in, she can't get out on her own, not without a special collar.

'We both work, and were away last night. We left extra food down for Tangy, but wondered if Houdini would find her way in.'

'So how's she doing it?' Sally asked.

'We couldn't work it out either,' the other woman said, taking out her phone, 'at least till Josh set up a webcam on the cat door. Here, take a look.' She started the video clip and held the phone out for them to see.

Sally watched, then laughed. 'Oh, that *is* clever!'

Tangelo appeared first. As his head pressed against the transparent plastic flap, the presence of the collar triggered the release switch and he was able to push his way inside, but before the flap fell shut again, Bluebelle pushed in behind him.

'Unless she follows him straight out, she gets stuck inside,' Josh said.

'Well! See that, Dylan?'

'Anyway, let's not stand out here talking,' Caitlin said. 'Come inside. You two look like you could use a cuppa.

'That'd be lovely,' Sally said, 'but can you give me a minute? I'll just check on Bluebelle, and I'd better give her owner another call.'

*

Reaves made a slow circuit of the block around Araton's house, finding nothing. Not that he expected to. The woman who'd kicked him would hardly be standing around in the pissing rain, waiting for him to return. She'd be holed up somewhere, hiding, watching him pass by with his awkward walk and sniggering to herself. On the other hand, the exercise had helped his injury. His natural inclination had been to curl up somewhere dark and warm and wait till the throbbing ache had eased, but actually getting out and moving about seemed to help, and by the time he returned to Plover Place he was moving almost normally. Drenched from head to foot, but almost back to normal.

A new Mercedes C-Class swung into a park behind Burdon's car, and Rosten got out. He was wearing a smart woollen overcoat and shielded his head with a folded copy of the Telegraph. He scuttled up the footpath like a fat crab and clambered into the front seat of Burdon's car.

'Prick!' Reaves muttered under his breath as he followed him up the road. That front seat was his. *He* was in charge.

Resisting the temptation to tear the door open and toss the fat prick in the back, Reaves took the rear seat for himself, landing in it with a dull squelch.

'Well?' Burdon's eyes quizzed him from the rearview mirror.

'I've been round the block, checked both sides. No sign of her. Front gardens. Parked cars. She could be hiding anywhere. We'd need a big team for a proper sweep.'

'Forget her.' Burdon's voice was throaty, like someone with a heavy cold. Even in the narrow mirror, he could see the swelling and the blackening bruises beneath her eyes. 'Her presence here suggests Araton's on his way, and he's the one we're after.

'According to the map, this whole estate is enclosed in a one-way system, so I want it under three-car surveillance. The road in,

239

the road out, and here outside his house. Rosten?'

Rosten reached into his overcoat and handed Reaves a walkie-talkie.

'We stay in touch at all times. Any movement, anything. If a dog shits on a lawn, I want to know about it.'

'What if Child or Healy get in the way?' Reaves asked.

'You're armed, aren't you? Collateral damage. Araton's our priority.'

Collateral damage, he thought. He'd certainly like to teach that little bitch about collateral damage.

'What if we don't find them?' Rosten asked. 'Before we pick up Araton, I mean?'

'Then you find them and deal with them afterwards or you don't get paid,' Burdon replied. 'The "how" is up to you, but I want them dealt with.'

Reaves grinned and licked his lips.

They ran checks on the walkie-talkies. Rosten tucked his back inside his overcoat saying, 'I'll take the inbound lane, you take the exit.'

Like he was in-fucking-charge of this operation!

Reaves said nothing, not in front of the client.

Rain pounded on the car roof. Rosten glanced back at his companion. 'All right?' He regarded his drowned-cat appearance before adding, 'I was going to offer you half my newspaper, but there doesn't seem to be much point.'

He was out, shielding his head and trotting back to his car before Reaves could summon a reply.

*

Jane knew in an instant. And in that same instant, Araton saw she knew.

Something, at least.

Her gaze lingered on the things on his desk for a moment too long. Not her things, the advertising flyers, and the bill he'd brought down with him.

He leapt to his feet. 'What? What is it? What do you know?'

Jane turned her eyes on his and shook her head. 'Nothing. Noth—'

He seized her by the jaw, bony fingers digging into her cheeks, and bellowed into her face. 'Tell me!'

Jane's hands were bound behind her, but her feet were free. For a moment, she was tempted to kick him the way she'd kicked the tattooed man, but she didn't want to rile him. Not with help close at hand. He could still hurt her badly with that lump of wood. Instead, she just shifted sideways and pulled her head away.

Araton turned back to the desk, speaking slowly as he connected the dots. 'The keys. My sister's keys. You knew she has keys to this place. You've used them, haven't you? Been here before. When? *When?* What did you do?'

Jane had put it all together.

How would Araton's buyer communicate with him when he was in hiding at an unknown location without phone or internet? The old-fashioned way. The same way Araton had communicated with his sister when asking her to deliver him supplies.

By mail.

It wouldn't take much. An innocuous postcard delivered to his house. At some point, once the intensity of the search died down, he'd sneak back and check. Or his sister would collect it for him and pass it on. Confirmation received, he'd make an anonymous phone call full of keywords and code phrases, and arrange his escape from the country.

That explained his patience – his equanimity about not having heard yet, despite the two-week setup period being over. Mail deliveries weren't like instant messages: they took time. A day or two at least. It explained his remark about them spending a couple of days together. Today was Saturday. The mail had been delivered. There'd be no more deliveries till Monday.

It also explained Burdon's interest. She'd been sent to England to collect him, only to discover things had gone pear-shaped, that Araton had been tumbled and forced into hiding. Someone – one of her old CIA contacts or whoever she was working for now – had got wind of MI5 employing outsiders, so rather than track him down herself – a foreigner in a foreign country – she decided to let Matt and Jane do the work for her.

Now she was here, waiting outside, anticipating Araton's return because the tests had proved successful and the communication had been sent.

And received.

Jane had seen it herself in the mail she and Matt bundled up and sent back with Araton's key. A postcard from London with an indecipherable signature and the message, "Everything well. Expect to see you soon."

Araton moved to the bed and took out a holdall from beneath it. Digging down one side then the other, he found what he was looking for and drew it out. A pistol. A Markarov, the same vintage as the NBC suit in the wardrobe upstairs. It was old, grimy, and its smooth sides were speckled with chips of rust, but it still looked deadly.

He rummaged further, deeper, and extracted four rounds of 9x18mm ammunition which he loaded into the magazine with shaking hands. Then he slammed the magazine home, cocked and aimed the gun at Jane's forehead.

'*What did you do?*' he repeated, his rage barely under control. 'Tell me. Now. *Everything!*'

'Your sister gave us the key. We came in.'

'When?'

'Thursday. Thursday morning. We took a look around, talked to your neighbours, then I gathered up the mail and sent it back to your sister with the key.'

'The mail. What was in it?'

'Bills, a flyer, and a postcard.'

'A postcard of what?'

'Tower Bridge in London.'

'*Jesus!*' he muttered. 'Describe it. The postcard. The picture!'

'Just ... Tower Bridge.' Araton waved the gun. 'A ... a nighttime shot. All lit up. Cars and buses going across it.'

'So the vehicle deck was closed then? No ships going through?'

'No,' Jane replied, puzzled.

Araton lowered the gun and pocketed it, his expression transformed, his voice no longer anxious. 'That's it then! Thursday, you say? Jesus Christ.' He gave a bitter laugh as he looked about the place then untangled the laptop's charger from the overloaded socket on the wall. He dropped it into the holdall, added the laptop, took one last look around then made for the ladder.

Pushing the bag ahead of him, he climbed out, paused then looked back down. 'Excuse my manners, Ms Child. You have been most helpful. And something of a hindrance, I must say. Two whole days, wasted! Still, all's well that ends well, eh?'

Sitting on the floor above, his legs swinging in the opening, he took out the gun again, reached into a side pocket of the holdall and began screwing a long black cylinder onto the end of the barrel.

'It's nothing personal, but I don't want any loose ends.' He pointed the gun at her. 'If what you told me is true, then no one knows where you are. You should probably thank me. Better this way than slowly starving to death down there, eh?'

He took aim and fired.

37

Brolly in one hand, a fistful of Pinkerton's Supa-Gro Rooting Hormone in the other, Matt tapped on the locked office door.

'Whaddya want?' Ryan, the heavy, stepped up to it.

'I need the loo.'

'He means the bathroom,' Horovitz interpreted. 'Stick with him.'

Ryan unlocked the door and ushered him out. 'What's with the stick?'

Matt leaned on the umbrella. 'My knee's playing up. Old war wound.'

'Huh!' Ryan sounded sceptical.

As he drew near, Matt gave a short gasp of pain. Ryan looked directly at him, and Matt let fly with the handful of fine, greyish powder. Without waiting to see its full effect, he rushed straight at Horovitz, the blunted ferrule of the brolly aimed at his belly.

An explosive cry of 'Christ!' sounded behind him. Horovitz looked up, saw Matt coming, lurched backwards, and stumbled over his chair. Matt reversed the umbrella, used it like a bat, and slammed the handgrip against the side of Horovitz's head.

Taliq rose from his seat, digging beneath his jacket with his right hand, but Matt was ready for him. Brolly abandoned, moving at full speed, he kicked out at the trestle table separating them. The top slid off its supports and straight into Taliq's stomach. He went down with a grunt as computers and comms gear hit the floor around him.

Matt paused to snatch up his phone then bounded for his car, the only vehicle left since the others had gone to look for Jane. The keys were still in the ignition. He started it up, looking at the confusion in the rearview mirror. The Special Forces guy was on his knees, grey-faced, coughing, hands cupped over his streaming eyes, trying to clear them. Taliq was doubled over, holding his stomach. Horovitz was on his feet bellowing orders.

Matt jammed the car into reverse and accelerated.

Horovitz let out a startled cry as the car rocketed towards him. He dived to one side, straight into an open fertiliser bay, but Matt wasn't aiming for him. He pushed the shift into Drive and headed for the fallen trestle table, grinding over computers and comms gear before accelerating away.

*

Jane kicked backwards as Araton aimed the gun. An automatic reaction. Pure instinct, but a rather pointless one. As if you could outrun a speeding bullet or dodge aside like a matador confronted by a charging bull. As she did so, as her chained hands slid along the water pipe, her shoulder clipped the single power outlet with its overload of multiple adapters.

The cellar lights went out as Araton fired.

Poh!

The silenced muzzle flash looked like the spark of a short-circuit.

Jane fell, and the pain was excruciating. In her back, just below her left shoulder blade. She lay gasping for several seconds before realising it was only coming from her back, not her front, yet she'd been facing her attacker. Thinking of exit wounds and bullets tumbling as they tore through a body, she drew some slack on the chain around her right wrist and gingerly touched her fingers to her back. She could feel nothing.

Was she numb?

No, there *was* nothing. No blood, weeping wound, no stabs of pain. Not so much as a tear in the fabric of her shirt.

She rolled to one side, and immediately the pain in her back eased.

Overhead, Araton closed the hatch and replaced the carpet. The darkness in the coal cellar was complete, so it took her several more long seconds to realise she hadn't been hit at all. That as she'd leapt back, she'd fallen on one of the plugs dislodged from the plugboard and landed on its three stabbing prongs. Painful, and an interestingly shaped bruise, but they hadn't even broken the skin.

Still, she didn't quite trust herself. She'd heard about shock and delayed reaction, and carefully checked herself out, feeling around as far as she could reach. She drew an exaggerated breath and flexed her limbs. Arms, legs, hands, feet, fingers, toes all present and in working order. She turned, twisted, and sat upright. She was unscathed.

How the devil had he missed?

The dark, she guessed. A moving target. An unfamiliar weapon. Had he even fired it before? Who knew? Best not question her luck.

But was it luck?

She thought of Araton's last words to her. He was right. No one did know she was here, not even Matt. She'd heard Araton overhead, replacing the things in the hall cupboard after he closed the hatch. No one knew about this place but the three of them, and if something had happened to Matt ...

*

Terence Araton took a moment to double-check the positioning of everything before closing up the hall cupboard. No doubt DSTL Security would be back for another look around with their forensic cameras. No point alerting them to his hiding place. Or his crime.

Flexing the fingers of his right hand, he relieved the residual ache from working the old gun. He didn't know much about crude mechanical weapons like this and hadn't maintained it very well. It had always had a heavy trigger pull, but there was no doubt he'd hit her. That cry of pain over the muffled retort was unmistakable. Even if only wounded, she'd die soon enough.

He felt elated. He'd never killed before. Not a human being. Not directly. Laboratory animals, of course. Mice, rats, rabbits, dogs. Thousands upon thousands of them over the years. Experimental subjects to ingest or inhale his compounds, or have them dripped onto shaved skin or into eyes or mucous membranes, wriggling and writhing as they howled in agony and terror. But not an actual human being. A vigorous young woman too. It was almost ... sexual. If she hadn't kicked out the lights, he'd like to have watched her death throes.

With an effort of will, he dragged his mind back to his escape. All he had to do was find a phone, call the number he'd memorised weeks earlier, and give the right reply to the passphrase. Would they send someone for him? It was the least they could do, considering what they were getting.

He took one last look around his house, thinking how little he'd miss any of it, then paused at the front door to look out at the quiet street through the rain-smeared window. Dusk had arrived early thanks to the storm. He reached for an umbrella then recalled that he really must leave the house undisturbed.

Steady now.

His exhilaration and excitement had almost got the better of him. It was the little things, the tiny slip-ups that brought down mighty empires. Like that damn spring tide.

Think!

We. The young woman had said *we* several times. She and her partner. Was he or she out there somewhere, watching the house? It would make sense. Only a fool would go down into that cellar without backup, despite what she'd said. Or perhaps someone else was out there. One of Wyatt's goons. Or MI5's.

Araton drew his hand away from the lock. Going out the front was foolish. Tempting fate. Discretion was always the better part of valour. Better to slip away out the back and over the fence.

*

Jane couldn't stop crying. Relief, rage, the sheer bloody terror of having a loaded gun aimed at her – and fired – with the deliberate intention of ending her life. She still couldn't quite believe she was untouched. Still half-expected searing pain and a sudden collapse. The darkness made it worse. Utter and complete. It was like being blind or having no eyes at all. Perhaps he really had hit and killed her. Perhaps she was already dead, and this was what it was like afterwards ...

What, you mean I'm going to spend eternity fastened to a wall? Because this damn chain feels solid enough.

It was that thought that finally brought her round.

Wiping her cheek on the shoulder of her shirt, she forced herself to take a series of slow, steady breaths and assess her situation as calmly as she could.

Water pipe. Hands chained. Pitch black. What else do you need?

She thought of the muffled muzzle flash. Perhaps the last thing she'd ever see ...

C'mon girl, get a grip!

Araton was gone now. Straight into Burdon's arms, or the arms of the authorities. Or perhaps one and then the other. Her message to Avery would kick things off. They'd come, check out the house. She had only to wait.

But none of them knew about this place, just Matt. His words came back to her: "Only three of us know where Araton is, and one of them's the man himself."

Matt. Was he OK? Where was he? What had happened to him?

A hundred possible scenarios flared in the dark recesses of her mind. Everything from a simple traffic accident to a nefarious double-cross by MI5. She almost wished he hadn't told her about Penny after all.

OK, worst-case scenario: Matt doesn't come. She could simply shout for help. Of course, there'd have to be someone up there to shout to, someone nearby, preferably with their head in the broom cupboard ...

She tried it, just for the sake of experiment, just to hear something other than the sound of her own breathing, but her cry felt dull and flat in the confined space. As if the walls were lined with sponge and her words were made of water.

Well, that won't work. But Matt will come.

Not if he's in a coma, or a prison cell, or worse. Besides, would he imagine, even in his wildest dreams, that she'd go down into Araton's cellar?

This wasn't getting her anywhere. Speculation was foolish. So was waiting. She could be down here hours, days. Forever. Waiting for help was *not* an option.

A proper assessment of my situation then ...

The chain had been wrapped around each wrist and secured with what felt like a pair of rusty padlocks. In between, it had been looped around the water pipe with just enough slack to let her move from side to side. The full span of her movement was about ten feet between support brackets. Enough on one side to reach the chemical toilet, enough on the other to almost reach the far wall. The pipe was copper; three-quarter inch; the mounts thick and solidly fixed to the wall.

The chain then. Any weak links?

She felt along it link by link. Nothing. Even if there had been a break, it would be impossible to lever a link apart without proper tools; heavy-duty tools too. The chain felt like quarter-inch steel.

Any chance of getting some light back?

None. Her backward lurch against the overloaded socket had torn everything out. Apart from the plug she'd been lying on – which felt like the clunky adapter for a portable CD player she'd once had – the rest was out of reach. But perhaps if she kicked off a shoe and felt about with her foot ...

Wait. Copper pipe. Copper was malleable. A galvanised pipe would be impossible to bend, but copper ...

Logically, the weakest, most bendable point would be equidistant from the mounting brackets.

She slid from side to side. It was impossible to tell exactly where she was in the dark, so she measured the distance with her feet. She was size 8. That meant her shoes were probably nine or nine-and-a-half inches long. Thirteen steps between the brackets meant a ten-foot length of pipe, so half of that – six steps back - should put her about dead centre ...

Clasping her hands around the pipe, she leaned forward experimentally and gave it a tug.

No movement at all.

Not that she'd expected any. This was going to take some effort.

Bracing one foot against the wall and gripping the lengths of chain to protect her wrists, she kicked away, throwing her full weight against the narrow section of chain wrapped around the pipe.

That must have done something!

She felt about in the darkness. Yes, there was a slight kink on the inside of the pipe where the chain had bitten and – was she imagining it? – a tiny increase in the space between the pipe and the wall.

She tried again. Harder.

A little more?

There was only one thing for it; she worked again and again and again until her hands ached and her arms felt like they were pulling off her shoulders. The pipe was definitely bent now, no doubt about it. It felt like a bow under tension. Something must give soon.

Soon? That had to be an understatement. For a long time, it seemed like she was making no further progress, then, quite suddenly, there was a faint hiss and she felt a fine, misty spray coming from behind her. Pausing to inspect it, she felt what was now a sharp kink caused by her wrenching on the chain. Where the once-round pipe had been flattened to an oval, there was now a tiny tear in the stressed metal.

The discovery spurred her on. She worked harder and harder. The spray turned into a hissing jet blasting against the brickwork and showering her with grit and dirt and fragments.

Oh great, just as I was drying out!

She didn't care. She laughed aloud.

Time for a change of angle. She backed up, taking up the slack in the chain until she was right on top of the hissing break. Then she kicked her legs away and let her full weight drop against the chain. The pipe, pulled down, bowed. The gap widened, the hiss became a roar, but it took two more weight drops before the jagged edges parted, and she landed with a dull splat on one of the soggy scatter rugs.

Ice cold water jetted out. She gasped in shock and pushed away from its chilling blast.

Now I'll either freeze to death or drown, she thought. But at least I'm free. *I'm free!*

38

Before the old aircraft hangar vanished in the mist in his rearview mirror, Matt was on the phone to Avery.

'The mighty Matt Healy is finally returning my calls. I'm honoured.'

'It's a long story, Col. Have you heard from Jane?'

'Indirectly, yes. I got a call from a desk sergeant at Wiltshire Police relaying an urgent message from her. She said you'd cracked the case, but that we should proceed with caution because there were at least two members of an interested party outside the target's house.'

Matt swore under his breath. What had he dropped Jane into?

'I relayed the details to Marius Fennel. He's getting things rolling from his end, but there's some confusion about who this interested party is and what they're doing outside Araton's house.'

'That's my fault. Jane thought she was adding to information I'd already supplied. I got waylaid.'

'She suspected that. Said if I hadn't heard from you already, you might be in trouble. Were you? Your geolocate came up in the middle of nowhere.'

'I was kidnapped by the CIA. You can tell Fennel that. It seems they also have an interest in Araton.'

'Is that who's staking out his house?'

'No, I think that's the Saudi GID.'

'What? Bloody hell, Matt, what have you got yourselves into?'

'You tell me. You're the one who got us into it! Look, I've got to go. Tell Fennel what I told you about the CIA and the GID, and that Araton is hiding out in the cellar of his own house. If he pops his head up, we'll lose him. Probably forever.'

Matt tossed the phone aside and focused on his driving. He thought about Jane. How she'd been abandoned at that dreary bus stop for hours now, but she was still sticking to their plan. Tenacious, or what? What a partner! But the news about the other "interested party" bothered him. He turned the wipers up to full speed and pressed down harder on the accelerator.

*

Bartram Horovitz looked like a pale green ghost. And a very angry one. Whatever he'd dived into to avoid the rapidly reversing car now clung to his hands, face and dark suit like mildew. He spat and wiped the back of one hand across his lips leaving an angry-looking gash as he bellowed instructions into his phone. Taliq rummaged amongst the smashed laptops and comms gear, salvaging what he could.

Horovitz cupped a hand over his phone. 'For fuck's sake, leave that shit and call Tasha. We've got to intercept Healy.'

'No need, chief.' Taliq found what he was looking for: his mobile phone with the tracker app. He switched it on. The screen, though cracked, lit up. 'I put a tracker on his car, just in case.'

Horovitz uncupped the phone. 'Change of plan, boys. We're tracking the bastard. Don't intercept. Repeat, do *not* intercept. Keep your distance. Let's see where that sucker goes.'

*

Terence Araton closed and locked the back door of his house and stood surveying the rain-soaked garden. Rain. He smiled. How very English. A fitting departure in a way. It was hard to believe he'd spent more than twenty years in this place and that in a matter of hours, he'd be off to sunnier climes. Reborn. A new man, quite literally. A new man with a new identity.

His surveillance wasn't nostalgic. On the contrary, if there was any regret, it was that he'd taken so long to come to his senses. The history of mankind was one of conquest and killing. From animal bones to rocks and spears, to bows and arrows and then guns, men had always sought better, more effective means of murdering each other. Even now – perhaps, particularly now – with the world on the cusp of irreversible ecological ruin, they continued their stupid macho games. He was just a cog in the wheel. What did it matter which country learned his secrets? Hundreds, probably thousands of scientists like himself were engaged in similar research. Any one of them might make the same breakthrough tomorrow. The only sane response was to cash in while he could, turn his back and walk away. Live out the rest of his life in quiet luxury and seclusion, insulated by money while the world outside devoured itself.

Scaling the back fence should have been easy: the posts and rails were on his side. But ten days underground had told on his condition, and the capping was slippery with rain and moss. His descent into his neighbour's back yard was less than graceful – more like a controlled crash – and he squatted beside a dripping rhododendron while he caught his breath.

At least the rain kept her yappy dog inside.

He checked the gun in his holdall. He'd like to put a bullet in the stupid thing. Its owner, too, the silly bitch, with her prissy little garden and complaints about the weeds coming through from his side of the fence. "Here's what I think of your whining." *Pop!* Right between the eyes.

A foolish fantasy. Hardly the anonymous getaway he'd been planning, but a satisfying fantasy. It would be nice to leave Stratford-sub-Castle with a middle finger raised at its inhabitants.

He made his way around the side of her house. Distracted by his thoughts, he stepped too close to the edge of one of the garden plots cut neatly in the lawn. The sodden ground gave way, and he went over, rolling on his ankle.

'*Aaarrgh!*' He clenched his teeth to stifle a string of expletives and gripped his ankle in both hands, rocking backwards and forwards as the pain surged briefly then settled back into a pounding throb.

Not broken, sprained, that's all. Just sprained. But shit, damn and fuck!

The snappy dog gave a single, tentative bark from inside the house. The rain surged briefly then stopped altogether.

Araton massaged his ankle. The pain was around the ligaments at the top of his foot. It was swelling already, and his shoe was starting to feel tight. Should he loosen it or keep it tied? He couldn't remember which was best.

He tried to stand.

Oh, Christ. Not without support!

A stick of some sort. Something to lean on ...

A yard broom stood against the side of the garden shed. He half-hobbled, half-crawled across and seized it like a drowning man might seize an overhanging branch. Reversed, with the bristly top wedged under his armpit, it made a makeshift crutch.

Perfect!

He lengthened the strap on his holdall, slung it over his other shoulder as a sort of counterweight, and hobbled out into the street.

Not quite the glorious exit he'd imagined, but what did it matter? It was still an exit. He was free. And the horizon held a hundred million consolations.

*

Jane stepped through the loop of chain that bound her wrists and brought her aching arms out in front of her, flexing her shoulders and groaning with relief.

Water hissed from the broken pipe, but the floor was barely damp. The cellar would take hours, even days, to fill. She had plenty of time. Besides, Araton might still be in the house above. Best not confront him with her hands still chained together.

Flaunting every health and safety regulation in the book, she felt about in the streaming water and located the collection of plugs that had been in the wall socket. Drying them as best she could, she tried one after the other until, with a faint pop, the overhead lights came back on.

Relief flooded through her, even as she squinted at the sudden influx of light. The dingy cellar with its bare walls and makeshift furniture really was a welcome sight.

Her wallet and things were where Araton had left them, scattered on the desk, and it only took a moment to locate the fake Visa card with the sliding top and its collection of lockpick tools.

The padlocks that secured her wrists should have been easy. They were cheap, pound store things that probably only had three different keys per ten thousand locks produced. She'd picked the sophisticated lock on Araton's back door in less than a minute, but damn it, her fingers were cold from the drenching, and surging adrenaline didn't help. Besides, the angle was awkward too ...

Click!

Once one was done, the other took only seconds. Now she really was free to get out.

She unplugged the light again then ascended the ladder. Easing open the trapdoor, she glimpsed twilight beneath the door of the broom cupboard. Was Araton still about? She stopped and listened. A good ten minutes had elapsed since he'd shot at her. More than enough time to make his getaway. Still, she opened the door carefully and looked about.

The house was silent, undisturbed. She closed the door again softly – no point alerting him if he was still about – and tiptoed to the lounge. Streetlights had come on outside, and it looked like Burdon's car was still parked out front. Was that possible? Was she mistaken? She tiptoed upstairs and peered down from the box room window. No doubt about it. Araton, unaware of her presence – or perhaps careful of who else might be out there -- must have gone over the back fence. The same way she'd come in.

Perched on the rear fence, Jane felt the rain ease, leaving the air still and misty. She saw where Araton had landed, dropped lightly beside the impact point, and followed his trail of footprints across the sodden grass. Round the side, she found a confusion of prints by the edge of a flower bed and concluded he must have fallen, perhaps even injured himself. There were only a few more prints before he reached the gravel drive, but the left foot was much heavier, more solidly placed, while the right one was being dragged after it.

He was injured all right. Hobbling. She might catch him yet!

39

Rosten had driven back to the start of Plover Place, then turned left instead of right, so he faced the flow of traffic coming up Goose Green Grove. Not that there was any traffic to speak of – all he'd seen so far was a sodden cyclist coming up the hill in a green raincoat – but parking this way was easier than studying oncoming traffic through his rearview mirror. Lights off, seat back, heater on, Radio 3 playing softly in the background, it was a struggle to keep awake. It had been a long day, but dozing off really wasn't an option right now.

He hit a button on the console and lowered the passenger window slightly to let in some fresh air. In the wing mirror, he spotted an old bum shuffling along the pavement towards him, walking with the aid of a stick. He looked closer. Not a stick, a broom. The old bugger was using a broom as a crutch!

He thought of calling it in on his walkie-talkie. He'd called in the cyclist – and been roundly rebuked by Reaves as a time-wasting twat – so maybe not.

He chuckled to himself and lowered the window further so he could get a proper look as the old bugger passed. Then, out of devilment and boredom, he called out the pre-arranged passphrase. 'Excuse me mate, do you know the way to Tower Bridge?'

The bum stopped, startled, unaware the parked car was even occupied, and turned to the open window.

'I beg your pardon?' His voice, in contrast to his damp, muddy, dishevelled appearance, was unusually cultured.

Rosten grinned, not surprised at his surprise. 'Tower Bridge, mate. You wouldn't know the—?'

'I believe it is a popular spot with tourists.'

The smirk froze on Rosten's face. He leaned across the passenger seat and squinted at the limping figure in the twilight street.

'Jesus! I mean, Dr Araton?'

'Who are you?'

'Mick Rosten.' He unlatched the passenger door and pushed it open. 'We've got a team out looking for you, sir.'

The interior light came on, and the old bum dropped gratefully into the seat, casting aside the broomstick as he did so. 'Well, now you've found me.'

Rosten snatched the walkie-talkie from the centre console and started the engine. 'Got him!'

'What? Who's that? What's your call sign?' the walkie-talkie crackled back as he swung out from the curb to do a three-point turn.

Oops! She was right. The walkie-talkies used a public frequency so he should have identified himself first. He could imagine Reaves listening in and sniggering.

'Big R here. Target acquired. *Shit —!*'

As he swung across the narrow road, he caught sight of a running figure racing down the hill towards him. Moving at speed. In the middle of the road too.

'Jane bloody Child!' he said, aborting the manoeuvre and swinging back hard on the wheel, scraping the sides of two cars parked opposite before powering away. He ignored the squawking from the walkie-talkie and looked for another cross-street to get back to the right side of the road, all the while keeping one eye on the rearview mirror where he saw the sprinting figure drop far behind.

Ha hah! Eat my dust, girlie.

A cry from Araton alerted him to the danger, but by then it was too late. The oncoming vehicle was also travelling at speed. All he caught was a glimpse of headlights as his foot stabbed the brake.

The other driver had better reactions and threw his vehicle sideways. It skidded on the wet road and slewed to one side, but even with power steering and anti-lock brakes, there was no way Rosten could avoid the impact. He didn't even have time to brace himself for the crash.

*

Matt took the corner into Goose Green Grove way too fast. The back of the Astra skidded briefly on a spot of loose gravel, and he corrected the drift with a flick of his wrist before powering away up the hill.

'Not far now, Janey,' he told himself.

Plover Place was the first cross-street on the right, but as he rounded the bend in the one-way road, he found a pair of headlights racing towards him. Even with his advanced police driver training, there was no time to avoid a collision. All he could do was minimise the impact.

He threw the car sideways in a controlled skid. The front of the oncoming vehicle ploughed into the far side's rear passenger door and shunted his car sideways down the hill. In the millisecond before the Mercedes' airbags exploded, Matt caught a glimpse of the driver's face by the light of a street lamp. The Laputa driver; the man from the BB Inn; and beyond him and his car, a running figure. Jane. Heading down the hill towards them.

In in an instant he took it all in. A frozen slice of time before the world came rushing on again with the tearing graunch of twisted metal and a shower of broken glass. And somewhere amongst it, Jane's voice; shouting.

Matt fought through the rapidly deflating airbags around him, his ears still ringing with the impact and their explosive detonation. As he struggled to open the driver's door, Jane's voice cut through the deafening silence, and he came quickly to his senses. 'He's got Araton!'

Behind her, he heard the roar of another engine and tyres

skidding in the wet. A second vehicle appeared from the corner of Plover Place; sideways on for a moment, then the skid was expertly righted. It kept accelerating, hard, heading the wrong way down the one-way street, aiming at the running figure now silhouetted in its headlights. Jane. It was heading straight for Jane!

40

Shitty Limey drugs! You couldn't get anything decent in this country.

Rosten had found her a half-used blister pack of paracetamol in the pocket of his overcoat. Burdon had swallowed the lot, but they'd done little for the ache from her splinted wrist and the throbbing pain of her broken nose. She needed something decent, something with a kick, not this over-the-counter shit.

Where the hell's the target? What the hell is Jane Child doing here? Where is she now?

Despite the regular check-ins and updates from Rosten and Reaves, the long day and the throb of her injuries were taking their toll. She'd catch her eyes closing for seconds at a time, or feel her head lolling back against the headrest. Then she'd jerk awake, shake herself and punish her flagging body by pressing at the swollen flesh around her nose. The pain was like an ice pick shoved up a nostril. It made her senses reel and her eyes water, but it kept her awake.

The walkie-talkie crackled. A garbled message. An excited voice: 'Got him!'

What kind of shit message was that? Goddam amateurs!

Reprimand delivered, Rosten clarified: he had Araton.

The pain vanished. Burdon was instantly awake. She started her car, and as she did so, she heard Rosten's explosive coda – 'Shit, Jane bloody Child!' – and glimpsed someone sprinting past the intersection of Plover Place.

Two plus two made trouble. Without demanding clarification this time, Burdon swung the car around and raced after the running figure.

Forgetting her own rules for radio traffic, she bellowed into the walkie-talkie, 'Reaves. Start of Goose Green Grove. Come in from the entrance. Pincer movement,' then dropped the handset to take the corner with both hands on the wheel. It was then that she saw Jane Child, caught like a rabbit running down the middle of the road ahead of her.

Got you, bitch!

Burdon accelerated.

*

Jane paused at the front gate of the house on Dotterel Drive and looked warily left and right. Araton might be limping, but she didn't know how badly he was injured. Plus, he was armed and had already taken one shot at her.

The footpaths were clear in both directions. The street was quiet.

Which way would he have gone?

A bit of muddy scuffing on a curbstone suggested left. That made sense. It was only a short distance to the inbound side of Goose Green Grove, and there were shops and a payphone at the bottom of the hill. She couldn't imagine him waiting for a bus.

Jogging lightly, she reached the corner in time to see a shambling figure with a walking stick pause beside a parked car partway down the hill. *Was that him?* The misty air and early evening twilight didn't help. Then the car door opened, and the interior light came on. *No doubt about it!* Jane broke into a run.

The car was parked facing the wrong way on the one-way street, so the driver began a three-point turn. That was her chance. All she had to do was get the make, model, and index number as per Matt's instructions, but the bins were out on the footpath, and at least one had blown over. A zigzag path with added hurdles was too slow. The road was clear. It would be considerably quicker.

The driver must have spotted Jane's approach in his peripheral vision as he executed the first part of his three-point turn because, as the car's brake lights came on, his face suddenly turned her way. She was close enough by now to recognise the tubby guy from the BB Inn, and he evidently recognised her because, instead of putting the car into reverse for the next part of the manoeuvre, he abandoned it completely and accelerated away down the hill, scraping the sides of several parked cars as he did so.

Momentum carried Jane on past the entrance to Plover Place. She had all she needed: a silver C-Class Mercedes and the registration plate. She was slowing down when she saw a pair of headlights suddenly swing around the bend at the bottom of the hill. A moment later, the oncoming car was skidding sideways, and a second after that, the Mercedes hit it.

Matt?

She picked up speed again, thinking it certainly looked like the Astra Estate she'd rented yesterday.

Matt!

Araton was armed. Matt might be injured. She had to warn him!

The sight of the skid, the sound of the crash and its aftermath of broken glass propelled her pounding steps.

At first, she didn't notice the silhouette dancing ahead of her. Her own silhouette in the headlights of a car coming up behind. Then she realised: *another* car heading the wrong way down a one-way street. It could only be one person, especially as it seemed to be accelerating.

Jane accelerated too, she had no choice, but she couldn't outrun a car. Fortunately, she didn't have to. Two crashed vehicles now blocked the road ahead, and all she had to do was get beyond them.

Talk about hurdles! The car behind was almost upon her when she leapt the bonnet of the skewed Astra in a single stride, aiming for a smooth touchdown on the other side.

It didn't quite happen.

The chase car was travelling too fast, and the road was wet. It braked and skidded and smacked into the Astra's bonnet. Which rather spoilt Jane's landing.

Her outstretched leg should easily have cleared the far side, but she'd reckoned without the car moving sideways beneath her. As she came down, her heel clipped the left wing, she lost her footing and cartwheeled over in the road.

Shaken, stunned and bruised, Jane lay for a moment, working through a mental checklist. Nothing seemed to be broken. She had grazes on top of grazes now but felt mostly intact.

She got to her feet and looked back in time to see Burdon struggle from the car, raise the gun in her good hand and aim it at her. She dropped to the ground again as Burdon fired, and saw the bullet pass through the wing of the Astra. Straight through two layers of metal. Entry and exit wounds. A small neat hole and a ragged tear. Still, the car was her nearest cover.

Jane kept low and scuttled towards it as yet another vehicle raced towards them – travelling the right way on the one-way road this time, coming up the hill. It skidded to a halt a few yards behind where she was crouched, illuminating her with its headlights and, hopefully, blinding Burdon.

Matt's backup at last!

She turned and yelled a warning. 'Look out! She's got a gun.' But her words faded as a tall figure stepped from the car, clearly unconcerned. Jane shielded her eyes, squinting at the glare of headlights as the man stepped into their beam. He moved towards her, reaching behind as he did so to draw something from his belt. Something he raised and aimed at her as she cowered by the car. Another gun.

He stopped three feet away, just beyond kicking distance, grinning down at her.

The tattooed man!

'Got her, boss,' he called.

Burdon's cold reply came back. 'Kill her.'

41

The chassis of the Astra had twisted from the impact, causing Matt's driver's door to stick. The second, lighter impact didn't help matters, so, releasing his seatbelt and kicking free of the deflated airbags, he dropped his seat back and clambered into the rear.

The sound of a pistol shot from the front startled him, and he threw himself to the floor just as a pair of headlights illuminated the downhill side of the car and came to a skidding halt a few yards off.

Just car lights. No blue-and-reds, no sirens. No other vehicles from what he could make out. And the shooter, who he could now see through the front window lit by the stopped vehicle's headlights, seemed unperturbed.

He stayed down, stayed where he was, one hand on the rear door release ready for a quick exit.

He heard Jane's warning shout, then, "Got her, boss!" and Burdon's cold instruction. Without another thought, he threw the door wide, clipping the man's wrist as he fired, knocking the gun from his hands and sending it skittering away across the glistening tarmac.

The guy was quick. He reacted fast, swinging a tattooed elbow that clipped the side of Matt's head. He followed it with a swift left to his midriff. Matt tensed his muscles just in time, but the impact was still shuddering, and he fell back against the car, taking a right hook to the jaw. He saw stars this time. And flashing lights. A whole line of them; red and blue; somewhere in the distance down the hill. But too far away. Too far ...

Gasping, he struggled to stay upright, his head spinning, then looked in surprise at a second figure outlined by the headlights. The silhouette moved behind the tattooed man and swung a foot at him. It looked a silly, inconsequential thing to do against such a formidable opponent, but it caught him between the legs and seemed remarkably effective. The guy let out a thin, high-pitched shriek. His knees buckled, and he staggered then pitched forward, coming down on top of Matt and pinning him against the car.

*

Some odd atmospheric effect amplified the red and blue flashing lights in the distance. Beacons in the mist, Burdon thought, abandoning her vendetta. She was a professional. She had, perhaps, two minutes before they arrived, and she still had a job to do. Still, as she moved to the crashed Mercedes, she couldn't help feeling a certain satisfaction at the sound of the pistol shot that must have ended Jane Child's life.

The front of the vehicle was badly crumpled. Neither passenger had been wearing a seatbelt. The airbags had saved them from serious injury, but they'd been bounced around, and both still looked dazed. She tore open Araton's door, wincing as she forgot her injured wrist, then waved the gun at him. 'You! Out! Now! My car.'

'It's all right. She's with us,' Rosten told him blearily.

Araton looked bewildered then fumbled with a deflated airbag tangled round his holdall.

'Is that essential?' Burdon snapped. He shook his head. 'Forget it then. We don't have time. Move!'

As Araton hobbled to her car, Rosten made to follow them.

'Not you,' she said, and shot him.

The gun's retort shook Araton. He obviously didn't know who she was, but it was clear she now had his full attention. He scrambled into the passenger seat of her car, pulling on the seatbelt, his eyes fixed on her battered face as she climbed in the other side.

'Not pretty, huh?' She slammed the door, extinguishing the interior light. Despite that, she could still feel his eyes on her. 'I'm just a courier, here to get you to safety.'

If he was reassured by that, he didn't show it.

The engine was still running. Careful now of her injured wrist, Burdon put the transmission into reverse, backed up and swung the wheel to execute the three-point turn that Rosten hadn't managed. There was some damage to the front of the car. Glass, paint and plastic came away, littering the street. The inside headlight was out, but one was enough. The blocked road and bodies would occupy the police for some time. Time enough to ditch this and find another vehicle.

She shoved the shift into first and drove away.

*

Reaves buckled like soggy cardboard, whimpering and drooling as he fell against Matt, but Jane had no time to help her partner right now. Burdon was still back there somewhere, with a gun, and wanted her dead. So was Araton. He too was armed. Three shots in her general direction in the last half-hour, and all of them had missed. She didn't fancy her chances against a fourth.

Diving down again, keeping behind the cover of the Astra, she rolled, snatched up the tattooed man's pistol, and came up in a crouch beside the car's front bumper. Peering around it, she saw Burdon had lost interest in her and was focused instead on the Mercedes.

Another pistol shot. Jane flinched and ducked, but this clearly wasn't aimed her way. Then two car doors slammed, and when she looked up again, she saw Araton had been bundled into Burdon's car.

Reversing lights came on. Burdon backed away.

The tattooed man's gun was unfamiliar. The light was bad, the visibility poor, and the target was moving too. But she knew the safety-catch was off and that she'd only get one shot.

The car paused. The reversing lights went out, and it began to move forward again to complete its turn.

Jane stretched her arms across the bonnet, steadying the pistol clamped between both hands. She checked her aim, eased out her breath, and gently squeezed the trigger.

The bullet made neat round holes through the side window and the front windscreen. Then the car accelerated, skidding slightly on the wet tarmac before it turned into Plover Place and drove away.

Jane sank back down against the bumper and dropped the gun. Matt had finally freed himself from the groaning dead-weight of the tattooed man. He secured the man's hands with a zip-tie handcuff then hurried to her side.

'My guardian angel! Are you all right?'

Jane nodded.

He glanced at the tail lights of the departing car. 'Don't worry, the cops'll get them.'

Jane looked at him blankly. Said nothing.

A moment later, a beaten up Toyota sedan skidded to a halt, followed by a white van. Not the police. But they weren't far off. The sirens were getting louder, the lights brighter.

Jane blinked. The scene felt fractured, like a half-remembered dream.

A young woman leapt from the car. Someone Matt seemed to know.

'What happened? Where's Araton?'

'Gone,' Matt replied.

'Where? Which way?'

'You tell me. You're the ones with all the tracking gear.'

The young woman cursed him then looked around at the residential street. Blinds were up, and curtains pulled back in nearby houses. Someone peered from a partly opened door. Someone else held out a camera phone. Behind her, the sirens' pitch grew louder.

She gestured and yelled something to the van driver as she raced back to her car. Mounting the kerb, digging wheel ruts in the grass verge and clipping a privet hedge, she drove around the crashed vehicles and continued up the hill. The van followed. Twenty seconds later, the first of half-a-dozen police vehicles came to a screaming halt and armed officers fanned out to secure the scene.

Matt squeezed Jane's hand. 'It's over, Janey. We did it. Don't worry about missing Burdon. Araton won't get far.'

'No,' she said flatly. 'I don't expect he will.'

42

The next fifteen hours went by in a blur. Jane felt as if she'd been awake for every one of them. Now she lay watching as the room slowly lightened, listening to the sound of Matt's steady breathing. He'd had a good night for once. *Lucky Matt.*

Salisbury Cathedral chimed the hour. Six crisp tones. Each note seemed to hang in the air, motionless, till it was swamped by its successor. When the last one finally faded, a great sadness welled up inside her, and it was all she could do to stop herself from crying.

Matt slumbered on.

After medical examinations, interviews, and preliminary statements, Wiltshire Police had put them up in a tourist hotel near the city centre. A beige, brown and ochre place as bland as its residents, but by that stage of the evening neither of them cared. After a near-sleepless night the night before, it was all they could do to swallow a few morsels of food before crashing into bed.

But sleep had been elusive despite her weariness. Jane dozed, fitfully, not restfully, and the more she tried to put her thoughts aside, the more forcefully the recollection of events came back to her.

Too many movies and TV shows, perhaps. Too many slow-mo action sequences. She couldn't possibly have taken in all those details, but her mind kept replaying them regardless ...

The reversing car, Araton in the passenger seat, his startled face looking around wildly. The tattooed man's gun, warm, comfortable, feeling like an extension of her own body, nestled in her outstretched hands and supported by the bonnet of the Astra.

The sights lined up as the reversing car slowed, bringing Araton before them like a gift. A gentle squeeze. He'd turned her way. Had he seen her? The muzzle flash?

The kick of the gun was surprisingly gentle, its retort no louder than a ruler smacked on a wooden desk. She knew the muzzle velocity must be something like 800 miles an hour, but somehow she could see the bullet in flight, a silvery spheroid spinning from the rifling of the barrel. She watched it star the glass as it passed through the passenger window, saw a small dent, and a spot of blood as it struck the side of Araton's head, then a larger one spraying the interior of the windscreen simultaneous with the bullet's exit and onward flight. And the man, already dead, rocking forward then back again as the car accelerated away.

'Don't you want that bacon?' Matt asked her over breakfast.

'No, go ahead.'

He helped himself, adding, 'Come on, Janey. Got to keep your strength up.'

She watched him demolish it with relish as she nibbled at a slice of toast. He finished, sat back, studied her, and took up his mug of tea. 'I know what it is. I know what you're going through.'

Jane felt something fall away inside her. 'What do you mean?'

'Post-case blues. Especially one that ended like that. All the build-up, all the action, all the excitement, then ... *blah*. You spend hours sitting around giving statements and writing up reports. It's like the end of a holiday, only much worse.'

'Yeah.' She forced a smile. 'That's what it is.'

MI5 sent a car for them, which was thoughtful, but the real reason was that Marius Fennel wanted a full debriefing. They'd told Wiltshire Police as little as they could get away with, and Colin Avery's NCA shielding had helped deflect some of their more pressing questions. The tattooed man's gun? Yes, she'd picked it up, but only to put it out of reach ...

There were a collection of Sunday papers in the back of the car, and Jane found her eye drawn to executive recruiting ads for banks, insurance companies, and finance houses. There were plenty of opportunities for someone with her experience and skill-set, but things changed rapidly these days. She wouldn't want to get too rusty.

'Don't tell me you're looking to go back to your old job?'

She looked up. Matt was smiling.

'No, just ... you know ... keeping my eye in.' She turned the page, feeling her own smile leak away as she did so.

The car took them straight to Thames House on Millbank. There was no waiting around this time. A guard met them as they cleared the security checkpoint and escorted them straight to Marius Fennel's office. He bounded from his chair and greeted them with warm handshakes.

'Do I even need to say it? Well done, you two! A splendid outcome. Couldn't have been better.'

'Did they get Burdon?' Matt asked.

'You haven't heard? They stopped her car on the A30. She gave herself up without a fuss. Apparently, driving around with a dead body didn't hold much appeal.'

'Dead?' Matt said. 'You mean Araton?'

'A single bullet wound to the left temple. Preliminary ballistics show it came from the gun you took off a freelancer by the name of Roger Reaves. Not that he's talking, but his associate is. It seems that losing a couple of yards of intestines did wonders for the man's cooperation.'

Matt stared at Jane. Jane said, 'What does he have to say?'

'Nothing very coherent after the crash, but he's given us full details of his recruitment, their employer and their assignment.

'We also recovered Araton's laptop. It seems he left his holdall behind when he fled. The tech team are hard at work on it. They've only found personal stuff so far: address books, scanned photos, family documents, and so on, but it's early days yet.'

They won't find anything more, Jane thought. At least, not what they're hoping to find.

'As for what Araton was actually up to, even I'm not cleared to know the details. His seniority at DSTL gave him free rein to work on whatever he liked, but I understand their people are piecing things together from his notes. No doubt they'll work out exactly what he was trying to sell to the Saudis.'

Oh no, they won't. It was all in his head. He told me so. The head I put a bullet through.

'No Mr Harroway?' Matt remarked as Fennel showed them out after the debriefing.

'Sebastian is currently spending time with his mother,' Fennel said.

'Is that an MI5 euphemism?'

'For what, Mr Healy?'

'For having one's security clearance reviewed.'

'I don't know what you're—'

'Oh, come on. Araton's buyers just happened to be clients of his arms-dealing brother-in-law?'

'Yes, well, I'm sure that's nothing to do with Sebastian, but no doubt questions will be raised.'

He gave them more warm handshakes at the exit, and they crossed the road to a narrow wedge of park beside the Thames. The trees were losing their leaves, and the sky was grey. Matt said, 'Is there anything you want to tell me, Jane?'

Jane shook her head.

'I know I'm not one to talk, but remember our agreement? No secrets.'

'Is it a secret?' she asked, looking up.

'I suppose not. Not now. Not between us. And we don't have to talk about it. Not until you're ready. Or ... never, if that's what you'd prefer.'

Jane took a breath. 'What was I supposed to do, Matt?'

He put his arm around her. 'Precisely what you did do. The right thing.'

Jane burst into tears.

They got off the tube at Elephant and Castle and headed home.

Matt said, 'There's something I haven't told you. I think Araton was a marked man anyway. Horovitz, the CIA guy, had a trained sniper and a sniper rifle with him. My guess is that if the Americans couldn't get Araton, they'd decided no one else would get him either – including us.'

'Is that supposed to make me feel better?'

'No, just ...' he shrugged. 'You know ...'

Jane nodded. They walked on.

As they approached a pound store, Matt held up a hand and ducked inside, emerging a minute later wearing a smug grin and patting the inside pocket of his jacket.

'Oh no,' Jane said, 'not more!'

'We've been away for days. Bluebelle will have lost the others by now.' He put an arm around her shoulders, and they carried on. 'Bugger this holiday business. You know what I fancy most of all? A home-cooked meal – it's my turn – an evening with my best girl, and a game of pingers with our cat.'

Jane smiled properly for the first time in what felt like an age. Hardly the most romantic words ever spoken, but she reckoned they would do.

If you enjoyed this book ...

... you can make a big difference.

I'm an independent author and don't have the muscle of Big Publishing when it comes to getting attention for my books. But I do have something powerful and effective: a committed and loyal bunch of readers..

Honest reviews help bring my books to the attention of other readers, so if you enjoyed Private Nightmares, I'd be very grateful if you could spend a minute or two leaving a review on this book's Amazon page. It can be as short as you like.

Thanks very much!

Geoff

About the Author

Geoff Palmer is an award-winning novelist and technical writer based in Wellington, New Zealand.

You'll find him online at:
geoffpalmer.co.nz

On Facebook at:
facebook.com/geoffpalmerNZ

On Twitter at:
twitter.com/geoffpalmer

Also by Geoff Palmer

The Bluebelle Investigations series:

DEAD MEN'S SHOES
A Bluebelle Investigations prequel

Jane Child's career is going nowhere. Stuck in the headquarters of a large London bank, she's in the slow lane heading towards a middle-management dead end when her boss becomes a basket case. The new job comes with a laptop that contains something more than official, bank-authorised software. When Jane cracks the computer and discovers her boss's tawdry secret, she inadvertently stirs the murky waters of the criminal underworld, and some very big, very nasty fish swim out.

PRIVATE VIEWING

When Jane Child falls under the spell of her new boss, the wealthy but mysterious Damien Trotter, she finds herself trapped in a web of intrigue, vile secrets and murder, where even her most intimate moments are no longer her own. Now she must confront the shadows in her past and the deeper, darker shadows in her present. Shadows that may cost her the man she loves, her happiness... and her life.

PRIVATE LIVES

Jane Child's first case: a missing cat. How did she get the boring one? Partner Matt Healy's is far more interesting: someone's counterfeiting top-notch coffee. But sometimes less can be more. More complex, more frightening and much, much more dangerous.

PAYBACK

Solikha Duong lives the carefree life of a village girl in northern Cambodia until her world is torn apart by "truck men" from the south. But Solikha is tough, resourceful, and won't give up without a fight.
Alice Kwann is on vacation when she's attacked by thugs at a stopover in northern Nevada. But Alice too is tough, resourceful, and won't give up without a fight.
What binds these women is a shocking secret and a desire for revenge. Because sometimes your past won't let you go.

Non-fiction:

HOW TO WRITE A BOOK
12 Simple Steps to Becoming an Author

The complete guide to writing your first book. And your next one.

Of all the creative arts, writing a book is both deceptively easy and surprisingly difficult. There are plenty of How To guides about creative writing, but precious few deal with the actual day to day process of becoming and being a writer. This practical, self-help guide is an exception that will unlock your potential, your creativity and your genius.

www.ingramcontent.com/pod-product-compliance
Lightning Source LLC
Chambersburg PA
CBHW052034240626
47153CB00006B/2083